A Crooked Arrow Christmas

A MILITARY SWEET COWBOY ROMANCE IN BIG SKY COUNTRY

JENNA HENDRICKS

Dedication

I want to dedicate this book to all of our servicemen and women who bravely go out there day after day and do whatever is needed to ensure our country stays free.

There are a lot of men and women who will never get the recognition they deserve because they serve in the military intelligence field. Those service members, and veterans, have to stay secret. But rest assured, they are working hard behind the scenes to bring intelligence to our military leaders, and eventually, to the President.

Thank you for your service!

Books by Jenna Hendricks (Clean & Wholesome Romance)

<u>Triple J Ranch</u> –

Book 0 - Finding Love in Montana (Join my newsletter to get this book for free)

Book 1 - Second Chance Ranch

Book 2 – Cowboy Ranch

Book 3 – Runaway Cowgirl Bride

Book 4 – Faith of a Cowboy

Book 5 – Cowboy Blessings

Book 6 – The Cowboy's Game

<u>Big Sky Christmas</u> –

Book 1 – Her Montana Christmas Cowboy

Book 2 – Her Christmas Rodeo Cowboy

Book 3 – Her Mistletoe Cowboy

Book 4 – Her Sleigh Ride Christmas Cowboy

<u>Crooked Arrow Ranch</u> –

Book 0 - Wounded Hearts Ranch (join my newsletter to get this free)

Book 1 – A Broken Heart Mended

Book 2 – Hope's Healing Love

Book 3 - Love's Healing Balm

Book 4 – A Crooked Arrow Christmas

<u>Standalone Novels</u> –

Christmas Crazy in July

Rebel Hearts Anthology

See these titles and more: https://JennaHendricks.com

Contents

1. Chapter 1 — 1
2. Chapter 2 — 7
3. Chapter 3 — 15
4. Chapter 4 — 29
5. Chapter 5 — 37
6. Chapter 6 — 47
7. Chapter 7 — 61
8. Chapter 8 — 69
9. Chapter 9 — 77
10. Chapter 10 — 85
11. Chapter 11 — 95
12. Chapter 12 — 101
13. Chapter 13 — 107
14. Chapter 14 — 113

15. Chapter 15 119

16. Chapter 16 127

17. Chapter 17 135

18. Chapter 18 143

19. Chapter 19 155

20. Chapter 20 163

21. Chapter 21 173

22. Chapter 22 181

23. Chapter 23 187

24. Chapter 24 197

25. Chapter 25 203

26. Chapter 26 211

27. Chapter 27 219

28. Chapter 28 227

29. Chapter 29 237

30. Chapter 30 243

31. Chapter 31 249

32. Chapter 32 257

33. Chapter 33 263

34. Chapter 34 269

35. Epilogue 283

Character Page 285

Cranberry Meatloaf Recipe 288

Author's Notes 291

Newsletter Sign-up 293

Acknowledgements 295

Contact Me 297

Chapter 1

"What's with that pig?" Marnie Gallagher, the newest Crooked Arrow Ranch resident, pointed to a miniature pot-bellied pig with a black spot over one eye that looked more like a pirate patch than a spot.

Megan, the ranch's counselor, smiled and waved at the pig and his owner. "That's Pirate Spot, and Malachi McKinley. Pirate is a sort of mascot." She giggled. "You should see the Fourth of July parade. He sits on a float with a patriotic pirate costume and looks out at everyone as though he knows he is the cutest thing around. It's a lot of fun."

Unsure about this new town, Marnie didn't say much. She grunted her understanding and turned away. But the pig had sensed her attention and since he rarely walked around with a leash, veered off from his current path and headed directly towards the two women.

A sound caught Marnie's attention and she turned her head to see what, or who, was making it. A totally off-key song was being sung by a group of three teenaged boys. "Jingle bells, Batman smells, Robin laid an egg."

She shook her head and wondered if she had fallen down the rabbit hole, or was sucked up in a vortex and transported to a completely different plane of existence. Who sang Christmas songs in the middle of November? And half the town already had their festive Christmas lights and décor up. This was one strange place.

"Megan, it's good to see you again. I guess Pirate Spot wanted to come and say hi." Malachi grinned at Megan, then turned to smile at the tall woman standing next to her. "Are you going to introduce me to your friend?"

"Of course." Megan motioned toward Marnie. "Marnie, this is Malachi. He's in school to become a veterinarian. And in case you haven't figured it out yet, he's a big fan of little pigs with giant personalities." She then turned to Malachi and waved at Megan. "And this is Megan, she's new to town and the ranch. Recently she served in the Air Force."

Malachi put his hand out to shake, then hesitated when he noticed her right hand was resting on a cane to help keep herself upright. "It's nice to meet you. How long have you been here?"

Marnie moved the cane from her right hand to her left, then reached out to shake his hand. She paid close attention to his face, but he didn't seem disgusted or put off by her handicap. Instead, he just seemed unsure if she would shake his hand. "Nice to meet you, as well. I've only been here long enough to see the Christmas lights begin to go up. What's with all the Christmas? It's not even Thanksgiving yet."

Both Megan and Malachi laughed and nodded.

If there had been any tension when he realized her use of a cane, it was gone when they began talking about Christmas.

"Yeah, we go a little crazy here in Frenchtown for Christmas. I think a few years ago someone put out a petition to rename us 'Christmas Town'. Did you know that Santa Claus and his wife live here?" Before

Malachi could say anymore, Pirate Spot snorted. "Forgive me, and this here is my trusty sidekick, Pirate Spot." He motioned toward the pink pig with black spots. That day, the pig was sporting a red ugly Christmas sweater with a little pirate and the words "Pirates love Christmas" crocheted in green lettering.

"He's so adorable." Marnie gushed. "Does he like wearing clothes?" She tilted her head and considered how a pig must feel about wearing a sweater. She herself enjoyed wearing sweaters when it was cold, which it was. In Montana during November the weather could shift from sunny and in the low sixties, all the way down to below zero with a horrible blizzard.

Luckily, that day, it was a cool forty-one degrees with billowy clouds in the sky and blue patches breaking through quite a bit. All in all, a good day to be out and about. As long as a human was wearing a sweater, jacket, gloves, and possibly a hat. And apparently, a pig, too.

Then she noticed what Malachi was wearing. He wasn't very tall, for a man. A bit shorter than she was. And she was five feet eight inches tall. However, he was good looking with a boyish smile. But what really caught her attention was the fact that he wasn't wearing a jacket or even a beanie. He had on a cowboy hat, like most men did. Instead of being all bundled up like she was, he only wore a light blue and gray checked flannel shirt with blue jeans and cowboy boots.

Marnie figured he was accustomed to the weather for when she finally noticed the other men in town, they were dressed similarly. In fact, she was one of only a few women who were all bundled up for the cold - which brought her back to the little pig. When her eyes looked back down at the pig, she could have sworn he smiled and waggled his tiny, curly tail, almost like a dog.

"Yes," Malachi nodded. "Pirate loves a good costume. Plus, it's a bit cold for a small pig like him, to be out without something to warm him up."

Marnie expected Malachi would lean down and pick up the pig, but he didn't. Instead, Malachi waved and said he'd catch them later. Then the two left and began walking toward a group of teenagers who ended up gushing over the cute pig.

"Are there a lot of barnyard animals wearing costumes and masquerading as pets through town?" Marnie arched a brow and watched the rest of the people meandering through the sidewalks and even across the street.

Megan took a moment to think about the question. "Well, Pirate is the only pot-bellied pig that's a pet. But, there are quite a few horses, ponies, sheep, and other animals that have become pets. I think in a rural farm and ranching town like Frenchtown, you should expect to see things you wouldn't see normally in a city."

She didn't say much, only nodded and looked around. "So, where is the wonderful coffee bar you told me so much about?"

"Ah, yes." Megan waggled her brows and smiled from ear to ear. "The Frenchtown Roasting Company is just a few doors down. Follow me."

Marnie was grateful she didn't see a bull running around all wild and free, like the pig. While she wasn't accustomed to farm animals, she knew enough to know to stay away from bears and bulls. That thought pulled her up short when Megan opened the door.

"There aren't bears in town, are there?" With trepidation, Marnie looked around and prayed she wouldn't lose the toes on her other foot, or her entire foot, to a wild animal. Or a feisty barnyard animal. "Do I need to carry some sort of animal deterrent?"

Not wanting to scare the newest resident to the ranch, Megan stayed quiet. Instead, she decided to change the subject. "What is your favorite kind of coffee?"

"Bear-free coffee." Agitation was a new feeling for Marnie. Before her Air Force accident she had been a happy and carefree sort of person. Even having to spend almost an entire year at the Defense Language Institute in Monterey, California, studying Russian hadn't caused anxiety. Well, nothing more than the normal pre-test jitters most students had. She had seemed to have a way with languages, and it usually showed in her test scores.

Megan laughed. "Good one. But not to worry, bears don't come into town. And with it being so close to winter, you won't have to worry about them anywhere. Just don't go wandering around the forest on your own and you'll be fine."

Chapter 2

Declan Walden couldn't hold back his smile. He'd overheard part of the conversation between Megan and the new lady. Bears in town? She must have been a city girl. That was all he could think.

But to be fair, there was that one incident with a bear inside of the dog trainer's house a while back. Although, from what Declan had heard, that was a very strange case of vagrants luring the bear inside in order to trap it and then have shooting practice. He shook his head in disgust. The things bored youths got up to lately was enough to have him spittin' mad.

He wasn't much older than the kids who played that type of cruel game, but he was much smarter, and nicer than those kinds of kids. Declan had wished there had been a way to identify the culprits. He wasn't the only one who thought shooting up a trapped bear inside of a house, and then leaving it there to rot, was more than cruel. It was downright criminally insane.

Declan didn't mean to keep eavesdropping on the duo, but he couldn't take his eyes off of the beautiful new girl. She wasn't as tall as he was, but with heels she would be close to his six feet, two inches. Her long hair was a shiny brown with hints of red and gold. He couldn't be sure but thought it would be called auburn. While he wasn't close enough to see her eyes, he guessed they'd be something like a deep chocolate brown, or maybe blue.

So, without a conscious thought, his legs moved him closer to the ladies. Only so he could see her eyes, and maybe get her name. But in his excitement to get a better look at her eyes, he didn't notice they had stopped at the back of line and just about ran into her, with his coffee cup in hand.

With an abrupt stop, the coffee in his porcelain mug sloshed around the top and a few drops crashed over the edges of the cup and down his fingers. He cleared his throat. "Sorry about that. I must have been wool-gathering." He flashed a crooked smile and shrugged. The eyes that stared back at him were worth the mess on his fingers, and the chagrin he felt at almost bumping into her.

The woman had the deepest pools of coffee-colored eyes with hints of gold flecks surrounding her irises. When she tilted her head, he caught sight of bits of a deep green that looked almost like the color of emeralds. Instead of introducing himself, like the gentleman his mother raised him to be, he just stood there mesmerized by her perfect features.

When a sound finally broke through his haze, he realized that Megan was laughing at him.

"Declan, anyone home?" Megan waved a hand in front of his face. He ran a nervous hand through his head of hair. "Right, sorry."

Marnie noticed the way his eyes crinkled just a tiny bit when he smiled. She figured he was used to smiling since he had little wrinkles.

There was no way he was old enough to be wrinkling up already. Unless, well, maybe ranchers spent too much time outside in the sun and their skin wrinkled early? She guessed he couldn't be much older than she was.

The man staring at her was wearing the standard Wrangler work jeans, brown cowboy boots with splashes of mud on the tips and sides, a very large belt buckle that had to be uncomfortable for his stomach when he sat down, and the same shirt she'd seen on just about every cowboy she noticed while walking into the coffee shop – a black and deep blue checkered button down.

She moved her cane from her right hand to her left and put her right hand out and smiled. "Hi, I'm Marnie Gallagher, newest resident of the Crooked Arrow Ranch."

Declan's smile faltered, only a bit, but it was enough for Marnie to see it. She pulled her hand back before he could shake it.

"I'm sorry. Where are my manners? I'm Declan Walden. I run the local alpaca ranch here. I'm going to be stopping by your ranch later today to discuss wool production with Jerod and the guys." Declan scratched his head. "Well, I guess gals, too."

Megan must have noticed the coolness for she stepped in to rescue Declan before Marnie could turn back around. "Marnie, Declan also raises sheep and he's been very helpful to the ranch, assisting Jerod with finding a small herd to bring in for us to care for. He's a nice guy." She nodded her head once and tried to catch Marnie's eyes, but she had lost interest.

It was always the same, men would smile at her and flirt. Well, until they noticed that she was a cripple. It wasn't like she had lost her entire leg, or anything like that. Most people would never even know she had a problem if it wasn't for the cane, which she was going to learn how to leave behind very soon. No one would ever see her disfigured foot with its missing toes. Or even, see the prosthetic she wore on her foot in place of the toes that had been blown off by someone else's stupidity.

But somehow, he had already put two and two together and come up with her being broken. They always got that look in their eyes. The one where the light dimmed and the space between their eyes crinkled and their lips pursed together. She saw his pity before he could mask it. The nicer ones did try to hide their disgust, but in the end, it was always the same. After the introductions were over they would make some excuse and walk away never to talk to her again.

Or worse, they'd want to hear gory war stories.

Marnie blinked and looked at Declan. "Nice to meet you. I'm sure I'll be seeing you around." Since the line had moved quickly, it was her turn to order so she turned her back on the rude cowboy and walked up to the counter. She held her head high and used her cane. So what if her gait was a little off. If her injury made Declan uncomfortable, he could leave. Marnie had stopped caring what people thought about her, or so she thought. Now, she wasn't sure if her feelings were hurt, or just her newly acquired pride.

After the accident and loss of her toes, she had dealt with crippling depression. The Air Force doctors helped her somewhat, but it was her faith in God that eventually helped her to heal and move on from the emotional scars, if not the physical ones. Those would never go away. The Air Force sent her to the ranch to learn how to walk better, and to stop being so dependent on her cane.

She could do it, too. She'd learn to walk properly again and then no one would ever know what happened to her - especially rude cowboys.

"What can I get for ya?" A young woman behind the counter smiled at Marnie, even after she noticed the cane.

It was probably the first time someone outside of the VA, or the ranch, hadn't changed their expression when they noticed her injury.

That was a first. And one she greatly appreciated. In fact, it caused her to smile in return without even thinking about it. "I heard there were special holiday drinks? Can you tell me about them?"

The young woman's grin grew even larger, if that was possible. "Oh, yes." She licked her lips. "My favorite drink is the peppermint mocha." She sighed and her eyes drifted closed. "It tastes like Christmas in a cup."

"Mmm, that sounds wonderful. I'll take a large one of those, please." Marnie nodded, then turned to look at the pastries.

"Wonderful! I told the owner that most everyone wanted Christmas drinks before Thanksgiving. Normally, we don't serve the peppermint mocha until next week, but lately she's been open to starting earlier." The barista laughed and looked around the coffee shop that had already been decorated for Christmas.

"We also have peppermint and chocolate chip scones available, if you're interested in the Christmas treats." The barista pointed to a pastry in the case that looked like it was full of chocolate chips as well as tiny bits of peppermint candy.

Marnie's mouth watered at the image of that scone. "Sold! I'll take one of those as well." Once she paid for her order, she moved down the counter and waited for it.

Once Megan had finished giving her own order, she joined Marnie. "So, what do you think?"

"I love the scent of cinnamon, chocolate, and coffee all mixed together. I'll hold off on any real comments until I get my order and can tell you more." Marnie watched as another barista finished concocting her peppermint mocha.

"Here ya go." The second barista put the drink in front of Marnie, who gladly picked it up and smelled the alluring scent of chocolate, coffee, and sweetness through the opening on her lid.

"Hmm, this does smell like Christmas in a cup. Now for the taste." Marnie put the cup to her lips and sipped. While it was hot, it was also the best thing she'd ever tasted. "Oh, wow. This beats the peppermint mocha that the chain stores sell." She took another sip and sighed in bliss.

"Wait until you try the scone." Megan chuckled, then reached for the plate that Leena, one of the coffee shop employees, handed them. "I got one too." She took the plate with two Christmas scones on it to an empty table and sat down waiting for her drink order.

"Thanks, I'm so glad you brought me here." Marnie set the cane against her table and sat down. Sitting wasn't ever an issue for her, just getting up and walking. For some strange reason she could never understand, the toes helped a person to stabilize themselves when standing and walking. She had heard several explanations about the big toe acting as a counter to the way a human naturally stood, but that was about all she could grasp. The rest seemed silly to her.

"I hope you like the scones as much as I do. We'll have a large order of these for the day after Thanksgiving. Since most of our residents are male, and don't really buy into the whole Black Friday shopping, anyone who stays behind at the ranch will be on their own for food that day. But don't worry, Dana always ensures there's plenty of food in the fridge. All you'll have to do is throw something together and nuke it."

"And the scones? Where do those come into play?" Marnie quickly put a second piece into her mouth and sighed as the melted chocolate mixed on her tongue with the spicy peppermint candy. The buttery scone in and of itself would be wonderful, but with the added sweetness of the candy, it was to die for. It looked like Marnie was going to have to find a new way to exercise if she was going to make it through the next six weeks without gaining any weight.

Megan grinned, wickedly. "Anyone who goes shopping gets the Christmas scones. Plus, we stop in here for a drink order to go. We'll place it in advance since they'll be so packed that day, but it will be hot and ready for us when we arrive."

"Ah, I see." Marnie snorted. "It's a bribe."

Megan put her hand to her chest and blinked big, innocent eyes. "Who? Me? I'd never bribe anyone to go shopping."

"Yeah, right." The man laughed. "Can I join you?" Declan didn't wait for an answer.

The chair next to Marnie made a scraping noise, catching her attention. Declan sat down and Marnie could feel her joy evaporating.

Marnie rolled her eyes heavenward and said a quick prayer asking God to give her the strength to be nice.

"And what would you know about it?" Megan teasingly pointed to Declan. "You've never been involved with a Black Friday event at the ranch."

One thick eyebrow arched over Declan's left eye. "And how would you know since you're one of those crazy shoppers who is up before the cowboys and hanging out in long lines fighting other women all day long for a three-hundred-dollar TV set you don't even need?"

"Pft. Shows what you know." Megan shook her head and they continued to tease each other back and forth. They sounded like brother and sister going at it on a Sunday after church supper.

If Marnie were back home with her family, she would have stopped her younger siblings from fighting, but since she wasn't responsible for these two, she sat back and enjoyed her treats... without saying a word.

Chapter 3

"You know, you could have jumped in anytime to help a sister out." Megan grinned as she and Marnie made their way back to the ranch's truck after their morning outing.

"Why would I want to?" While Marnie wasn't anti-social, she was anti-rude jerks. Well, that might be too strong of a descriptor for Declan. He did seem to be surprised by her cane, but otherwise he was nice. And he made an effort to talk to her once they were all seated.

Marnie knew she should give the guy a chance, but why did it even matter? She was here to finish her recovery. Then she'd be off somewhere else. Her aunt wanted her to come and live with her. She was getting on in years and wanted someone else in the house with her, just in case. Aunt Trudy was tough, but she was pushing seventy. Marnie had never seen the woman slow down. If she wasn't of an age, Marnie would think that Aunt Trudy just wanted to take care of her, not the other way around.

So, making nice with the locals wasn't really necessary. No, she'd be polite moving forward, but not worry about making friends with anyone. Well, except for maybe whoever it was that created the most wonderful scone she'd ever tasted. That was one person Marnie could be friends with. Maybe they could even swap recipes.

Who was she kidding? The person who baked the goodies at Frenchtown Roasting Company was on an entirely different level than she was. Sure, Marnie knew how to make cookies and brownies that everyone seemed to like, but scones were a different story. Her only time making them had been from one of the fancy red and white checked boxes. The kind she bought from the grocery store.

For just a moment, she wondered if she added chocolate chips and peppermint crunches to the boxed scones, if they would be close to the one she had that morning. Then she shook her head and almost laughed out loud. Nope, it wouldn't work. Well, it might be okay, but it wouldn't taste anywhere near as good as what was happily lounging in her stomach. Just the thought of tasting another one of those scones put a smile on her face. Probably the first one since Declan pushed his way into her and Megan's brunch.

"What's with the smile?" Megan grinned and moved a tad closer to Marnie. "Are you thinking about a pair of fine green eyes by any chance?"

"Huh? Green eyes?" Marnie scrunched her nose and glanced sideways at Megan.

"Oh, please. Don't tell me you didn't notice those sparkling eyes every time they landed on you." Megan put a hand over her mouth to hide her chuckle. "I think a certain cowboy has a crush."

This time, Marnie did laugh out loud. "What? You're kidding, right? There's no way he has a crush on me. You saw how uncomfortable he was when we first met."

Megan stopped dead on the wooden sidewalk outside the general store and slightly pulled on Marnie's arm to stop her as well. "Now listen here, I'm only going to say this once. Not everyone you meet is appalled by a cane, or even a disability. Especially in this town. Everyone here has welcomed all who stay at the Crooked Arrow with open arms, no matter how they look, or what their condition is."

Remorse zinged up Marnie's back and caused her neck to tingle. Her head lowered and she thought about those she had met so far. The baristas at the coffee shop were super nice and they didn't even bat an eye at her cane. In fact, most of the people they walked past that day in town smiled and nodded at her. The only person she noticed who seemed disgusted was Declan. But was it disgust? Or was he just uncomfortable because he tried to shake her hand that held her cane?

Marnie sighed. "You're right. I know for most people a cane is nothing. Even for a young person. But for an airman it is a big deal. I was booted from the Air Force because I'm deformed, unfit for duty. And that is something that I'm still coming to grips with."

A softness covered Megan's face that spoke to Marnie. "I know. And that is one thing that we are going to work on while you are here. It is important for you to realize that just because you had an accident that caused you to lose some toes, it doesn't mean you are unfit for life. The military, all branches, have a different outlook. Did you know that not even someone with eczema is fit for duty?"

Marnie scrunched her nose. "What? Are you serious? But that's just a skin rash, isn't it? How does that make a person unfit?"

Megan shrugged. "All military personnel must be fit for combat. You can't be on a regular medication just in case you are out in battle so long that you can't get a refill, or not taking your medication could distract you from your duty. Even those who aren't considered combatants."

"That's stupid. Most of the Air Force aren't considered combatants. Most will never directly see war." Marnie hadn't been in a war zone herself, but she had known a few of her airmen buddies who had been in Iraq. The closest they got was the occasional rocket that would land close to their base. But they were so far from the fighting, to keep the fighter jets safer, that it was rare.

"But," Megan lifted a finger. "All are required to be ready and able to fight. You've seen the news reports of truck drivers caught in a firefight. Nurses and doctors under fire. And so many other non-combat roles being pulled into the battles."

A memory came to the forefront of Marnie's mind and she realized the truth behind that statement. In the Army there were some units that had women in combat roles. And of course, the Air Force had female fighter pilots who had been shot down over enemy airspace. But those women chose those roles. The one that stuck out to her was a young Army private who drove a Humvee in Iraq during the earlier days of the war in the Middle East. The girl ended up in an Iraqi hospital and the terrorists tried to take her from there, but the doctors protected her. Finally, the US Army rescued her. She was banged up very badly and of course given a full medical discharge with one hundred percent disability. That was when the military started to really look at the non-combatant roles in a war zone as a possible combat role.

She had even received extra training once she made it to Germany since she could be deployed to any hot zone around the world if her interpretation skills were needed. "I guess that makes sense. For me, even though I have prosthetic toes, balance will always be an issue, won't it?"

"Come on, let's get to the truck and head back to the ranch where we can have more privacy to continue this conversation. But I must say, I'm impressed with how well you are comprehending the situation right now." Megan smiled and urged them both on toward the truck.

Declan stood outside the coffee shop and watched as Marnie and Megan stopped to have an intense discussion. He also noticed how those walking past gave them a little more space than usual. He, as well as most of the townsfolks, knew who Megan was. And if she was talking to a new woman in town, that had to mean that the newbie was a ranch resident. Since Megan was the counselor for the Crooked Arrow Ranch residents, all knew to give them some space.

Except of course for the few gossips in town. He heard, more than saw, that a couple of the regular yabbermouths were watching with interest and talking about them.

"Come on, let's go see who this new girl is." Gladys pulled on Maybell's arm.

But as they came up next to Declan he put an arm out to stall them. "Ladies, good morning. So nice to see you." He smiled at them both.

Good manners forced them both to stop and greet him in return, but Declan noticed how Gladys kept eyeing Marnie.

"Why Declan, so nice to see you again. How are those cute little sheep doing?" Maybell asked with a syrupy smile. The woman had to be at least seventy, but she tried her hardest to look younger, and acted younger as well.

Sometimes Declan wondered if Maybell wasn't a cougar at heart.

"Miss Maybell. I'm doing fine and so are my sheep. Thank you for asking. How are the plans for the Thanksgiving dinner coming along?" Declan knew that bringing up the biggest event, other than Christmas, for the year would get their attention away from Marnie. That poor young lady wasn't ready for the whirlwind of these two gossips.

Gladys, and her pink pouf, bounced with glee when she turned her gaze back on Declan. "Oh, Declan, just you wait and see. I think this year is going to be our biggest and best town dinner ever." She clapped her hands together and smiled from ear to ear.

It always amazed him how the woman's hair was so high, and so pink. Gladys loved her bouffant and she kept it in such great shape. He and his ranch hands had once thought that it was a wig, but Declan himself had seen her getting her hair washed once at the beauty salon. It was real.

And Maybell dyed her gray hair a dark brown in an effort to look younger, and flirt with all of the single men over the age of twenty-five. Declan grinned when Maybell sidled up to him and put her arm through his.

"Declan, sweetie, do you have a date for the Thanksgiving dinner yet? My niece will be in town." Maybell batted her eyelashes.

He could feel the heat coming up his neck and into his cheeks. All of the older women in town were always trying to matchmake him with their daughters, nieces, or granddaughters. He wasn't interested in any of them. "I'll be sure to stop by your table and say hi." He extricated himself from the ladies the moment he noticed Marnie and Megan moving on.

He had done his part in saving Marnie from two of the town's biggest gossips. And he had a lot of work to get done if he was going to enjoy the Thanksgiving weekend.

When Declan made it home safely, he sighed. "Matchmaking women make me nervous." He shivered.

A laugh preceded the man who walked into the barn where Declan was trying to shake off the effects of the matchmakers. "Hey, boss. I take it you just met up with the local gossips?"

"John. You have no idea." Declan shook his head and rolled his eyes.

"Well, if you were to get married, like I did, then you wouldn't have to worry about Gladys and her gang." John laughed.

"Gang is the correct term alright. But enough about the pink-hair brigade. How're things going here today?" Declan put his work gloves on and headed toward his horse.

John tried to stifle his laugh, but it came out sounding more like a raspberry. "Pink-Hair Brigade? I love it. Although Miss Gladys is the only one with pink hair."

"True, but she is the ringleader." Declan pulled his saddle out of the tack room and hoisted it over the top of the stall where his horse was patiently waiting for him.

The moment a chocolate-brown head appeared over the stall door, followed by its well-arched neck, all stress evaporated from Declan. "Ransom, my boy. Good to see you. Are you ready for a work-out?"

The smart horse whinnied his desire to get out on the open fields and let loose.

"Yes, today you will get to ride like the wind. I think we both need a little recklessness." Declan put a hand up with some oats for an offering. The horse gently ate the treat and then waited to be saddled.

With only a few moments of impatience, Declan was able to get his horse ready for a good ride. "John, I need to give Ransom his head for a bit. Which field would be best right now?"

Declan's ranch raised both sheep and alpaca. But he also had a few head of cattle, mostly for the ranch's needs. Several pastures were full of his main animals and several were always empty. But today they were supposed to rotate the cattle to field five. If they had already done so, then Declan would ride through field four. But if not, then he would let Ransom loose in five. Both fields were smooth enough to let a horse have its head without worrying about rocks or holes. His hands went through them on a regular basis to ensure the safety of all of his stock.

"The men are in the process of moving the cattle to five." John removed his hat and scratched his head. "Sorry, but we had an issue with the alpaca today. It seems Titus decided he needed to assert his dominance over the entire herd."

Declan snorted. "I take it Damien didn't like that."

"That's an understatement. I think we need to separate some of the herd to give Titus his own herd to manage. He's been fighting too much with Damien." John put his hat back on and winced. "Damien isn't taking too well to having one of his own offspring trying to take over as the alpha of the herd."

With a nod, Declan finished cinching the saddle and mounted Ransom. "I agree. The herd is large enough to split off into two now. Which is what we needed in order to protect the growing flock of sheep." He started to move Ransom out of the barn then stopped. "Wait up John. How about we hold off on separating the herd for now. I'd like to have some of the residents from the Crooked Arrow come and watch. They want to start raising a small herd themselves, and I think this could be a great teaching moment for them."

A huge grin spread over John's face. "Boy howdy! That's a great idea. I was hoping we'd get to work more with them. You know I always enjoyed Skeeter and his antics." The cowboy laughed.

"I think everyone enjoys working with Skeeter, but remember, he's now the foreman over at the Henderson Ranch." Declan flicked the brim of his hat and headed out.

The moment he was in an empty field, he clicked his tongue and gently kicked Ransom's sides with the heels of his boots. "Heeyah! Have your head my friend." Declan loosened the reins, signaling to his Morgan horse that he could ride with the wind. Both horse and rider moved as one and enjoyed the twenty minutes or so of freedom. When Declan sensed Ransom needed to slow down, he pulled back just a bit on the reins and his horse slowed, if only a little. They were in more of a regular gallop versus a free hard ride. Then they continued to slow down until they were at a standstill.

Declan ran his hand down Ransom's neck and told him what a great job he did. The entire time they were riding, Declan could only think about the horse, the ride, and the passing scenery. He loved moments like this, when nothing entered his mind other than the pure joy of the ride. It was inevitable that his mind would start to think about work, which was fine. He loved his job. It was his calling and his life. But lately, other thoughts had started to creep in, thoughts he never thought he'd want.

A wife.

A child.

Maybe even a large family.

Someone to whom to leave his growing ranch. A son perhaps? Or even a daughter if she loved the ranching life. He knew women were just as good at ranching as men were. In fact, some were better. He might not openly acknowledge that fact, but he'd seen a few women outride some of his friends. Which made him wish he could raise a daughter who would do just that, out-ranch all of the male ranchers in the region.

When an image of a certain woman crossed his mind, he had to shake his head. He barely even knew her. And she certainly didn't seem interested in getting to know him. Declan couldn't blame her for being upset with him. He was such a fool.

Of course, the pretty new woman with Megan would be a new ranch resident. It wasn't that he didn't think women needed help recovering from war. It was that he hated the idea of a lady getting injured. It might be sexist of him, but he was raised to cherish women. To take care of them, open doors, and do the fighting so they didn't have to. That's not to say that women can't do all of those things, for they can. It's just that he has too much respect for women in general to expect them to do that sort of work.

He knew that he was living in a generation where he didn't fit. But when he saw that Marnie had a cane to help her walk, he felt like a heel. Here he was totally fit and could have served, but chose ranching instead of serving his country.

Declan could still remember being in grade school when the Twin Towers were taken down. That night he told his parents he was going to join the Marines when he graduated. They were so proud of their little Marine, as they called him. But when it came time, they challenged him to get his college degree first. The Marines were paying the student loans for men and women who joined after college. It seemed like the smart thing to do, so that was his plan.

But when his father took ill, he decided he needed to stick close to home and he quit college to come home and take care of the ranch. Now, his parents were retired in sunny Florida and his dad was as healthy as an ox with a pacemaker. And he was in his childhood home taking care of the family ranch, which he loved.

He had to stop thinking about a family. It would happen in due time. He was only thirty-one after all. He still had a lot of time before he needed to settle down.

All it took was remembering Maybell and her niece and his heart froze up and he shook his head. "Never in a million years."

Ransom flicked his head and whinnied. The act and sound brought Declan back to reality. "What is it, boy?" He looked around and noticed a coyote running away. "Yes, I see him. That's rather brazen of him, isn't it? It's only mid-afternoon. He must be checking to see if we have any unprotected cattle his pack can attack." He patted his horse's neck. "Good boy. Extra scoop of grain for you tonight."

Declan turned his horse and headed back to the barn. He'd have to let everyone know that coyotes were on the prowl. They'd have to set up guards and ensure that the lambs were all protected, and the alpacas were ready to guard their sheep. He might even have a patrol of ranch hands out for a while.

With the nights growing colder and colder, the coyotes must be having difficulty finding wild prey. It was normal for them to come and try the ranches and see if any unsuspecting cattle could be easily caught. They would stay clear of bulls and larger animals. It was the babies they would go after. Even some of the older sheep they would try and attack as a pack.

Which was why the alpaca were great guards. The noises they made were loud enough to scare off most coyotes. And it was also loud enough to signal to the herd that danger was near.

The way animals worked together to protect each other still amazed Declan. God must have created them that way. He sent up a quick prayer that God would protect his herds from the coyotes. Instinctively, his hand reached down to pat the shotgun he always carried on his saddle. His scabbard was attached to the front of his saddle on his right, since he was right-handed.

All of a sudden, a gust of wind blew up and he felt the chill of winter creeping in. "Well, Ransom, looks like winter is finally approaching. For a moment, I thought we might not get any snow for Thanksgiving." He looked up into the sky and noticed the thick, dark clouds moving in. The tops of the fir trees around his ranch began to sway and he could smell the snow coming. A slow smile crept across his lips and Declan clicked his tongue to get Ransom to go faster. He wanted to be in the barn before the first flurry fell.

Not that he minded being out in the snow, but there were preparations to make if they were going to have snowfall overnight. That, and he needed to make sure that his men were prepared not only for the snowstorm headed their way, but also for the coyotes that were sure to come by. Even in a snowstorm those predators would come looking for food if they were hungry. And from the look of the scrawny animal, they were starving.

The moment the barn was in sight, Declan put two fingers between his teeth and whistled loud and long.

Several ranch hands moseyed outside to see what was up.

Juan was the first to greet him, "Hey bossman. What's up?"

"In case you hadn't picked up on it yet, I wanted to make sure everyone was ready for the snowstorm about to blow in." Declan stopped his horse close to the entrance of the barn. "And to warn you that coyotes are on the prowl."

At first, no one said a word, but they did nod their understanding of the weather. But the moment Declan said "coyotes", they all began to moan.

"Really? Tonight?" Luis, a younger ranch hand who enjoyed going out to the local honkey tonk and dancing with all the young ladies slapped his hat against his thigh. "There goes my night."

Declan and John both laughed.

"Sorry, Luis. It's going to be a long, hard night. But cheer up, next Saturday is the town's Thanksgiving dinner. It should be a perfect night for dancing with every lady in town." Declan waggled his brows and grinned at the cowboy who was barely a man at only nineteen.

The snowstorm came just as all of the men began to prepare for a cold night. They were set up to work in shifts. Declan set up the large, institutional coffee maker and had filters all ready to go with the correct amount of ground coffee in them. He knew it was going to be a long night.

"I'll take the midnight to four am shift." Declan left the men to sort out their own shifts and headed back inside his house to fix a quick dinner and watch the weather report.

On the TV the local weather girl was wearing a dress that fit her body like a glove. She looked like one of those California party girls he'd seen on some reality show and he shook his head in disgust. Where were the men in suits? Or even women in suits? Nowadays it was all about trying to grab people's attention, mostly men, with hot chicks barely even dressed.

"This is why I rarely watch TV anymore," Declan announced to the empty room. A snowstorm was here and the lady on TV looked like she was ready to head out to a warm, balmy night out on the town, instead of below freezing temps with wind chill that could cause toes to fall off.

The weather reporter showed satellite images of the storm and gave their projections for a foot of snow to fall by morning. It was going to be a tough night out on the range. Declan had heard of women who wore jeans lined with flannel. This was the sort of night something like that would be nice. However, he was a Montana rancher, and all of his kind had sub-arctic weather long johns they could wear when needed. Tonight he'd get out his Jed Clampett long underwear and be prepared with his GORE-TEX jacket and snow boots.

Chapter 4

When the incessant ringing of his alarm woke him from a warm bed, Declan groaned and wished he'd have moved to warm, sunny Florida with his parents. This was the only part of being a rancher he didn't like. If it weren't for the snowstorm blowing out there right then, he wouldn't have minded getting up in the middle of the night to take his turn shepherding his flock.

Declan chuckled at his little joke. Jesus was the true Shepherd of Life. But Declan was given a little flock of his own to care for. And he would get out of bed and take the best care he could. With Jesus as his guide, he'd know what to do.

Before getting out of his warm bed, Declan grabbed his phone off the charger on his nightstand and checked the weather app. "Of course it's a *small* blizzard out there." The app had said that it was below freezing, which was expected, but the thirty miles per hour winds were not what he wanted to see. But he knew that God would take care of them. Whatever happened was in His hands, not Declan's.

With that thought in mind, he got up and dressed in as many layers as he could to help keep him warm. He even decided to put on some chaps. The thick leather would keep out most of the biting wind on his legs. His GORE-TEX jacket and matching gloves should help his torso and hands. But even with a thick gaiter rated at below zero, his face would still suffer from the wind. The cold would be fine, but the wind chill is what would get him.

Bracing for the worst of it, Declan opened his back door and exited his warm house, head down to block some of the wind. He had to struggle to get his door to stay closed, but once that was done, he headed to the barn where a fresh pot of hot coffee waited for him. He prayed.

The moment he stepped inside that barn, he released a sigh of pleasure and pulled the neck gaiter down from over his face so that it only covered his neck. The barn was always kept warm during the coldest of nights. It wouldn't do for his horses to get ill. They could handle the cold weather much better than humans could, but he loved to take care of his animals. Declan's face tingled as it warmed up and headed straight to the coffee bar.

"Hey, boss man. I'm so glad to see you." John, his foreman, who had the shift before him, grinned. His face was red from the cold wind, but his eyes sparkled. He loved this weather. "You were right about the coyotes, I heard them calling to each other."

"Did you see them? Please tell me you shot them all. Then we can all go to bed and not worry anymore for tonight." Declan knew it was wishful thinking, but he still had hope for an early night.

John shook his head. "Sorry. They weren't too close. I called over to the neighboring ranch and let them know I heard the coyotes coming from their land. They were already out on patrol, too."

"Yeah, I called Sheamus before dinner to warn him of what I had seen." All of the ranch owners had each others' numbers for just such an occasion. Declan appreciated it when others called to warn him, as well. He realized this would be something the ranchers at the Crooked Arrow would need to start checking on as well. He made a mental note to talk to Jerod about it the next day.

"Alright, so I take it all is fine, except for the creepy coyote calls?" Declan hated the sound of coyotes when they were on the hunt. Their high-pitched laughing sound reminded him of some cartoon hyenas he watched as a kid, it still gave him the creeps.

"Of course, and here's a hot, fresh mug of coffee. To get you going." John handed Declan a mug that said, "Cowboys get it done" with the image of a rider on a bucking bronc - the image that most people thought of when they thought of cowboys or rodeos.

"Thanks, man. Much appreciated." Declan took his coffee black on nights like this and when he sipped the hot java, he sighed as the hot liquid warmed him up from the inside out.

While Declan drank his mug of hot coffee, John filled a thermos and closed the top. "Here ya go, for the road."

"Thanks, have you seen Luis yet? He's supposed to be on watch with me, isn't he?" Declan craned his neck looking to see if his young ranch hand was around yet.

Before John could answer, he heard the wind forcing the barn door open behind him. Then he felt the chilling whip of the wind roil through the building.

"Ooooh, eeee that's cold." Luis stomped his boots once he had the door closed. Then he shook the snow off his jacket. When he looked up at Declan and John, he grinned. "Is that coffee? And is it fresh?"

"Of course, but you better hurry up and get some, we need to get outside and check on the herds. The coyotes are out there on the prowl." Declan was interrupted before he could say more.

Luis shivered. "I know, I heard them before my alarm even went off. Horrible creatures. Why in the world were they ever created?"

"Beats me, but I'm sure it has something to do with the circle of life." Declan grinned behind the rim of his mug as he thought about the cartoon from his childhood and watched as Luis must have been thinking the same thing.

The kid shivered like someone had thrown a snowball down the back of his shirt. Then he went straight to the coffee pot and poured a thermos for himself. Luis tended to put a ton of sugar in his coffee, and that night was no exception.

"Hey Luis, want a little coffee to go with your sugar?" John joked.

"Very funny. I know you're just jealous because your wife has you on a low sugar diet because you're getting old, man." Luis could give just as good as he got. Then they both laughed.

Declan held up his hand. "Wait, did you say you heard the coyotes calling out from your bunk?"

Everyone quieted down the moment realization dawned on them. The coyotes were close - too close - if they could be heard loud enough to wake a heavy sleeper in the ranch hand quarters.

The full-time ranch hands had a cabin not too far from where the sheep were currently bedding down for the night. And the alpaca herd was right there with them.

"I'll head back out; my horse is still saddled. You two hurry up and join me," John called out and he ran for his horse who had been waiting to be rubbed down and put away for the night. "Sorry, Benson, but we gotta work some more." John jumped up into his saddle and hightailed it out of there.

Both Declan and Luis woke up quickly and got their horses saddled as fast as humanly possible. Thankfully, they both remembered to put their thermoses of hot coffee in their saddlebags.

Neither said a word as they worked, focused so hard on the task at hand. When they left the barn Luis was the one who closed the barn door, so he was behind Declan by only a few strides when they arrived at the sheep pen.

The alpacas were in an uproar, as were the sheep. The bleating and screeching could be heard well before they saw the chaos.

Normally, Declan's three work dogs would be out there all night helping to guard the herds, but with the snow, he had left them behind in the barn. Their legs were a bit short to be running around in the new fallen snow. He noted there was already at least five inches on the ground. Selfishly, he wished he would have left the dogs out there, they could have helped to deter the coyotes.

John had put up a standing battery-operated torch that lit the area a little bit. Declan pulled a handheld flashlight from his saddle and pointed it toward the area where the most activity was sounding from. Sure enough, there were at least six coyotes trying to get inside the circle the sheep had created to protect the young lambs. And around them were the alpacas spitting and head butting the coyotes.

One of the older alpaca males had a coyote trying to nip at his legs, but the alpaca was spitting and kicking at the oversized rodent.

Declan pulled his shotgun out and fired into the distance. The sound combined with all of the light that was shining on the coyotes got their attention. Now that humans were here, they knew they were in trouble. This wasn't the African plains where one didn't worry about the wild animals who preyed on other wild animals.

No, this was a ranch where the animals who lived here weren't wild, they were mostly domesticated. They relied on the ranchers to protect them. And the ranchers relied on the animals for their livelihood, as well as in some cases - food. It was man versus predator and man would prevail. He had to.

John and Luis both took out their shotguns as well and Declan heard a few shots ring out. He prayed that none of his stock would be shot in the confusion of the chaos unfolding on his property.

When Declan caught sight of Titus, he grinned. The young alpaca was going to make a great alpha. He had actually taken a bite out of a coyote who turned and ran away, limping.

Declan had a rule, don't shoot a retreating wild animal, unless it's absolutely necessary. In this case, it wasn't. But once the dust settled and they had gotten the herds quieted down, John reported that there were three dead coyotes in the mix.

"It's too bad the Cattleman's Club isn't still offering rewards for dead coyotes." Declan frowned when he realized that they would have to deal with the carcasses. And they would have to do it then so as to keep other predators from finding it and making an even bigger mess. "Luis, head back to the barn and pick up a few of those tarps. We can use them to wrap the bodies before we move them to bury them."

"Why don't we just burn them? With the cold ground, digging a hole isn't going to be easy. Especially in this snow." John was his foreman for good reason. The man made a great point.

"True, but we still need the tarps to move the carcasses to a different pasture. I don't want to burn them where the sheep or alpacas might get hurt." Declan looked over his herds to see if anything was amiss. His shoulders drooped when he realized that there was a good reason for his sheep to still be bleating out their discontent. One of the lambs didn't make it.

John followed his gaze and he too, felt the loss. "Oh, man. I'm so sorry." He ran a hand down his face and took a deep breath. "Maybe we bury her?"

For just a moment Declan considered the idea, but decided John had been right the first time, the ground was too hard to dig. And if they didn't dig a pit deep enough, then it would attract the attention of other wild animals who liked to eat dead carcasses. "No, we should burn her, too."

John put a hand on Declan's shoulder. "Right. Of course. Again, I'm so sorry we lost one."

"Considering how long those coyotes had to have been here in the pasture with the herds, I'm surprised we didn't lose more. We'll have to reconsider how we handle this in the future. But not now. Now, let's get the fire pit going and then get to bed. The next team can keep an eye out on the herd when they get here." Declan turned his mount and headed to the pasture next to the sheep.

"Wait up. You still think the coyotes are a danger tonight?" John followed his boss through the gate in the fence separating the two pastures.

Declan nodded. "I do. They didn't get to take away their prize. I would bet they'll be back once they think it's safe from humans and try to get their dead lamb."

Declan and John found a spot away from the simple covering used to protect the sheep and alpaca from the worst of the sun and rain. Once the fire was set, Declan sent John home to get some sleep. "You've put in more than your fair share tonight. Go, get some rest. I'll stay here and watch the fire."

"I'll stay with you, boss." Luis dismounted and tied his horse to the tree nearby, but far enough away to ensure the smoke wouldn't hurt his horse.

Chapter 5

Marnie woke to the sounds of chatter. She moaned and turned over, looking at her clock. "What!" She jumped up out of bed and almost fell flat on her face, forgetting for just one blissful moment that she wasn't an invalid. Thankfully, she caught herself quickly and leaned back on the bed.

She kept her prosthetic toes on the dresser next to her bed. The VA did a pretty good job with the look, but it wasn't comfortable enough to sleep in all night. Plus, the doctor said her foot would need the nightly reprieve. So, she always took it off when she went to bed, or got in the shower. As she sat there trying to wipe the cobwebs from her brain, she took another look at the clock on her nightstand. It was already past eight in the morning. She never slept in like that. Normally, she was up the same time as the guys, about five A.M. It was the same when she was in the Air Force, the alarm went off at five and she was up and ready to go.

But, she didn't sleep well that night. Too many strange sounds and weird laughing kept interrupting her sleep. It was like a trip she had taken to the zoo when she was a child. The hyenas laughed a lot like what she heard during the night. It was high-pitched and had an ominous feel to it.

However, she knew that the Montana mountains didn't have laughing hyenas. Bears, bobcats, and a whole assortment of other beasts that might like to take a chunk out of her, or even out of her other foot. But no hyenas. Or at least, that's what she thought until last night.

Every time she fell asleep, the peace and quiet only lasted for twenty minutes or so, then the squealing sounds would start. For a moment she thought something had gotten into the hen house, or maybe the pigs got loose? But she listened and didn't hear anything close by. It was definitely a distant noise.

Her MOS in the Air Force had taught her ears to pick up on a variety of nuances. Distance was one thing she was good at with a live sound. One not on headsets.

Marnie quickly got ready and put her prosthetic toes on. They were almost like a sock, but they had a nylon strap that went around the back of her heel to keep the piece on. Once she put her boots on, she felt better, as though no one would be able to tell what was wrong with her. Well, at least not until she used her cane.

But that was what she was here for, right? To learn how to walk without her cane. Then, she could see about finding a job. One where they would never know about her issues.

Marnie walked into the kitchen to a raucous group of men and three women. All were talking at the same time so it was difficult to understand them.

"Oh, good. Marnie, did you hear the coyotes last night?" Dakota Monahan jumped up and pulled the chair next to her back. Dakota was a recent addition to the ranch, and it turned out really well for her. They thought she had severe depression and PTSD, but it turned out she had Multiple Sclerosis and just needed a whole new set of medications. Once she was taken off the anti-depressants she really changed. Or so she told Marnie.

Marnie had only been at the ranch for a week, and didn't know Dakota back before the correct diagnosis. If only Marnie's diagnosis could have been changed as well. But, it's hard to mis-diagnose toes blown off. At least she didn't have to deal with PTSD and the after-effects of being in a war zone.

"Was that what I heard? I could have sworn it was a pack of hyenas. They woke me up too many times to count. What happened?" Marnie bit her lip, praying that no one would say they lost any animals.

"It was wild!" Skeeter Murphy, who was the foreman next door, but a recent graduate of the Crooked Arrow Ranch program, beamed with excitement. "A large pack of coyotes was out on the prowl, during the blizzard, too. They scoped out a few different ranches, but ended up attacking Declan's little herd of sheep." He stopped and his eyes changed to a look Marnie could only interpret as sadness.

"Oh, no. They didn't?" Marnie knew what was coming so she prepared herself for the worst of it.

Skeeter, and everyone else nodded. All a bit solemn now.

Jerod was the first to finish the story. "Thankfully, they only lost one lamb, but one of the alpha alpacas was slightly injured. He'll make a full recovery, but Declan thinks that one is going to be trouble." A slight laugh escaped him.

"The alpaca? Or the coyote who hurt him?" Marnie was confused and she felt the little space between her eyes tighten.

"Oh, the coyote is gone. I don't think they'll have to worry about any coyote attacks at that ranch for a while." Skeeter chuckled. "No, the alpaca." He paused long enough to put his elbows on the table. "Do you know much about alpacas?"

Marnie shook her head. "Nope, I can't tell the difference between an alpaca and a llama. I heard there is an obvious difference, but I can't tell." She shrugged.

"Well, alpacas work sorta like giant guard dogs. They are territorial creatures. And they have worked to protect the herd of sheep that Declan's raising." Skeeter paused to drink some coffee.

Jerod interrupted, "That reminds me, Declan was supposed to come over today to talk about raising sheep and alpacas here on the ranch. I'm not sure if he's going to make it." He pulled his cell phone out of his pocket and sent off a quick text.

Skeeter pursed his lips and shook his head. "I thought phones weren't to be used at the table?"

Jerod grinned. "That rule only applies to the residents. I, as the owner of this exquisite ranch, can text whenever, and wherever, I need t o."

Marnie picked up the coffee mug that someone had placed in front of her and smiled. The way everyone at the table bantered, it felt like she was back with her Air Force friends shooting the breeze over breakfast before heading off to their assignments for the day. It felt natural, almost like home.

She missed her friends.

While listening to the back and forth was fun, she was sorta interested in learning more about the alpaca and sheep. Also, what ended up happening with the coyotes was something she really wanted to know about. However, she didn't want to ask how many animals died. It wasn't that she had a bleeding heart, but any animal that died was s ad.

"Okay, okay. Quiet down guys." Dana interrupted the group. As the wife of the ranch owner, she could get away with anything. Plus, she was a fantastic cook. These guys would never say a bad thing about her. And they would put up with a lot of glares if it meant they got their meals hot and on time. "Please, someone tell Marnie the rest of the story."

Of course, the resident jokester who was no longer an actual resident jumped right in. This time, no one interrupted his story until he got to the gory parts.

"Alright, Skeeter, we are all still eating our breakfast." Dakota, his girlfriend, gave him the stink eye as she put her fork, still full of scrambled eggs, back down on her plate. "Please, don't ruin the wonderful breakfast. You know how important it is for me to eat the entire plate."

Skeeter put his hand on hers. "I'm sorry babe, I just got caught up in the telling of the tale." He turned his eyes on Marnie and she noticed his pink cheeks. "I'm sorry. I shouldn't have gone into so much detail. But suffice it to say, only one lamb died. The rest of the herd, both herds actually, only had a few scuffs and scrapes. Nothing that will cause lasting harm."

"That's really good to hear. But how do you know all of this already? With the snowstorm out there, I can't imagine anyone has been into town yet to tell the tale." Marnie decided she'd go ahead and eat the bacon on her plate. She knew that Dana prepared their own meat that had been raised on the ranch. Part of her thought she'd have a difficult time eating meat from animals they raised, but she didn't. Maybe it was because she hadn't known this pig or any of the animals that had already been butchered before she arrived.

That was one thought she didn't want to dwell on. No way was she going to assist with the butchering. Not in a million years would she even get close to the barn on those days. Or wherever they did it. Marnie didn't need to know any more about how the meat was prepared than what spices were used when cooking it - thank you very much.

"What about the humans? Did any of them get injured?" Marnie wasn't exactly thinking about Declan, but since she had only met him the day before, she was curious. And of course, she didn't want anyone to get hurt.

Dakota sat up straight in her seat. "I can answer that one. I was the one who answered the phone today and Declan and his men are just fine. Not even a scratch on any of them. Of course, they all did have a rough night out in the cold keeping watch, but other than some windburns, they're fine."

Marnie breathed a sigh of relief. She hadn't realized she was nervous for the answer until then.

Megan winked at Marnie. She just shook her head. Marnie was positive Megan was trying to play matchmaker, which was crazy since she had only just arrived and needed a lot of therapy. There should be no time for men. And Megan, as her therapist, should know this better than she did.

"Oh, hold up." Jerod raised his hand when he looked at his phone. "Declan said he'll still come by, just later in the afternoon. They have a lot of work to do this morning."

Megan grinned. "That's good. I think it will be nice to hear what he has to say about us raising alpacas, and maybe some sheep, just for the wool."

Not wanting to get goaded into Megan's matchmaking, Marnie turned back to her plate and realized that she'd already finished off the four slices of bacon she had along with half of her ham and cheese omelet. She must not have been paying much attention to her food as she ate.

"Marnie, when you're done in here, let's meet in my office. I wanted to go over your therapy plan before we start." Megan was all business now, gone was the sparkling eyes and teasing comments.

Marnie hoped that meant the therapist would stay professional in all of their meetings. The last thing she needed was to be locked in a room as the woman tried to rope her into being some cowboy's girlfriend. And for what? A couple of months, or weeks? Not her speed.

Some women liked to move fast and cycle through as many men as they could get their expensive manicures on. But that wasn't Marnie Gallagher. No siree. She liked to take her time, get to know a guy. Be friends. Her parents always said that the best foundation for a relationship, other than both being believers in God, was friendship. Her parents were friends first, then came dating. And they were the happiest couple she'd ever seen.

That was what she wanted, maybe. One day?

Marnie ate as quickly as she could, while listening in to the tall tales the men were spinning about their various encounters with coyotes. One thing Marnie knew about military men, was that when they told their stories, they usually embellished them. Like her dad when he told his fish stories. The fish was always twice the size of what he actually caught. And he would always say that he had to throw back too many great fish since he always caught over his limit.

She smiled thinking of the simpler days with her family. Since she joined the Air Force, her parents had been a bit distant. Oh, they supported her, but they always feared for her safety. So when she was injured in a training exercise, they weren't very happy with her. But that didn't mean she never missed them.

It was times like this that she missed her dad the most. He would love these tall tales of heroism that most likely weren't very accurate. But totally made for great stories.

"Remember when someone tried to scare everyone with the glowing eyes in the yard outside our rooms?" Skeeter grinned. That had been one of his pranks early on. And still to this day no one suspected it was him.

"I thought there were coyotes out there. All the prankster needed was a recording of the coyote's call and it would have seemed real." Dana shivered when she remembered that night.

Marnie put her fork down and looked at everyone. "I heard there were pranksters here, but glowing eyes outside your bedroom window? What, is this an elementary boarding school?" She did her best to hold back her laugh. The prank was funny, but she didn't want anyone to think she'd appreciate being the butt of their pranks. She would enjoy hearing about them, but not being the target.

Skeeter sniffed and sat up straight. "I resemble that remark."

This time, Marnie couldn't hold her laughter in. She let it go and enjoyed a good, cleansing laugh. "Really? You're taking pride in being called a little boy?"

Dakota put a hand up. "Don't waste your time, Marnie. Skeeter loves all attention, even when you call him a little boy."

Marnie snorted and shook her head. "Good to know." She stood, "Well, I gotta get going. Thanks for the laughs and the tall tales. Have a great day."

"Tall tales?" Tony frowned and shook his head. "These are all the truth. Just ask Dana. She can vouch for us."

Once Marnie was comfortable on her feet, she looked to Dana, who shrugged. "Yup. Things around here are pretty much as they described it. We do have a problem with coyotes, so if you're out late at night, just keep an eye out. Usually, shining a light on them or waving a large stick at them will do the trick."

Not sure what to think, Marnie's eyebrows shot up past the end of her bangs. "Good to know." As she made her way to the counselor's office, she wondered just what she had gotten herself into.

The VA therapist who signed her up for this program told Marnie that it would be relaxing and safe. So far, it wasn't either.

Chapter 6

Lunch had been a rather rambunctious affair. The men of the Crooked Arrow were all full of rumors and gossip from the neighbors.

"Did you hear about the tree that fell on the old Brown barn?" Tony Sullivan, who was still recovering from his last round of surgical skin grafts, turned bright eyes to Jerod.

The leader of the Crooked Arrow arched a brow. "Tony, you aren't excited about someone else's misery, are you?"

Tony sat back and furrowed his brow in response. "Not even close. But the Brown's had been wanting to get that barn pulled down for quite some time. They just didn't have the extra money needed to pay someone to take it down. Thanks to the storm, their insurance company is going to get rid of it for them."

Dana piped up, "Only the Lord can turn something sad into a blessing. I'm glad the Browns will get that old eye sore taken away now."

Tony, who was hard of hearing in one ear thanks to almost being killed by a suicide bomber who didn't take too kindly to women learning anything at all, least of all how to use computers, watched Dana as she spoke. He had been learning how to read lips as well as listen in with his one good ear. As long as there weren't a lot of people talking at once, he could follow along in a conversation.

But when he went anywhere, he took his service dog, Buffy, with him. She was more than a service dog, she was his true partner. She walked on his left side, the one where he lost most of his ear and hearing, and she notified him of anything coming from that side so he could turn his good ear toward it.

"Well, I for one, am glad that the good Lord tore their barn down. It was a real hazard. Any animal could wander in and a light wind could have blown the barn down on the animals." Tony took a sip of his hot coffee and continued to share town gossip with everyone at the table.

Marnie had learned her lesson earlier, with breakfast, and now she was paying more attention to her food, which was so much better than anything she'd ever had while in the Air Force. She only turned half an ear to the gossip. The fate of the buildings and animals of their neighbors was interesting, but she wasn't really invested in the folks of Montana. At least, not yet.

A rancher crossed her mind for only a second, but she wasn't interested in what happened to him, either. He was a friend to Jerod and the rest of the cowboys, and cowgirls, here at the Crooked Arrow, but that didn't mean she had a vested interest in his health and safety. Last she had heard he was well and his ranch only lost one lamb. Which sounded really good after hearing all of the horror stories over lunch.

No, she'd done her part and wished a man she had only met once health and happiness. Marnie no longer needed to think about that one cowboy.

If only God had gotten the memo.

The sound of a truck stopping close to their front door sounded in the dining room, as everyone was picking up their plates. Marnie had offered to help Dana with cleanup since there really wasn't much she could do outside after a storm like the one they had experienced. The guys said that all they were doing was checking on the animals and making sure all were fine and fed. The next day they would pull out the only four-wheeler they had and check the fences.

Marnie didn't give the sound outside much thought; several neighbors had already stopped in to make sure all of the wounded vets had survived the storm. She shook her head when she realized that the local ranchers and farmers were actually quite nice.

When the first neighbor stopped in, she thought he was coming to get an eyeful of injured soldiers. Marnie had figured the neighbor was interested in passing on gruesome gossip. But the locals weren't like that. She had discovered that by the third visitor, a Mr. Henderson, the ranchers all looked out for each other. Which included those on the Crooked Arrow.

As a city girl, all she knew was that gossip was how people passed the time, especially during a winter snow. But she had learned firsthand how wrong she had been. And if she were honest with herself, Marnie would have to admit that she was glad to know how hard everyone worked on a ranch and farm. The people here were real and honest. Almost like something out of a movie, but nothing like what she had seen on the big screen lately.

So, when she turned around after having unloaded an armful of dishes, she was very surprised to see a certain cowboy standing behind her. His light brown hair and intense green eyes sent a shiver down her spine. Marnie sucked in a breath and held it as he looked her right in the eyes.

"I'm glad to see you're alright. What did you think about our little snowstorm last night?" A slow smile spread across Declan's face and he rested one hand on his overly large belt buckle while the other one ran through his mussed up hair.

Before Marnie could speak, she needed to let the air out and take more in. After a couple of deep breaths, she shook her head. "I'm not in Florida anymore, Toto."

The deep chuckle that escaped the sexy man standing in front of her was smooth - and nice. Marnie had met many men while in the Air Force, but none of them had affected her the way meeting Declan had. One moment she disliked the brute, the next she felt all girly and wanted to swoon in his arms. She'd never do it, but the image had run quickly through her mind.

"That's for sure. Did you sleep through it?" Declan asked.

"Actually, the snowstorm wasn't what kept waking me up, it was the coyotes." Marnie instantly regretted her words the moment she saw the look of pain cross over Declan's features. "I'm sorry, that was insensitive." She bit her lip to keep from saying any more. The man had just had a whole pack attack his herd. He'd even lost a baby lamb. She needed to be nicer. Even if he had been rude when they met, she should do what Jesus would do.

Declan shook his head. "Don't worry about it. I did ask you. So, I take it the town gossip mill is in full swing already?"

Marnie sighed and nodded. "Yup. We've already had several local ranchers come check on us and they each shared different stories about what happened last night."

"Yeah, same here." Declan rubbed the back of his neck. After disposing of the coyotes he had thought to get some sleep, but after only an hour, he was back up and working again. Life on a ranch was never slow - or boring. Even in a huge snowstorm, there was still a lot of work to be done. "So, what do you think of winter in Montana? This has to be like another planet to you."

A small chuckle escaped Marnie as she recalled her first winter in Germany. "Actually, I've seen some pretty heavy snowstorms before. Just not in Florida."

"Really?" Declan's brows rose and he waited for her to continue.

"Yup, I served in Germany for a few years before my, ah, accident, sent me home." Marnie hated talking about what happened to her, even if it was just a tiny reference. She hadn't been injured in combat like the rest on the ranch had. No, she had been hurt in a stupid training accident. The sort of thing that should never have happened.

"Wow, I heard they have some really great skiing in Germany. Did you ever get the chance to experience it?"

Marnie pursed her lips. Skiing was one of those sports that she absolutely loved. But without a special device, she'd never be able to do it again. At least not without a lot of falling. She was still amazed at how much five little toes did to keep a person upright. She knew someone who had lost their little toe, and other than not wanting to wear sandals again, it hadn't affected his life one bit. Or his equilibrium. But for Marnie, it was almost like losing her entire foot. She couldn't walk more than a couple of steps without the help of her cane. But, with help, she was going to re-learn how to walk on her new toes without a cane.

"Yes, I used to ski." Marnie hoped that would be the end of that, but the man didn't seem to get the hint. Not even when she grabbed her cane and started to walk away.

"What mountains did you ski? I heard the military has its own ski resort somewhere in Germany. Garmish something or other?" Declan followed her back to the dining room and he even picked up the last of the plates and followed her back into the kitchen and put them on the counter next to the sink.

The last thing Marnie wanted was to talk about her favorite sport that she'd never get to participate in. At least, not without a huge outlay of cash for a special ski. Then she stopped her train of thought and realized that with her prosthetic toes, she might actually be able to ski again with regular ski equipment. Until that moment, she hadn't thought it was possible. But if she could learn how to manage her balance without a cane, she could ski. Especially if she used the ski poles to help her with balance when she needed it. The long skis should work to counter her imbalance issues. Maybe she could ski again. She made a mental note to ask her doctor the next time they met.

"Garmisch-Partenkirchen is a wonderful resort in Bavaria. I've skied there before and loved it." She winced but reminded herself she might be able to go back one day. Marnie closed her eyes and took a deep breath. Images of the brown gingerbread-like cottages famous in the Bavarian region flitted through her mind and she thought about the last time she had been there.

A group of female airmen had made the trip with her and they all skied their days away. The powder was unreal after the first night's snowstorm. Then the blue skies dotted with billowy white clouds had made the days perfect, but the nights were very cold without cloud cover to keep the heat from the sunshine in.

Declan tilted his head to one side and stared at the woman in front of him. He noted her tiny smile and the way her nostrils flared a little bit when she breathed out. The woman was beautiful. Especially when she was remembering a better time and place. He didn't know her story yet, but one thing was for sure, he wanted to know more about Marnie Gallagher.

Jerod cleared his throat. "Declan, good to see you. How's your stock? I heard you lost one. Are the rest alright?"

Declan practically jumped when a strong hand landed on his shoulder. He blinked twice before turning to the large man who ran the ranch. Declan was a big guy in his own right, but he'd heard the scary stories about the former special ops soldier. Even though they stood shoulder to shoulder, Declan knew if the man wanted to take him down, he wouldn't even break a sweat.

"Jerod, always good to see you." Declan nodded. "Yes, we lost one lamb, but the rest will be fine. A few scrapes and a couple of angry alpacas, but all in all, it turned out well for us. Could have been much worse." Declan had grown up in the area, so he knew from experience how dangerous a pack of hungry coyotes could be. And any animal that went out in that storm had to have been starving. Normally, the coyotes stayed away during blizzards. So he thought it odd that they came to his ranch looking for food.

"I understand that the alpaca herd worked to protect your sheep. Is that normal? Is that why you have them both?" Jerod motioned for them to move to the chairs at the dining room table. "Care for some hot coffee?"

Declan nodded. "Yes, please. It's still freezing cold out there."

As they sat down, Marnie went to the counter and poured out two mugs of fresh, hot java. Out of the corner of his eyes, Declan watched her walk along the counter, without the aid of her cane. However, he did notice that her hip seemed glued to the counter at all times. While he didn't know exactly what her issue was, he figured it had something to do with her balance. Maybe she had a knee injury? He wanted to ask, but knew that it wasn't any of his business, so just before Marnie picked up a tray, he turned his attention back on Jerod.

However, something told him to look back at the pretty veteran. When he did, he jumped up so quickly, his chair fell backwards.

Marnie had the tray wobbling in one hand while her other held onto her cane for dear life. "Oh, boy. This was a mistake." The tray teetered back and forth and coffee sloshed over the edges of the coffee mugs.

"Here, let me help." Declan took the tray out of her hands before she could drop it. He smiled at her and then put the tray down on the table in front of Jerod. When he turned back around to see if she was alright, all he saw was her backside racing out of the room as fast as she could hobble.

Declan looked from Marnie to Jerod. He scratched his forehead and asked, "What? Did I do something wrong?"

Jerod stood up and sighed. "Around here, we don't assume someone needs us to come in and rescue them. We ask first."

Declan threw a hand in Marnie's direction. "But, she was about to lose the tray, with full mugs of coffee on it."

Jerod nodded. "And she would have cleaned up the mess, like any soldier, or airman, would have."

"But..." Not knowing what to do, Declan ran a hand down his face. "I took the tray so she wouldn't have to drop it and then clean it up. I don't understand why that was a problem."

"Look, everyone here is injured in some way. Whether it's a physical injury, like Marnie's, or they are dealing with PTSD. But all of them have one thing in common." Jerod looked past Declan to where he could no longer see Marnie.

"What's that?" Declan asked.

"They are all military. In the military we have been conditioned to think we are weak if we can't do something without help. Men and women alike go through this. And those who come here seem to have it even worse. There's something about being injured and then kicked out of the service for not being a whole person any more..."

Declan interrupted. "No, that's not true. You are all whole people. And just because you can't do some of the stuff you once did, doesn't mean you are any less of a person. Everyone needs help from time to time. I've never been in the service, or had more than a sprained ankle, but I have times when I can't do things all on my own."

"And that's just it." Jerod stared at Declan.

The way Jerod glared at him, directly in his eyes, made Declan squirm. It was like he was a kid again and the principal was about to get after him for one of the pranks he had pulled, and got caught for. "What's *it*?"

"You never served. You can't understand what it's like for someone in the military to come back home injured." Jerod blew out a breath. "We are trained to be larger than life. We are these weapons of war. Even the women are taught they are invincible. But then, when we come face to face with our own mortality, or limits, we realize we aren't what the Army, or in Marnie's case, the Air Force, conditioned us to b e."

With a shake of his head, Declan blinked and opened his mouth, but shut it again. Then he said, "you're right. I can't understand. Why would the military make you think you were invincible, when no one i s?"

Jerod took a moment to gather his thoughts. "When we enlist, we go through basic training. We all receive the same training at first. The military, no matter what branch you join, breaks you down and rebuilds you in their image. When we enter the service we are a group of individuals who have had different upbringings, different experiences."

"Yeah, but that's what makes everyone so unique. And those traits bring a plethora of experiences, which in turn adds value to the group of humans." Declan stopped talking and thought about what he had just said. "If we were all the same, then we'd be like vanilla ice cream, with very little flavor."

Jerod chuckled. "Hey, I happen to like vanilla ice cream. But yes, in the civilian world, having so many differences does make for a better world. But in the military, we have to be able to act without thinking. And no matter where we trained, or what our specialty training becomes, in war we must all know exactly what to do. And know that those around us will be doing the same thing. It's how our military has been so successful."

"Well, that and all of the money. Right?" Declan grinned.

Jerod shook his head. "The money is very important - I mean look at the Russian army - they are falling apart because they don't have enough money to pay for upgraded equipment. Shoot, even the US military had a lot of issues with the first Gulf war when we sent our troops over without personal protection such as bullet-proof vests. When units were finally outfitted properly, that was when the tide turned in our favor."

"So, the money is the key then." Declan stated.

"No, not exactly. Like I said, money is important, but the heart of the warrior is more important. Look at the insurgents. They don't have a lot of money, or even training. But they all believe so fully in their cause. And they have been brought up with their beliefs since they were babies. They are all conditioned to think one way. If anyone turns against their religious beliefs, they are killed." Jerod paused, waiting for Declan to catch up.

"So…" began Declan, "when a group of warriors all believe the same thing, and think that God is on their side, or whatever deity they believe in is backing them, they are more powerful?"

"Well," Jerod tilted his head from side to side. "Something like that. What the military does is teach us how to fight the same way. We are taught that as the US, no one is greater than us. We are given a sense of importance and strength. Even those who enter the service with very little self-confidence are usually very confident in their ability to fight the enemy and win. It's why so many other countries come here to train. Sure, we have numbers and great equipment, but it's here," Jerod pointed to his head, "and here." He pointed to his heart. "That makes us superior to all of the other forces out there. Well, maybe the British and Jewish military forces are close." Jerod chuckled.

"Thank goodness we are allied with both of those nations." Declan grinned and waggled his brows. "But, back to what you were saying about Marnie. She got upset and walked away without one word just because I took the tray from her arms? But shouldn't a gentleman help a woman carry things?"

A loud roar of laughter and a clap of Jerod's hands startled Declan and he stepped back.

"Declan, you still have so much to learn about women." Jerod shook his head. "Today's woman can do it all without us men. Chivalry is dead."

"Oh, I don't know about that." Dana entered the room and put her arms around her husband's torso. "I can do it all, but I don't always want to. I still love it when you open the doors for me, or carry my bags. But," she put a finger in the air, "when a woman is injured, her pride won't allow for chivalry." Dana turned her gaze to Declan who was watching intently. "Especially from a man who had already displayed a sense of pity to said injured woman." She arched a brow.

Declan put a hand to his heart. "What? Me? I don't pity Marnie."

Dana pursed her lips and nodded. "Yes, you do. She saw it in your eyes when you first met."

"But you weren't there." Declan narrowed his eyes and thought back to that day. It wasn't Dana standing next to Marnie, but Megan the counselor.

"I didn't have to be there to know about it." Dana tilted her head to the left and watched as realization dawned on Declan's face.

"She told you about meeting me?" When would Declan ever learn that women talked about so many different things? Men would say they met a pretty lady, but then let it drop. Women, his mother used to say, would talk about every little thing that was said and how it was said. Then talk about the clothes the men wore, or any other lady nearby. Women spoke in detail, while men spoke in general. Well, that was until the topic turned to sports. Then, women were usually casual and general while men were intense and detailed. Declan and his friends always chatted about their team's stats and who might get traded before the end of the season.

"I believe you looked interested in her until you saw her cane, then you took pity on her. Am I right?" Dana put a hand on her hip that jutted out at an angry angle.

Declan could tell that Dana was judging him in that moment, and he hadn't passed muster. "It wasn't pity, more worry for her. And if I'm honest, I felt embarrassed at putting my hand out to shake hers when she couldn't."

"Can I ask what happened to her? Why does she need the cane?" Declan knew better, but he was really curious.

Dana shook her head. "Sorry, you'll have to ask her. We don't talk about our resident's medical situations."

Feeling like a louse, Declan hung his head. "Of course, I shouldn't have even asked. You're right and it's really none of my business."

Jerod put a large hand on Declan's shoulder. "Hey, man. Let's go chat about the alpaca and sheep. I really am curious to know more about them and how they can help my ranch become more self-sustaining."

Dana watched the two men walk back to Jerod's office before she realized they never did get their coffee. She went to work making up a fresh pot and took it to the men in a carafe.

Once that task was done, she headed back to the kitchen where she found Marnie cleaning up. "Marnie, you don't have to do that. I was just about to clean up my own mess."

"I know, but I felt bad leaving you to clear all of this mess alone." Marnie shook her shoulders and looked down at her feet. "And I was hoping to apologize to Jerod for the way I ran away." In her eyes, she had taken the coward's way out. And that wasn't who she was.

Dana poured two small cups of coffee and handed one to Marnie. "Sit down and join me. I know I could use a little coffee break."

The two women sat at the table and drank without talking much. Then, Dana began to tell Marnie about how she and Jerod got together.

Chapter 7

"You know Jerod's story of suffering from PTSD and why he started this ranch." Dana didn't ask, she stated the fact.

"Of course, his story is part of our orientation. He was still suffering from severe PTSD when he started this ranch. He felt if he could help even one soldier recover, then he'd feel just the tiniest bit better. Plus, being out here in the middle of nowhere he could stay clear of most triggers." Marnie looked down at the coffee cup in front of her on the table. While she didn't suffer from PTSD, she understood it a little bit better having lived on the ranch for over a week now. She'd seen one of the new guys have a rough time of it just the day before.

Dana's grip on her coffee mug tightened and her knuckles turned white with the exertion. "Yes. We started dating not long after he arrived and it was...tough. To say the least. We had a few issues, but eventually he began to heal." She sighed.

"You really love him, don't you." It was obvious to anyone who saw the couple together. And Marnie wished she had someone who loved her the way Jerod loved Dana.

Dana's grip on her coffee mug loosened and she smiled the dreamy smile only a woman in mad love could do. "Yes, I'm so glad I decided to stick with him." She averted her eyes and chuckled. "I almost didn't. He tried to get me to leave him alone. But I saw that deep down he just needed to know he was loved. And not just loved by me, but also by God. That's when his healing began."

"I know that God can do a lot for anyone who trusts in Him. And I do trust in my Lord. But I don't suffer from PTSD, so things are a bit different for me." Marnie took a sip of her hot coffee.

Dana stood up to get the pot and top off their drinks. "You know, hurt is hurt, no matter the cause or effect. You are hurting physically, yes. But you also have an emotional component to your journey."

Over the rim of her coffee mug, Marnie said, "I don't understand."

Once Dana had filled both mugs, she sat back down. "Your injury isn't just about your missing toes and learning how to balance with the prosthetic."

"Ah, yes, it is. That's exactly why I'm here." Marnie furrowed her brows.

Dana shook her head. "If learning how to balance on your new prosthetic was all you needed, then the VA could have helped you from your home. You were offered the spot here for the emotional component. It's been what – nine months since your injury?"

"Nine months and eleven days. But who's counting." Marnie rolled her eyes. She wasn't sure why she kept counting the days, but she couldn't help it. That was the day that changed her entire life, and not for the better.

"Marnie, that there tells me everything and I'm not even a psychologist, or trained counselor. I'm a part-time barista and wife to a rancher. Even I can tell you need to get your mind wrapped around what happened to you and figure out how you are going to move forward. Until you do, you won't be able to find your balance." Dana sat back in her chair and sipped her hot coffee, watching her new friend over the rim of her cup.

Marnie took in Dana's words and realized that she was right. There was an emotional, or mental, component to her healing. No one had ever told her that before. At least not in a way she could understand. The VA did say she needed something they couldn't give her, but they didn't go into details. Or did they? The conversation was a bit hazy.

She was very angry when they told her she needed to go to a ranch for more help. At first, she thought they were just trying to offload her to someone else. So, she called her parents and asked if she could come home. At first, they were all for it. Until they spoke to her doctors. Then they agreed she should go to the ranch. Was this what they were all trying to tell her? That she needed to work on, what? Learning how to cope?

With eyes beginning to fog up, Marnie wiped at her face and looked back down at her coffee mug. She didn't say anything, or even look at Dana. Then she heard the soft scuffing sound of a chair moving on the floor and she looked up to see Dana leaving the table.

No one said a thing, and when Marnie was all alone in the kitchen, she let her tears fall.

"So, what you're saying is that with a little investment we can have a small herd of sheep and alpaca and then come spring we shear them for the wool? How little are you talking?" Jerod narrowed his eyes and sat forward with his arms on his thighs.

The number Declan stated was more than just a little. "But that includes the equipment you'll need to shear the animals, clean the wool, card it, spin it into yarn, and then dye it before weaving it into whatever you want to sell."

"That sounds like a lot of work. We don't always have a full ranch."

"Really? From what I hear you have a waitlist for this place." Declan grinned. "And, you can always just shear your animals and sell the wool at market until you think you are ready for more. Just starting out that might be best." Declan pulled out his phone and brought up his notes app. "I can sell you two alpaca and six sheep to start." He showed Jerod a number for the animals.

"That might be doable, to start. Megan is looking into ways we can get more money to start our own little herd. Apparently, there are grants for those who want to raise alpaca and sheep." Jerod shook his head. "I don't know where we would be without her help. She is the reason we have had so many success stories already. And have the money to keep going."

Declan chuckled. "Yeah, I heard that there was a betting pool on how long you'd survive here when you first started."

Jerod's nostrils flared.

"Whoa now." Declan put his hands up in defense. "I didn't get in on it, I just heard about it. And told them they were wrong to bet on someone failing. But," he sighed, "you know how some of these ranchers and farmers can be. They hang out at the Cattleman's Club and get bored. It's almost like they are those crazy gentlemen from the regency era who have nothing to do all day long. I heard they had betting books in their clubs on the stupidest things ever."

Declan's little rant seemed to have done its job and Jerod leaned back in his chair *not* looking as though he was about to tear the man's head off. "I know all about it. And I was quite happy when those who bet against me lost. But, that doesn't mean we are completely in the black. I have to keep the ranch full for at least the next year just to pay for what we currently have. Adding anything, like the alpaca and sheep, will require a full grant to pay for it all. At least until we can start turning a profit from the wool."

"And that means you won't be able to afford any of the other equipment this year. But you will need to ensure there is some sort of covering out in the pastures for the herd when we have inclement weather. Make a small lean-to if that's all you can start with. And put a drinking trough in it as well." Declan nodded. "Just know that I'm here to help you. I've already given you a price I would never give anyone else. I won't make any profit on the animals I sell you."

Jerod rubbed the stubble on his chin. "Then why are you selling them to me?"

"Because I want to do my part to help. I never served in the military, but I can help veterans out here and there. This is my small contribution." Declan felt his cheeks warm and he looked down, not wanting the big, bad special ops Sergeant to see him blush.

"Thank you, I really appreciate your help. And down the road, I'm sure we'll be able to help you, too." Jerod stood and held out his hand. "Now of course, this deal is contingent on us getting the grants."

Declan stood and shook hands. "Of course, I'll hold those animals we spoke about until you know one way or the other. And don't worry about helping me out, you and your residents do so much for our town. I don't know what would have happened to the Christmas tree farm if your guys hadn't helped out."

Now it was Jerod's turn to look down at the floor. "We do what we can. And besides, it is really great therapy to help others."

Declan cleared his throat. "Well, I must be getting back to my ranch. There's supposed to be another storm tonight and I need to make sure everything is ready."

Jerod led him out of the office and back toward the front door. "Does that mean you'll be keeping guard against the coyotes again?"

"No, I don't think we'll need to do that tonight." Declan shook his head and sent up a quick prayer that the coyotes would find shelter for the night instead of looking for someone's cattle.

A soft chuckle escaped Jerod. "I have a feeling after what you told me, they won't be coming near your herd any time soon."

"Well," Declan shrugged, "I don't know how smart coyotes are. Do they learn which ranches to steer clear of?"

"I guess we'll see." Jerod opened the door and was about to wish Declan a good day when he heard footsteps behind him.

"Hi." Marnie's tentative voice sounded just loud enough for both men to hear and they turned to look at her.

Declan took one step closer to the woman he'd hoped to see again, but stopped. He noticed her red eyes and prayed he wasn't the cause of her tears. "Hi. I'm sorry if I upset you earlier. I swear, that's all I seem to do since we've met." He held his Stetson in his hands and winced. He wanted to turn away from her so she couldn't see his own pain, but knew that she'd take it the wrong way.

"No, you don't need to apologize. It's me who owes you an apology." Marnie twisted her lips and stood taller. "I still have some issues to work through, but running from a tough situation, or conversation, isn't who I am. I'm sorry if I made you uncomfortable. I'll try not to be so soft moving forward."

Jerod cleared his throat. "I've got some paperwork to finish. Declan, best wishes with getting your ranch ready for the next storm." He waved and walked away.

Marnie turned to watch Jerod leave and wondered what that was about. "Are you having a tough time with the weather?"

Declan chuckled and the change in topic helped to ease the tension that had grown since Marnie spoke. "Not exactly with the weather, but with the coyotes."

Marnie's eyes widened. "Oh, that's right. You don't think they'll try again, do you?"

He shook his head. "I doubt it. At least for tonight. But I do need to get back and make sure all of my animals are prepared for another storm tonight. I hope to see you again, Marnie."

She smiled and Declan felt that last of the tension evaporate.

"I look forward to learning more about the alpaca and sheep. Sounds like we're going to be getting a small herd soon." With a wave and another goodbye, Marnie closed the door behind Declan.

She felt better for apologizing and dealing with her issue. Marnie knew she was a strong, independent woman, but sometimes she still felt like a little girl. Didn't matter that she was twenty-seven and had seen more than most people twice her age would see.

Dana had been right, she needed to get her head wrapped around her new reality. But more than that, she needed to *accept* her new reality.

Only a few hours later Marnie would wonder what, exactly, her new reality was when the wind whipped, and she heard trees falling outside the house.

Chapter 8

"Even being from Florida, where we have gale-force winds and hurricanes all the time, I still can't believe this storm." Marnie looked out of the back window at the trees blowing around the paddock and prayed Jerod and Tony would be alright.

Dana stood next to her and had a hand to her mouth.

In the next second time slowed and everything that happened had Marnie acting on impulse with no thought at all for her foot, or even her own safety.

A loud crash sounded just as a hefty wind ripped through the paddock and brought a tree down on the side of the barn.

Marnie ran for the door and the new resident who had only arrived a few days before was close on her heels. Somewhere in the distance she heard a scream but ignored it as her instincts to help kicked in.

Marty Winters, the new Air Force Tech Sergeant, passed her up as he bolted for the barn.

But Marnie wasn't the least bit offended or exasperated. In fact, it felt like Marty's speed only fueled her own run toward those in need.

It didn't hurt that she knew he had super long legs, so of course he would pass her up. But that thought only flitted through her mind for a second, then she was focused on getting to the barn as quickly as she could.

By the time she reached it, the barn door had been flung open and Marty was inside yelling, "Anyone hurt?"

Marnie ran in and looked around. She didn't see any humans, but she did see the hole in the roof of the barn and the cows bellowing their disapproval. She made her way to them and wished Mike Blankenship was still there. He was the cow whisperer and knew exactly what it would take to calm them down.

In front of her were five cows, all moving around and ramming each other. She never knew an angry cow could ram another cow. "Wait!" She held her arms up and looked around for somewhere safe to hide. One of the cows looked as though it was breathing fire and its eyes were laser-focused on her. "I'm here to help. Don't hurt me."

One second she was trying to find a way to get out of the path of the angry cow, and the next she was on the ground in a pile of hay with a man on top of her.

"Hey," Marnie pushed at the man lying on her only to realize that he wasn't moving. "Marty? Marty!" She yelled and pushed his shoulders. "Marty, are you alright?"

The man moaned and moved only a tiny amount, but it was enough for her to push him to the side. She realized that he had saved her from being bulldozed by another cow, one she hadn't noticed. It was now snorting and bellowing so loudly, the other cows had moved away.

Marnie rubbed her hand down Marty's back, looking for blood or broken bones. There were none, thankfully.

"Ow, that hurts." The man's eyes were still closed and his face was contorted with pain, but he did move away from her all on his own.

"What happened?" Marnie kept an eye out for the cow who had mowed them both down. The last thing either of them needed was to be trampled by the mad cows.

"Bertha was charging for you, but I knew you were too focused on the other cow in front of you. So I ran interference. Only, Bertha didn't like it so she hit me from behind." Marty took a few deep breaths and then sat up, wincing as he did so.

"Here, let me help you get up." Marnie stood and offered her hands to help him.

"Thanks, do you see anyone else in here?" Marty asked once he had dusted off the hay from his clothes.

Marnie reached for her cane, but then realized she didn't have it. She looked around her and then realization dawned on her, she had left it behind in the house when she tore out of there looking to see if she could help anyone who might be injured in the barn. The moment she realized that she didn't have her cane, she wobbled on her feet and put her arms out to stabilize herself. "Whoa."

"Where's your cane?" Jerod asked when he walked over. "And what happened to you two?"

In unison, Marnie and Marty both said, "Bertha."

"Ah, yeah. You gotta watch out for that one. She's fine until the storms hit." Jerod looked over to the cow in question and shook his head. "Shame on you. Attacking the newbies like that. You know better."

Bertha mooed and began chewing the hay she had pilfered. The rest of the cows were right next to her eating away.

"Well, I guess we don't need to worry about feeding the cows tonight." Marty laughed, then stopped and leaned over. "Ow. I think Bertha might have done some damage."

"Come on, let's get back inside. The rest of the guys can get the animals away from the part of the barn that's damaged." Jerod put a hand out to help Marty, then he looked at Marnie and quirked a brow. He said nothing, just looked at her as though he knew something was different.

She bit her lip. "I seem to have left my cane inside the house. I might need to hold on to someone to get back."

"Really? It seems to me that if you were able to make it out here without a cane, you can make it back without help." Jerod grinned, but then held his other hand out. "If you need help with your balance, hold my arm as we walk back."

"No, you're right. I can do this." Marnie nodded once and followed the two men. Not two seconds later she was regretting her decision. A gust of wind blew her and she fell backwards and landed hard on her backside. "I can't do this."

A set of gloved hands reached out to help her up, but stopped short of touching her. "Do you need any help?"

When Marnie looked up, she was shocked to see bright green eyes that she didn't expect to see again for a while. "Declan? What are you doing here?" Not wanting to look a gift horse in the mouth, she reached for his hands and let him help her up. Then she kept hold of his arm as though they were a couple out for a stroll in the middle of a sunny day, instead of in the middle of a blizzard.

"I thought I should come by when I heard about trees falling all over the county. I noticed earlier when I was here that you had a tree leaning over the barn. I had forgotten to mention to Jerod that he should have that tree trimmed, or even cut down. It's dangerous to have trees too close to barns for this very reason." Declan lowered his head as another strong gust tried to blow them both over.

Marnie held on for dear life and they slowly made their way back to the house. "Well, I'm glad you came by. But I think it's too late for the tree, and the barn."

"We can fix the barn to weather the storm tonight, and tomorrow, I'll bring a few guys over with some equipment to get the tree taken care of. And I'm sure we'll be able to help patch the hole, as well. We just need to make sure the cattle and horses are all safe for tonight." Declan opened the door and held on to Marnie as she timidly walked inside.

Dana was there at the door, handing Marnie her cane. "Here, I noticed you dropped this when you ran out."

"Thank you. I don't know what I was thinking." Marnie took the cane and breathed a sigh of relief when she put her hand on it and leaned into the stability of the wooden device.

"You weren't, you just reacted to a need." Dana took a step closer. "Are you alright?"

"Yes, I'm fine. But I'm worried about Marty. He was injured saving me from a charging cow." Marnie looked around and asked, "where is he?"

"Megan took him into her office to check on him. With this storm, getting to the hospital might be difficult." Dana bit her lip and looked in the direction of the counselor's office.

"I doubt anything was broken, but he might have some cracked ribs. The cow hit him so hard, it knocked us both down. I was very lucky he got in the way." Marnie knew she would have broken something if the cow had hit her from the side. Which is exactly what would have happened if Marty hadn't been there to shield her from the hit. Sadly, he took the hit meant for her.

"Let's pray that's all it is. With this storm, I don't know how long it will be before any emergency services will arrive." Declan looked from

Dana to Marnie. "And, well, I think I might need to shelter here for a bit."

Dana took a step closer to Declan. "I don't know what you were thinking, coming over here like you did in this storm." She put a finger up close to his face, then smiled. "But I'm glad you did. Thank you. And of course, you can stay as long as you need to. But what about your ranch?"

"This isn't our first blizzard. The ranch hands have it covered." Declan took his gloves off and his outer coat. "Where should I put these? They got a bit wet."

"Here, I'll take them and hang them up near the fireplace to dry off faster." Once Dana was in the other room, Declan and Marnie were all alone.

"Thank you, again for helping me." Marnie shook her head. "Winds and rain are normal for us Floridians, but all of this snow. I don't know how you do it. Especially when the high winds are involved."

Declan chuckled. "And I don't know how you handle hurricanes."

The back door opened and wind brought in more than snow, Tony walked in stomping his feet. "Did someone say hurricane?"

"Yeah, down in Florida those are something we regularly have to handle." Marnie took Tony's coat and held it for him while he took off the rest of his snow gear.

"Try earthquakes. Those things have no warnings at all and they can shake the sense right out of you." Tony shivered.

Marnie wasn't sure if his shiver was from the cold or the thought of an earthquake. But either would make her shiver, too. "No thank you. I think I'll stick to my hurricanes. At least with those we have a decent warning."

"What are you all doing out here? Dripping on the carpet and sharing weather stories? We've got work to do," Jerod practically bellowed.

"Sorry, boss. I just stepped inside. What do you need?" Tony was all business and his smile was long gone.

"I need everyone to check all of our doors and windows. Make sure everything is locked tight. Then check the wood supply and ensure we have enough wood inside for the night. I don't want to have to walk outside again, if we don't need to." Jerod turned to leave, but then turned back. "Tony, are the animals all battened down for the night?"

"Yup, and the cows were milked, too. We couldn't do much about the hole in the barn, but with the tree still there, it should keep out a lot of the wind. As long as it holds in place." Tony began to move toward the area where they kept their wet clothes before he headed off to check windows and doors.

"I'll go and make sure we have plenty of hot coffee and tea for everyone." Marnie turned to head toward the kitchen.

"And I'll check your wood supply," Declan offered. "Jerod, how's the new guy?"

"Marty?" Jerod shook his head. "I don't know. But I think he'll be fine without the hospital for tonight. Megan is on the phone with an ER doctor going over what all happened."

As Marnie walked out of the room, she heard the exchange and winced. It was her fault that Marty was hurt. Once she checked on the hot drinks, she would go and see if Megan needed any help. She only had basic first aid training, but she had done her share of tending to injuries in the field. It was amazing what airmen could do to each other, and themselves, just in training.

That thought had her going back in her mind to the day she was injured.

Chapter 9

February in Germany was more than cold, it was downright freez-ing. But that didn't stop the Air Force from training. Marnie's company commander never backed down in bad weather. He used to say, "War doesn't stop for rain, so neither do we."

So she wasn't surprised when her platoon had to train in the snow on a very cold February afternoon. The sun wasn't shining, it was snowing too hard to even think of seeing the sun. Not to mention the high winds. At times, the snow was blowing sideways.

If the airmen she was training with had been goofing off, it would have been one thing. But with the high winds and low visibility, they really shouldn't have been training with live grenades. She blamed her company commander, at first, for not canceling the training session. Then she just realized she had very bad luck.

And of course, there was an official investigation; it was standard operating procedure, or SOP. After any training accident it was re-quired. And since the incident caused her to lose her toes and get a one hundred percent medical discharge, that later the VA ruled to be a medical retirement, a long investigation ensued. One where the company commander was exonerated, as were those directly involved.

Marnie remembered talking to her VA counselor. "I suppose it makes sense to train in that sort of weather. Captain Mayfield always said if we held out when there was bad weather for training, we wouldn't understand how to fight in a real battle during horrible weather. The logical part of my brain understands, but my heart doesn't."

Marnie's counselor, Emily, helped her to accept the situation and to not blame anyone for what happened to her. Eventually, she realized that God allows bad things to happen to good people. She knew that on Earth she probably wouldn't ever understand it fully, but once she got to Heaven she would.

Before she could relive that entire fateful day for the millionth time, her memories were interrupted when Jerod asked her, "Hey, you here with us?"

Marnie shook her head. "Huh?"

Jerod chuckled. "You had that look that we all get once in a while. The one where you're going to somewhere in the past." He arched a brow.

Marnie looked down at the mug in her hand.

"Should you be going back to that memory?" Jerod took the mug out of her hand and set it on the kitchen counter.

Marnie noticed how the grout between the tan tiles were cracked in a few places and could use a good scrubbing - with bleach. She would have to do that once she checked on Marty. "Probably not."

"We all do it, especially the new guys. Forgive me, and gals." Jerod scratched the stubble on his chin. "I don't know what is passing through your head right now, but I can imagine it might have something to do with a certain snowstorm you experienced almost a year ago."

It shouldn't have surprised Marnie that Jerod knew all of the details, including the weather. She had signed off on the doctor's sending him her file. If he was going to help her, he needed certain information. Information that she didn't enjoy discussing. "I see you've read the report of that day. This is the first snowstorm I've been in since the accident."

He took a moment to consider her words. "I'm here, if you ever want to talk about it. I'm sure you've heard a little bit about my background."

Marnie nodded. She knew he had been dealing with PTSD, but didn't know where he was in his recovery. All she knew was that God and Dana had played a bit part in his turning things around.

"One thing that I've learned, and it seems to work for everyone, is talking about it. Trying to hide your feelings and keep them all bottled up only serves to make an explosive that will blow all over the place and cover your entire life with fire, like a Molotov cocktail. And if you don't feel comfortable discussing it with me, then find someone you trust." Jerod poured a cup of hot coffee into the mug and handed it back to Marnie.

"Thanks. And not just for the coffee." While Marnie didn't want to go into it all at that moment, she knew that everyone needed Jerod, she also knew that talking about it helped. Praying also helped. And later that night she planned on talking to God about what she was feeling. "I think that for now, I need to keep busy. So I'm going to see if Megan could use my help with Marty."

With a nod, Jerod watched her leave the kitchen. He startled when only a few moments later he heard the sounds of boots on the kitchen linoleum. When he turned, Jerod was surprised to see who stood there.

"Sorry, I didn't want to interrupt, but I also didn't want to eavesdrop." Declan shrugged. "I tried not to listen while I waited."

"You could have turned around and walked away." Irritation was evident in the tone of Jerod's voice.

"I could have, but I would have made noise. I think that moment between you and Marnie was important. I did try to think about something else while you were speaking. Honest." Declan grimaced and knew that he should have done something else, like maybe putting his fingers in his ears.

"How much did you hear?" Asked Jerod.

"Enough to know that snow is a trigger for her at this point in time." Declan had met enough of the soldiers who had come through the Crooked Arrow to know they all had triggers of some sort. It was inevitable. He had also learned that it wasn't just veterans who suffered from injuries and PTSD. He had friends who'd been in deadly car accidents that also had a version of PTSD. His high school buddy, Tim, called it survivor's guilt when his girlfriend had died in a car crash, and he only had a broken arm.

"I trust that you won't talk about this with anyone else?" Jerod eyed him warily.

Declan knew that if he wanted to do business with Jerod and his ranch, he could possibly learn about things that he had no business knowing. The types of things that he would have to keep quiet about. He nodded. "I'm not a gossip."

"Most gossips don't think they are, either." After taking a cleansing breath, Jerod sat down at the table.

Declan thought about what Jerod had said. He knew plenty of gossips around town. He had always assumed they knew exactly what they were doing. And either they didn't care they were hurting others, or they just didn't realize the affects their words and loose tongues had on other people. "I never talk about the things I see, or hear, when I'm here at the ranch. It's no one else's business."

After watching Declan for a moment, Jerod nodded. "True. I thank you for your discretion."

Wanting to change the subject, and maybe cut some of the thick tension, Declan took a seat after getting a cup of coffee. "So, your inside wood pile should get you through the night. There is also plenty on the back porch, covered with a tarp, should you need more."

"Thanks, Declan. I appreciate the help." Jerod stood up and headed to the coffee pot. He took down his favorite mug, the green one with a soldier holding a flag, and filled it with coffee. When he took his seat at the table, he noticed Declan was still there. "Something on your mind?"

There was something on Declan's mind, but he wasn't going to discuss it with Jerod. At least, not yet. "Just wondering how long this storm will last." He grinned over the rim of his mug before setting it to his lips for a sip of the hot java.

They spent the next few minutes discussing what they could do for the barn, once the storm had passed.

"I've got a chain saw back at my ranch. Once it's safe to drive home, I'll go grab it and bring it back. We can at least cut up the tree, for more firewood." Declan laughed. He had seen quite a pile of firewood. He doubted they would need any more until next winter. But he supposed one could never have enough firewood on hand.

"I think I have some wood we can use to patch that hole. Hopefully, that will be enough. I don't want to think what it will cost if we need to replace the entire barn." Jerod shook his head.

Declan hadn't thought the hole was that bad. "I doubt you'll need to do anything too major. You might need to replace part of the wall, and of course that section of roof, but I'd be willing to bet my truck that it won't take much more than that."

"Be careful, I just might take you up on that bet." Jerod grinned.

When Marnie left the kitchen after her discussion with Jerod, she found her way to Megan's office and said a quick prayer that Marty would be alright. She hated to think that anyone would be seriously injured because she didn't know what she was doing.

So, when she walked in and saw him sitting up and smiling at her, Marnie's heart beat double time. She hadn't noticed before how handsome he was. Or, was it just that he could rock that messy hair-do like no one she'd met before?

"Hi, how are you feeling?" Marnie practically tripped over her words. She wanted to add, again, how sorry she was for his injuries, but she bit her lip to keep from saying any more.

Marty was tall, she had noticed his height before when they first met, and figured he was at least six feet, two inches - maybe three. He had bright hazel eyes with hints of green and gold that almost made them sparkle. She even liked his beard. It wasn't full blown ZZ Top material, instead it was maybe a few day's growth and trimmed nicely. Just what she liked in a man.

Out of nowhere, the intake meeting warning hit her hard, like a rock to her gut. There was no dating allowed amongst the residents of The Crooked Arrow Ranch. Marnie had to clear her throat and in doing so, she missed what Marty said.

"I'm sorry, I didn't catch that." She felt like a dolt, or possibly one of those silly heroines in a rom-com that she had recently watched.

He chuckled. "I'm fine. No need to worry." Marty's smile was too large for someone who had just been hit by a cow.

She narrowed her eyes and glanced at Megan, who tried to hide a giggle.

"Sorry, I had to give him something for the pain. We don't normally do that sort of thing here, but in this situation…" Megan shrugged.

Another rule from her intake meeting was that they didn't want anyone getting addicted to pain meds, so if any were needed, then Megan was the only one who could administer them. And they had to be prescribed by a doctor. They didn't even allow pot or any forms of marijuana to be used, per federal regulations.

Marnie wasn't upset with any of the rules, she actually agreed with them. She sucked her lips in and tried hard not to laugh when she saw Marty waving at her. "Is he going to remember this?"

"I sure hope not." Megan shook her head and sighed.

"Right," Marnie turned her gaze back to Megan. "I came in to see if you needed any help." She wasn't sure if there was any help to give at this point in time.

"Thank you, but I think he just needs rest and time to heal. We did a telecall with an ER doctor and even though we don't have an x-ray, we both agree that Marty most likely has been badly bruised. At the worst, he could have a cracked rib. But other than rest and pain meds, there really isn't much we can do for him. I've already put a bandage around his midsection and put ice on it." Megan pointed to the big tan bandage wrapped around Marty's midsection. He was laying on his side so she couldn't see his back, where an ice pack probably was attached.

"Okay, do you need any coffee or tea?" Marnie wasn't one for sitting around while things could be done. Plus, she needed to keep busy in order to keep memories from coming back to her. Now was not the time to get upset, now was the time to be tough and get stuff done.

Marnie was surrounded by big, tough military men and she didn't want any of them thinking she was weak.

"Actually…" Before Megan could say anything else, Marty interrupted.

"Can I get some hot cocoa?" The words out of Marty's mouth weren't slurred, but it was obvious he wasn't speaking like himself. His speech was slower, and lower, than anything she'd heard coming from him before.

"Sure, I'd be happy to get you some." Marnie turned to Megan. "How about you?"

"I'll take a coffee. Two sugars and a splash of cream?" Megan asked.

"Be right back." Marnie closed the door behind her and tried really hard to stifle her giggles. Seeing a big, strong man like Marty Winters asking for hot cocoa the way he did just didn't jive with his image. Part of her hoped he didn't remember this the next day. He would probably be embarrassed.

She certainly would.

But, she had to remember he was in a lot of pain, and who knows how much of the medicine Megan gave him. She probably had to give him more since he was such a large man. Not that he had any spare fat on him, it was that he was very strong and had a lot of muscles. Muscles that had her smiling when she had seen him flex his arm muscles the other day.

The other two tough men in the kitchen sitting there drinking and talking surprised her.

Chapter 10

Marnie stopped short and quickly wiped the smile and dreamy eyes from her face when she noticed Declan looking at her funny.

"Are you alright?" Declan asked.

"Um...yes. I'm just fine." Marnie started and stopped, then moved to the kitchen counter where the hot cocoa and coffee stuff was kept. "Just helping with some hot drinks."

"Need any help." Declan stood and made to walk toward her, but she shook her head.

"I'm good. Do you two need more coffee? I'm going to make some more, looks like this pot is just about empty." Marnie held the pot up so the men could see there was only a splash left.

"I'll take a top-off, if you don't mind." With his cup in the air, Jerod smiled at Marnie.

"Here ya go." Marnie topped his mug off, then without looking at Declan, she began making a fresh pot of coffee.

For some strange reason she felt guilty. She didn't understand why she felt that way. Other than being the reason for Marty getting hurt, she hadn't done anything wrong. Okay, so maybe ogling the injured Marty wasn't the best thing to do. But she didn't need to feel guilty over it, did she?

While she went over the idea in her head, she felt someone behind her.

When Declan spoke, Marnie practically jumped out of her skin.

"Hey, are you alright?" Declan asked, again.

Marnie felt heat rising up her neck and into her face. "I'm fine. Why do you ask?" She glanced at him out of the corner of her eye but continued to work on making coffee.

"Well, for starters, you're pouring hot cocoa powder into the coffee maker." Declan pointed at the tin can she held in her hand.

Marnie blinked a few times and got her mind out of the clouds. "Oh, right." She chuckled. Then she sat the tin down and took the filter out that was full of cocoa powder. "I...uh...guess I wasn't focused. I'm going to make some hot cocoa and some coffee." She shrugged, not knowing what to say. All of a sudden, she felt nervous around Declan.

It wasn't as though the man could read her thoughts. No one knew she had been thinking about Marty in an inappropriate way. While she knew nothing could happen between her and Marty, she didn't think there was anything wrong with appreciating how nice he looked. Or how wonderful it was of him to save her.

However, with Declan, it was different. Her right hand reached down to her side and felt for the cane. At times, she would touch it when she was nervous, or just needed something to help her feel safe. In this instance, it was a nervous reaction to a man standing so close to her. A man, if she was being honest with herself, was very good looking.

In her mind she wondered why it was that she was surrounded by such good-looking men on this ranch. Sure, there were good-looking airmen, and soldiers, back in Germany, but that was to be expected with so many thousands of military men in the area. Here? On this ranch? It felt as though just about all of the men were good-looking.

She could even remember when she first met Skeeter and thought he was a nice-looking man. A bit young for her, but still nice looking. Marnie was also very glad when she found out Tony was taken. That man, even with his physical issues, was extremely handsome. It must have been because all of these men were military.

However, Declan wasn't military. So his green eyes shouldn't affect her so much. Especially when he stared intently at her.

"What has you so discombobulated?" Declan leaned his hip against the counter next to her and folded his arms across his chest.

The move emphasized the bulging muscles in his biceps. A little shiver went down Marnie's back. She couldn't figure out what was wrong with her. She had never been boy-crazy. But lately, all she could think of were the handsome cowboys surrounding her. Was it because they were cowboys? She knew that most women went weak in the knees around sexy cowboys, but these guys were all dressed appropriately for a winter storm.

Even in the kitchen, Declan wore long sleeves and his shirt was buttoned up all the way, except for the very top one at his neck. There was nothing provocative about his attire. He certainly wasn't dressed like some of those cowboys on sexy book covers. So Marnie couldn't understand why her pulse beat so erratically around him. Or even around Marty. Her hormones must just all be messed up with the rising barometer from the storm. Or something like that.

Marnie had never been a STEM girl, so she wasn't too sure about the science behind her crazy emotions, but she did know that she had to get a hold of herself. Maybe her emotions were going crazy because of the close call she just had in the barn?

It made sense to be attracted to Marty, he had just saved her from a charging cow. Something she never thought she'd have to worry about. She was from Florida, for Pete's sake. Who in Florida ever had to worry about a cow?

But her attraction to Declan made no sense. Just a day earlier she was hoping she'd never see him again. He had shown pity for her, and she didn't want a pity date, not ever. So why was her body reacting to his nearness like it was?

"Discombobulated?" Marnie shook her head. She had to get her mind back into what was going on around her, and not keep thinking about hot men. "I haven't heard that word in a very long time."

Declan shrugged. "Eh, I happen to like a variety of words. Would you rather I said, *What has your head in the clouds*?"

This time, Marnie heard him and laughed. "Okay, funny man. Why shouldn't I be, what did you call it?" She turned to look Declan straight in the eyes. "Discombobulated? I think I deserve it after the incident in the barn."

Declan's mouth twitched and his arms fell to his sides. "Yeah, I think almost getting run down by a cow would set anyone's mind to wandering. Sorry."

"Thanks, but it wasn't your fault. It was no one's really. I just feel bad for Marty." With her mind focused, Marnie set to making coffee. And this time, she pulled the proper tin full of coffee out. Then she put a kettle on the stove to make hot water for the hot cocoa. She checked out the cocoa powder in the coffee filter on the counter and shrugged. It would be fine. There was no reason to waste it.

"What are you making?" Declan looked over her shoulder, then stood back. "I hope you aren't planning to use hot water for the cocoa."

"Why? Isn't that how you make hot cocoa?" Growing up, Marnie always had hot cocoa from a packet of powder mixed with hot water. She'd even add those little marshmallows on really cold days. However, really cold days in Florida were nothing compared to really cold days in Montana.

In fact, before heading to Germany, her coldest cold had only been down to about forty. And that was an overnight low that rarely happened in the Orlando area. In Germany, she'd had days that were down to ten degrees. And the current storm in Montana had to bring the temps to close to that low.

With a chuckle, Declan moved to the fridge. When he opened the door, he smiled over his shoulder at Marnie. "I'll show you the proper way to make hot cocoa." He pulled out a gallon pitcher of milk.

Since the ranch had their own cows, the milk they drank came from their own Jersey cows. It wasn't processed and homogenized like what one would find in the grocery store. Instead, it was processed by hand over a few days. The results would generate milk, cream, and butter. In the summer, they also used the cream to make their own homemade ice cream.

"Do you know the process for making raw milk ready to drink?" Declan asked Marnie.

Marnie scrunched her nose and said, "Eww, raw milk? Aren't you supposed to pasteurize and homogenize it first?"

Jerod laughed. "Something like that. We have our own cows, as you know. And we milk them twice a day. Then we prepare most of the milk ourselves. However, since we have so much milk, we also sell some of the raw milk to our neighbors who don't have their own cows."

Marnie looked around the kitchen, then opened the fridge again. "I don't see vats of milk laying around anywhere. Where do you keep it?"

Declan, not knowing the answer, waited for Jerod to pipe up.

"Well, we have a room off the side of the barn where the milk goes to start the process." Jerod opened the fridge and pulled out a gallon size jug of white liquid. "This here mason jar is the only one that is being prepared for cream and milk." He put the sealed jar on the counter.

Once he had the lid off, he pointed to the thick, white cream on top. "This is the cream, it rises to the top." Then he pointed to a thin line where the milk below the thick cream had a lighter color. "This is the line, but directly above it is a thinner cream, mostly what is used for coffee creamer and a few other things that I won't get into now. It also gets mixed in with the milk to make a richer flavor. But the top part, the richest of the cream, is scooped out and set aside to churn for butter. With so many of us here, and with the fact that we make all of our own meals, we tend to go through a lot of butter."

Marnie nodded her understanding. "Okay, I can get that. I also read recently that healthy eating, and I mean organic and home-grown, is best for anyone recovering from illness or injury."

Declan added, "It's actually good for everyone, not just those at risk. I also tend to eat as much direct from a farm as I possibly can." He grinned. "Of course, I do my share of eating at the diner in town, too. But to be honest, most of their meat and produce come from area ranches and farms. So technically, it's not as processed as most diner f ood."

Not wanting to offend anyone, Marnie held her tongue. Instead she just nodded and looked at the glass jar. "So, how do you process the milk to drink here?"

"I'm glad you asked. Maybe this is something you can help us with while you're here." Jerod put the jar back in the fridge, then sat down at the table to describe in detail how to make raw milk ready.

"First, you have to make sure your hands are clean, as well as your work station, and any equipment you are using. It's very important to not add any bad bacteria to the milk while it's in process." Jerod took a sip of his coffee. Then he listed the steps.

"Cover the opening of your glass jars with a cheesecloth, you'll want to drain your milk through that first. It's to get any outside contaminants that may have floated in while milking the cow."

"Then you put the jars in a fridge for at least twenty-four hours to allow time for the cream to come to the top."

"After that, you scoop the cream out and put it into another clean jar. Put that aside."

"Then what's left is the milk with some extra cream, or fat, to give it a sweeter flavor. That milk can then be processed for drinking. Some will drink it as is, but we prefer to pasteurize it first. That entails boiling the milk at one hundred and sixty-one degrees for at least fifteen minutes."

Marnie couldn't believe all of the work that went into making their own milk. She shook her head. "I never knew how much work went into working a ranch. Do you buy anything from the grocery store?"

They all laughed, and the men nodded their heads.

"Well, we certainly don't make our own sugar or flour." Jerod stated.

Declan added, "there are quite a few ingredients farmer and ranchers don't make themselves but are used to make food from scratch on a daily basis. Our general store gets plenty of people spending their hard-earned money in their store."

"I guess that explains why the general store sells so many other things, besides groceries." Marnie hadn't really thought about it. Coming from a big city, she just bought her food stuff from the local grocery store. Once in a while she would go to a local farmers market and buy fresh produce and honey, but that was about it. All of her meat came from either a big box store or the local grocery store. The idea of growing anything herself, or raising an animal to butcher, had never crossed her mind.

"I can see from that strange look in your eyes you are finally starting to see what it is to live out in the country." Jerod stood up to fill his cup with the freshly brewed coffee. "The coffee is ready, you might want to work on the hot cocoa now."

"Oh, right." Marnie looked to Declan, then back at the soup pan on the stove. "How do I boil milk for hot cocoa? I always thought you weren't supposed to cook milk by itself."

Declan tilted his head. "Actually, we won't boil the milk. We will heat it up until right before it begins to boil. Then add it to the mug with the cocoa powder in it." He poured some of the fresh milk into the pan and put it on the stove.

Marnie's head was full of all of the new things she had learned in just one week on the ranch. The most important, was to always keep an eye out for ramming cows. Or was it charging bulls? Either way, she needed to keep a better eye on everything around her.

It was almost like being back in her listening center. Back in the Air Force, she didn't look at anything in particular, but her ears were always up and listening to any sound she picked up. She spent time monitoring various frequencies and listening for key words in English and Russian. Or any other language that might catch her attention.

If something was in a language she didn't understand, she would record it and flag it for someone else to listen to and then disseminate what was important. Most of what she heard wasn't very important. However, there had been times when she picked up enemy chatter. Those conversations were always recorded, translated if needed, and then forwarded on to the proper person in her chain of command.

Even though the Cold War was technically over, she had heard enough Russian conversations to know that it really wasn't. She hadn't realized it at the time, but she had picked up on early troop movements that aided in the Russian attack on a prominent Eastern European country that was working toward membership in NATO. Of course, it was also just before her accident.

Her former unit was still deep in listening mode with the war still ongoing. Marnie felt that was the hardest part about being medically discharged - she was no longer able to help her country assist with the war effort for an allied nation. She knew her friends were busy listening and translating all sorts of important data surrounding troop movements, battle plans, and possibly even the movements of high-ranking Russian officers.

Her counselor told her she needed to stop watching the news so much, and she had. Now, she just looked at weekly updates. But still, her ears itched to listen in on what was happening, as it was happening. The news always got it wrong. Or they were fed bad information. Either way, it wasn't the same as being in the thick of it.

Maybe, being on a ranch could be similar. She could learn to train her ears for the animals. Then, she'd never be blindsided again. And no one else would have to get hurt in her place.

She had made up her mind. "Actually, I was hoping to work more with the animals directly. Is that possible?" Marnie smiled at Jerod, praying that he wouldn't see through her motives. She wasn't really sure if the reason she wanted to work with the animals was a healthy one, but to her, it seemed logical. She had a skill. One that could be useful on a ranch. All she needed was some self-training.

Then maybe, just maybe, she could use her military skills for something on the outside.

Jerod frowned when he looked at her expectant face.

Or not...

Chapter 11

"Marnie, do you understand how physical the work is with the animals?" Jerod schooled his features and looked Marnie directly in the eyes.

She noted how he had sat taller when he asked her that question, and his face went blank. Almost like he was about to begin an interrogation, or something. Marnie wasn't sure what he was getting at, but she figured he had understood her motivation. Even though she had never talked about what she did while in the Air Force, or that she hated the fact she had to leave her career behind.

It really wasn't fair. She didn't need to walk normally. A military intelligence listener and translator didn't actually go into the field. They could either be up in an airplane flying around listening in on top-secret communications. Or they could be back in Germany sitting at a desk all day long listening in.

While Marnie had done both, she spent most of her time behind a desk. On the ground. Not using her legs or feet for anything. When she had made that same exact argument while still in the hospital, her commanding officer had reminded her that everyone in the Air Force, no matter their job, had to be battle ready. That was why everyone trained for battle. He had recognized the fact that most airmen never saw battle, but they still had to be ready.

In that moment with Jerod, it was almost as bad as the moment she realized there wasn't anything she could say, or do, to stay in the Air Force. Marnie stood tall and prepared to defend her desire to work with the animals. However, she didn't get the chance to say a thing.

Declan looked between the two and decided he needed to jump in. "You know, it's not common knowledge, and I'm totally not being sexist here, but a woman's touch always helps with the alpacas. They are very territorial and the alpha males don't work too well with alpha men." He glared at Jerod.

The former special ops soldier turned his head and opened his mouth, then closed it, only to open it again to say, "what? You think I'll scare off the alpacas?"

Declan laughed. He couldn't help it. "No, I think the alpacas might scare *you* off."

"Pft. That's absurd. No animal scares me off, not even our bulls." Jerod waved a hand in front of his face as though he was swatting a fly away.

Marnie arched a brow. The tension was ratcheting up again. One thing they didn't have in short supply was the feeling in the air that was as thick as pea soup when the men got on their soap boxes. She thought about it and nodded. "I don't take any offense to that statement. It's a proven fact that some animals do respond better to females. We send out a pheromone that can calm the wild beast." She grinned.

Now both men were laughing.

Declan chuckled and nodded his agreement. "That is so very true. Look, Jerod. I can help Marnie learn how to interact and take care of the sheep and alpaca if you agree." He paused, about to say something about her cane being a good thing, but thought better of it.

The shepherds of old used to use a shepherd's crook to help manage and protect their herd. While Marnie's cane didn't have the C-curve in the old shepherd's crook, it was still sturdy enough to fend off wild animals and also help to move sheep, or alpaca, where she'd want them to go.

However, he knew she was still closed off to anyone talking about her cane. Or maybe it was just him she didn't want to talk to about it.

Jerod's nostrils flared. "I don't want a repeat of what happened today. I know you aren't accustomed to being around wild animals, and it is dangerous. Even sheep can hurt you."

Marnie hung her head. She turned back to the stove to see that the milk had already begun to bubble up and she pulled the pan off the hot stove. Thinking about what Jerod had said, she began to pour the milk into the mugs for hot cocoa. She had also made one for herself, since it was so different from any hot cocoa she had ever made.

Once the cocoa was stirred and the mini-marshmallows added, she looked for a tray to help her carry the drinks back to Megan's office. She could have made two trips, but she didn't want to have to come back. Or look like she didn't know how to carry three hot mugs. If only she didn't need her cane. Just one more reason for her to really focus on whatever Megan was going to do to help her get rid of her dependence on it.

"Marnie," Jerod's voice was soft. "Please, let's discuss this. My first priority is to ensure everyone's safety here. I don't want you to get injured."

She slowly turned around. Marnie had one hand on her cane to balance her and in the other she had a mug of hot cocoa. She took her first sip and her eyes widened. "Wow, Declan, you weren't kidding. Milk really does make a difference."

It wasn't that she wanted to change the subject, it was just that the hot cocoa was that good.

"See, I told you so. Listen to me, kid and you'll learn a lot about life on a ranch." Declan winked and Marnie felt her stomach do somersaults.

She realized he really was a good-looking man. Not as handsome as Marty, but close.

"Okay, okay. I'll think about it." Jerod said as he watched the two and realized there might be something between them. He grumbled something under his breath, but the other two in the room didn't hear him.

"I have to get these drinks to Megan and Marty. If you'll excuse me." Marnie put the drinks on a tray and then she balanced it on one hand, just like a waitress would do in a busy restaurant. Using her cane, she kept her balance the entire time.

When she made her way to Megan's office, she realized that Marty didn't jump up to take the tray from her. Instead, he went back to the table and sat down to drink his fresh cup of coffee with Jerod. "Maybe he doesn't think I'm an invalid, after all."

Declan watched Marnie walk away with the tray perched on her hand out of the corner of his eye. He wanted nothing more than to jump up and take the tray for her. But he had learned his lesson. She needed to do this. And he needed to let her.

Jerod grinned wide and shook his head. "I should rename my ranch. Maybe call it the Lucky Hearts Ranch."

Declan turned back to the man at the table. "Huh?"

"Nothing." With a grin, Jerod took another sip of his hot coffee.

Chapter 12

By dinner, the entire house was restless. Normally, they would all be outside working, or in the barn, until dinner was ready. But with the snowstorm, all anyone could do was make sure there was enough wood on the fires in the rooms that needed it, and watch.

"I'm bored. Surely there's something we can do? Can we get started on repairing the barn yet?" Dixon had been at the ranch for a while now and was about to be released. Back in the Middle East, he had been involved in an explosion and lost one leg. In the beginning, he had a hard time with learning how to walk again. Then, he also had to deal with PTSD, something he would probably struggle with the rest of his life. But he was strong and more important, strong-willed, which helped him to begin healing and learning how to cope with his triggers.

Jerod stood up and paced the living room. He, too, had been a bit fidgety all day. "I hear ya. But we might want to look at this as a day of rest. We don't get too many of those here on the ranch."

With the animals all fed, there really wasn't anything left for them to do. The storm outside was still blowing too strongly for anyone to be outside if they didn't absolutely need to be.

"Why don't we try playing a game?" Dana stood up and walked to the cupboard on the side of the room. She pulled out a few decks of cards and a couple board games. "Does anyone like to play..." she looked at the games, "Settlers of Catan, Ticket to Ride, Monopoly, or Phase 10?"

"How about some poker?" Dixon asked.

"I love Settlers. Anyone else want to play?" Marnie grinned and walked over to take the box from Dana. "Do you play?"

With a shake of her head Dana stated she had never played.

"Really? Whose game is this?" With the box in hand, Marnie walked over to a card table that Jerod was setting up in one corner, near the windows that looked out back. She glanced through the curtains to see the snow was still falling, and didn't look to be letting up any time soon.

Declan walked over and joined her. "I've never played this one, but my family has been playing Ticket to Ride for years. Have you ever played that one?"

Marnie looked at the box in his hands and shook her head. "Nope, but how about we play one game of Settlers, then one of Ticket?"

"Sounds good to me." Jerod grinned and sat down at the table.

Dana joined them and took the box from Marnie and opened it up. "Should I read the instructions? Or can you teach us all?"

"If no one knows how to play this game, how did it end up here?" Marnie sat down and took the resource cards from the box and began separating them. Someone had mixed the cards all up and she had to separate every wheat, wood, brick, sheep, and ore before they could start playing. "Why don't you help me to separate the cards."

Marnie set up the different resources in the center of the table and everyone picked up a stack and started sorting.

"I take it this isn't part of the game?" Declan asked.

With a chuckle, Marnie shook her head and launched into the rules of the game and what the resource cards were for. "And you'll have to pick a spot to start with your first settlement. I generally like to be on wood and brick intersections to start. But it also depends on the numbers." She pointed out the numbers that she had put on each of the board pieces. "Sixes and eights generally are rolled the most on dice, so it is good to put a settlement on a corner of a six and an eight when you can." She placed one settlement on a corner that had three numbers touching it – a six, a nine, and a three.

Declan looked at the board and tilted his head. "So, when a six is rolled, you will get one wood resource card? Because the six is sitting on top of a wood?"

"Exactly." Marnie nodded and continued explaining the game. "Okay, for this first round, let's just play with our cards showing so I can help you all figure it out. After a few rounds if you want we can reshuffle the board and play for real."

Jerod shrugged and Dana grinned.

About halfway through the game, Marnie realized why the ranch had it in the first place. "Jerod, you dog! You are a Settlers fan, aren't you!" Marnie laughed and shook her head.

Jerod already had the longest road, with six pieces in a row. He also had three settlements and was about to turn one into a city. "Back when I was stationed overseas, we used to sit around and play this game for hours. It was the only thing that would take my mind off of what we just did, or were about to do." A dark cloud covered his face and he looked outside.

Dana put a hand on his arm and squeezed. "I'm here."

Jerod winced and patted Dana's hand. "Thanks."

Declan and Marnie exchanged a glance. No one said anything until Jerod broke the silence. "Sorry about that. Sometimes memories come back at the oddest times."

"Do you want to keep playing?" Marnie wasn't sure if playing this particular game was good for Jerod, or not. If it brought back bad memories, she didn't want him to have to play it anymore.

"Sorry, I didn't mean to be a downer. Let's keep playing. I have a lot of good memories with this game. That's why I bought it when I opened the ranch. The board always changes so you never play the same game twice." Jerod picked up the dice and rolled them. "It was my turn, right?" He grinned and chuckled when he noticed that his roll got him the ore he needed to upgrade.

Dixon walked over to the table and watched the game for a few minutes. "Say, Jerod, what's happening with the tree farm this year? And what about the town's Christmas celebrations? Will all of this snow hurt any of the plans?"

Everyone at the table stopped what they were doing and looked at Dixon. Marnie knew they had some Christmas events they were all going to help with, but she hadn't learned exactly what she would be doing yet. Her plan had been to work on the ranch and not be out and about all over the countryside during the winter.

Dana raised her eyebrows and looked at her husband. "Yeah, Jerod. What's the plan this year?"

Jerod practically snorted when he looked at the innocent expression on his wife's face. "Honey, you know exactly what the plan is. In fact, you had a hand in the planning."

Dana put a hand to her chest and feigned innocence. "Who? Me? I don't think so." She shook her head. "The Christmas celebrations off ranch have always been your domain, not mine."

Dixon chuckled. "Dana, we all know that you love Christmas just as much as everyone else. I'm actually surprised you haven't taken over all of the Christmas planning for the town."

"Nope, not me. I'm too busy with taking care of things here and working at the coffee shop in town." Dana grinned, but everyone knew she was having fun.

"Okay, so I'm the newbie here." Marnie held up a hand to interrupt the banter. "What all goes on for Christmas around here?"

The game had been forgotten and all of the ranch residents pulled up chairs or stood by the gaming table and started talking all at once. At least those who had been here for the past Christmas events.

The only two who hadn't been around for the last Christmas were Marnie and Marty. But Marty was asleep in his bed. Even Declan grinned as though he knew all about the seasonal events, and he wasn't even a resident at the Crooked Arrow.

"I sure hope you fill up the rest of your spots here at the ranch before Thanksgiving. Your help is what has made Christmas in Frenchtown so successful and fun." Declan stated.

"I don't know about that. We have our own Santa and Mrs. Claus here, so I think they deserve most of the credit." Jerod worked hard all year long, but the Clauses were the hardest workers of the Christmas season. While Jesus was the heart and soul, Santa and his wife were the visible faces of the season.

Dana practically bounced in her seat, anxious to tell everyone what they had come up with this year. "It's going to be so exciting! I can't wait for practice to start Thanksgiving weekend."

Now, Declan looked just as confused as Marnie felt. "What practice?" He narrowed his eyes and looked between the grinning couple.

"Dana, you tell them." Jerod waved at his wife to continue the story.

"Okay, okay. Quiet down everyone." Dana clapped her hands together and waited for all to give her their undivided attention, as though they were little kids, and not grown men and women.

Megan entered the room and sat down on a sofa near the group.

Before Dana could start, Marnie noticed her and asked, "How's Marty doing?" She bit her lower lip, hoping and praying that the man was healing.

Chapter 13

With everyone looking her way, Megan sat up straighter and cleared her throat. "Marty is resting comfortably. He should be good by tomorrow, just sore for a few days. I recommend light duty until his ribs are no longer hurting him."

"Good idea." Jerod added, "getting run down by a cow isn't something to underestimate. I've been where he is and it can hurt a lot."

Dana nodded. "I remember." Then she shivered.

"I won't soon forget the experience, either. And I wasn't the one hit by the cow," Marnie added.

Declan's nostrils flared. "No, but you were the one who was hit by the big man who had been hit by the cow."

"He did save me, didn't he?" Marnie nodded and grimaced. "But I'm fine, only a few scrapes and small bruises on me. Nothing like what Marty experienced."

"Thank the good Lord." Dana shook her head. "I'm just grateful that no one was seriously injured. In a snowstorm like this, we would have had a tough time getting medical help for anyone."

Megan clapped her hands. "Alright, now would be a great time to share the Christmas plans."

Marnie had to agree. The mood had turned rather somber, and she wanted the gaiety to return to the room. Even with the snowstorm raging outside, they had managed to have some fun, and everyone was joking and having a good time.

That was until the conversation turned serious. But Marnie didn't have to worry for long, since Dana was more than willing to talk about Christmas.

"So, we always help the Christmas Tree Farm out. The past two years we have had quite a few residents who could help out with cutting trees, selling trees, and various other needs around the farm. And we will still help where we can, but we have also agreed to help the city with their celebrations." Dana stopped to take a drink of her water.

"I know we don't have a full ranch today, but within the next week we will. Although, since so many are new to the ranch, I'm not sure how many will be ready to help, or even if they can physically do what's needed." Jerod jumped in where Dana left off. "I spoke with Cody and Joseph Makinaw, who own the tree farm, and they had planned to hire some of the local teens to help out this year since their farm was doing so much better now."

"That's good to know." Dixon had worked on the tree farm since his first Christmas at the ranch. "I really have enjoyed working on the Christmas Tree farm. Will you need me somewhere else this year?"

"Actually, I was hoping you would lead whatever team we have for the tree farm." Jerod rubbed the stubble on his chin.

Dana took over. "And I was hoping that Marnie might be interested in working with me on the new project we have this year." Her eyes landed on Marnie and lit up. "We are going to put on a live nativity at the community center in town!" Dana clapped her hands together and waited for everyone's reactions.

The guys smiled, but none of them seemed very excited.

However, Marnie grinned from ear to ear. "You know, I haven't seen a live nativity since I was a kid. That is so much fun! I can't wait to help out. Thank you."

"What's the difference between a live nativity and a regular nativity?" Declan asked.

Marnie chuckled, but didn't respond. She waited for Dana to answer since there were many ways it could be done, and she wasn't sure yet how Dana had it all planned out.

"Well, usually, instead of setting up fake animals, a church will do it outside, or in a barn, and use real animals. I've seen it done with live camels, sheep, goats, and even a donkey for Mary to ride on." Dana then went on to tell more about what she wanted to do and she even hoped they would have a real baby to use since Mary was going to be cast using a teenage girl, instead of a little girl like most plays did.

Declan began wagging a finger. "You know, there is a family who recently had a baby, and their oldest is a teenage girl. Have you spoken with the Pendleton family?"

"No, I don't know them. Can you introduce us?" Dana pulled out her phone and opened her notes app and began writing down the information Declan gave her. "Do they attend our church?"

"No, they are members of the Catholic church. But I'm sure they'd be happy to help. Have you cast your Mary yet?" Declan stood up to refill his coffee, then asked if anyone else wanted a refill.

"I'll help." Marnie stood up and followed him into the kitchen.

Dana was right behind them. "I haven't had the tryouts yet, I was planning on having them over Thanksgiving weekend. Since most everyone will be in town anyway, it would be a great time to do it."

"That's smart." Declan stopped inside the kitchen and waited for Dana and Marnie to get everything together for more coffee.

They all continued to chat about the details of the live nativity until Marnie asked about a camel.

"Camel?" Dana put a finger to her chin and thought about it. "You know, I don't think we have any camels around the area. That's a good question."

"You could use alpacas, as long as no one was going to ride them." Declan offered the use of his alpacas and sheep for the play.

"Thank you, Declan. That's very nice of you." Dana grinned and looked between him and Marnie. "I think the two of you should work on the animal part. See what we need and who can offer us the use of their animals. Then of course, work with them to make sure the play goes off without a hitch."

"Me?" Marnie pointed to her chest. "I don't know much about animals, especially barn animals."

"But Declan does." Dana nodded toward the alpaca wrangler.

"I know alpacas and sheep, but nothing about donkeys." The man took a step back and stared wide-eyed at Dana.

"The donkey is only needed for one scene. I think with your knowledge of horses, you can handle that much." Dana's eyes sparkled as she looked between the two. "Besides, you'll get to work with Marnie for the next five weeks."

He blinked a few times, then a slow smile spread over his face. "Okay, I think I can handle that."

The rest of the evening was spent with the three of them reviewing the script that Dana had received from another church who had put on a live nativity the past few years. Then the snow let up and everyone went outside to see the damage.

Jerod whistled.

Dixon rubbed his hip on the side where he had a prosthetic.

Marnie gaped, open-mouthed at the scene before her. "There must be five feet of new snow on the ground."

"I'm almost afraid to see the damage to the roof of the barn." Dana shook her head.

In the area directly behind the house, was a winter wonderland with a very light snow continuing to fall as all stood in place looking at white. Everywhere they looked it was white. Even the evergreen trees were covered in fluffy white stuff.

One couldn't even tell where the fence posts were unless you looked really hard. The outline of the barn could be seen, but that was mostly thanks to the protruding tree sticking out of the roof. Thanks to the steep angle of the blue tarp, there was little snow sticking to the slick tarp and it acted as a beacon for where the barn was located.

"This looks like something out of a Christmas movie." Marnie took a step off the back porch and raised her hand, palm up, to catch a snowflake as it drifted down. "I can't believe there is any snow left to fall."

Megan shrugged. "Well, it looks like we are going to have plenty of work for everyone to do over the next few days."

"But, Thanksgiving is less than a week away." Dana complained. "We still have so much to do to get ready for the community dinner, not to mention, our own."

"I think I can help. I'll see about bringing over a couple of my ranch hands tomorrow, as long as the roads are passable, and we can probably get the barn patched up in a day with all of us working on it." Declan pulled his phone out and noticed he didn't have any reception.

Jerod watched and almost laughed. "Yeah, out here when it snows like this, we usually don't have cell reception. Come on back inside and let's see if we have Internet. If so, you can hook up to my Wi-Fi and see if you can get a signal that way."

"Thanks." Declan raised his hand with his phone and followed the group back inside.

"Wow. Do you get those types of storms very often?" Marnie asked.

"Not too often, but a few a year." After taking her coat, hat, and gloves off, Dana offered everyone more hot tea, cocoa, and coffee.

It was already after nine at night, but most weren't ready to sleep yet. There was too much excitement from the storm, and everything they were going to have to deal with the next day.

Jerod put a strong hand on Declan's shoulder. "Well, it looks like you'll need to stay the night. There's no way the county will have the roads cleaned before dawn. I'll show you to an empty bunk."

Chapter 14

Declan didn't make it home until almost noon, thanks to the slow work by the snow patrol. Instead, he spent the morning assessing the damage to the roof of the barn and helping the guys at the ranch to get the tree moved and the tarp back on top.

"Thanks, Declan. Your help was greatly appreciated." The leader of the ranch smiled his gratitude.

"It's a good thing you had a chainsaw. Once I get home and get cleaned up, I need to check my place out, then I'll call you with an update on when I can be back to help fix your barn." Even though Declan was confident his place held up just fine, he still felt the need to check the place over himself. It was a very rare day when he slept away from his own ranch. He had great help, but he still didn't want to leave anything up to chance.

As Declan drove away, he kept thinking about one person in particular, and her dazzling hazel eyes. Marnie had stood by and said nothing when he left. But she did give him a small smile when he looked back over his shoulder before exiting the ranch. At least she had stopped scowling at him. So that was progress, he supposed.

The drive home was slow, thanks to all of the snow still on the road. Most of the roads had been cleared, but the one leading to his house hadn't been done yet. Thanks to his one-track mind, he hadn't put on the snow plow he normally drove around with before heading to the Crooked Arrow.

So, when he happened upon a snow drift taller than the hood of his truck, he had to stop and get out his snow shovel. Thankfully, he kept that in his truck all winter long. Declan hummed the tune of "Jesus Loves Me" while he worked on shoveling a path through the drift.

About thirty minutes into his workout, his ears perked up. When he lifted his head to see what the sound was that had caught his attention, a big grin spread across his face. His work would go much faster now that his snowplow was cutting a path for him.

Declan raised his shovel to let John Mason know exactly where he stood. The truck with his plow attached to the front stopped and a cowboy hat waved at him. Knowing that his ranch foreman would make short work of the snow, Declan jumped back into his truck and turned it on to get the heater going. He felt the pins and needles work through his fingers and then his hands, as the feeling began to come back while he rubbed them in front of the heating vents. "Oooo eeee, that's one cold day out there." He blew into his hands before putting them back up against the vent.

Within twenty minutes Declan was home and telling his tale of adventure to John and Juan. "I take it all went fine here? No issues with the herd or any falling trees?" Declan knew that if there had been any issues the men would have handled it. But more importantly, they would have called him.

"We lost power for a few hours last night, but that's normal. Luis started the generator and we all stayed in the main house with the fire blazing all night long in the family room." The ranch foreman nodded toward the large room where blankets and pillows still lay on the couches.

Nodding, Declan headed toward the room in question. "I'm glad you all stayed here where you could use the generator and the fireplace to stay warm all night." He eyed the mess the men left, but said nothing about it. Instead, he focused on business. "Has anyone been out yet to check on the animals?"

"Yes." John picked up one of the blankets and began folding it haphazardly before setting it on the couch. "Luis is out in the barn now ensuring the horses are all fine. Earlier this morning we all went out and checked on the herds. Their wool kept them warm."

Juan chuckled and added, "and a few of them huddled close together under the sunshade. It worked well to keep the snow at bay. There was snow all over, but at least most of the area under the covering only had a thin layer."

"Good to know it worked on that storm." Declan shook his head. "I need to clean up and then I want to take a look around. If everything here is fine, I'd like for us to head back to the Crooked Arrow and help them with the roof of their barn."

Juan rubbed his long beard. "I reckon we got enough lumber to help them. As long as the damage isn't too bad."

"That's what I thought, too." Declan headed toward his room. "Do we have hot water?"

Both men laughed. "There might be some by now."

The ranch's hot water tank was heated with propane, but it wasn't very large. If his men all showered at his place, it would take some time for the water to heat up, especially in this cold.

"Yee-ow!" Declan exclaimed and jumped out of the shower. There had been one little drizzle of warmish water, then it turned freezing cold. In fact it was so cold, he wondered if the water came directly from the well and bypassed his hot water heater.

In the distance, Declan heard his men laughing.

John yelled out, "Gotcha!"

Grumbling under his breath, Declan put on a clean pair of sweats and headed out to see what his bumbling ranch hands had done to his hot water. "Very funny." If he wasn't so cold, Declan might have laughed. They turned the hot water valve to 1 so that only cold water would come through.

"Hey, bossman. That's what you get for filling our coffee tin with used coffee grounds. Never mess with a man's coffee." Juan tsked and walked away, leaving Declan to fix the hot water heater all by himself.

While he waited for the water to warm up, Declan made a fresh pot of coffee and sat down to his lunch. Once he had finished his roast beef sandwich, cole slaw, and chips, he figured the water was warm enough to get started.

This time, he felt the stream of water before getting in his shower. While it wasn't hot, it was warm enough for a quick shower to rinse off the past thirty-six hours. Later that night he'd have to take a long, steaming hot shower to relax his muscles.

"Alright, let's agree to leave coffee and showers as sacred. No more practical jokes in those arenas. Fair?" Declan grinned, knowing he had gone overboard with his practical joke. He never should have messed with their coffee supply. A cowboy lives on coffee, especially in the cold months of a Montana winter.

But he would have to retaliate for their messing with his hot water. If he didn't then they would think they bested him, and he couldn't have them thinking that. He'd find a better way to get them back. A couple of worms in their stir-fry? No, that would only cause them to get him back via his food. He'd recently seen a video that went viral of a few pranks. He'd have to go back and check them out. The one with saran wrap looked like it might work. At least for Juan and Luis it would. John was a bit more observant than the other two. He'd have to come up with something special for his foreman.

All thoughts of pranks and videos left his mind the moment he made it back to the Crooked Arrow Ranch. Declan and his men knocked on the front door of the ranch and from the look on Jerod's face, he knew something was wrong. "What happened? Please tell me your barn didn't collapse after I left."

From behind him came a woman's voice. "No, even worse." Dana sounded as though she was about to cry. "Everything is ruined!"

"Come on in and I'll get you up to speed." Jerod stood back and opened the door all the way to allow the four men to enter. "I trust all was well at your place?"

Declan scowled at his foreman, but decided against telling anyone about the prank he fell for. The guys at the Crooked Arrow also had a real mean streak when it came to pranks and he wasn't about to share any secrets with those guys. He wanted to make sure he stayed on Jerod's good side. Who knew what some of those military guys would do if given the idea of messing with the hot water heater. "Yup, everything was fine."

Luis chuckled and under his breath he mumbled something about cold showers. But Jerod paid him no mind, he had other more pressing matters to think about.

"Come into the kitchen, and I'll get you all something hot to drink." Jerod led them to the large kitchen, where most of the residents of the ranch were already seated, hot drink mugs in hand.

Once the newcomers all had mugs of hot coffee, Declan turned his curious gaze to Dana and Jerod. "So, what happened while I was gone?" He then looked around and noticed all of the residents, including the injured guy Marty, were present. No one looked to be any worse for the wear, except for Marty. But the looks of pain in his eyes made sense. He had been rammed pretty hard by an upset cow only the day before.

"The pageant is ruined!" Dana flew her hands in the air and sank back in her chair.

Chapter 15

Unsure what she meant, Declan repeated her claim, "the pageant is ruined?"

Jerod put a hand on his wife's and squeezed. "Not exactly ruined, but the space is. Yesterday's storm did a number on the town hall. Thanksgiving dinner might have to be canceled, too. All of the plans for this year's holidays are going to have to be reviewed and changes made."

"What happened to the town hall?" Even Luis was paying attention.

Everyone who had been around for even one Christmas in Frenchtown knew that the entire town came together from Thanksgiving all the way through the new year with celebrations and festivals. For Thanksgiving, the town held a giant dinner. Anyone who wanted to have a festive dinner would come in on Saturday and bring a potluck dish. The town provided turkey and ham, while everyone else cooked up all of the traditional sides as well as some not so traditional ones. The celebration was over one hundred years old and everyone, including the town grumps, participated. It was the single biggest event of the year. Even bigger than Christmas.

Although Christmas in Big Sky Country was a glorious affair, it wasn't something everyone did all at once, and on the same day. Christmas was a season where everyone would do various activities. The city would put on a Christmas Fair that lasted most of the month of December.

The Christmas Tree Farm that was run by the Makinaw family would coordinate events so that some took place at the tree farm and the rest were in town, at the city hall. Losing the hall at this point in time would break so many hearts.

"The roof was set to be replaced this summer, but the snowstorm caused the entire roof to collapse and even the walls crumbled. It's completely destroyed!" Dana put her head in her hands and Declan watched as her shoulders shook.

Everyone around the table was quiet. Most looked down at their hands or in their coffee mugs.

Hesitantly, Marnie offered up an idea, "What about renting some large tents and heaters? We could put them all down Main Street. There should be plenty of room that way, right?"

Dana shook her head. "It's too expensive. All of the money that's raised from the festival and donations go to help the disadvantaged in our area. If we use any money on tents, there won't be enough to help those who really need it. And forget about college scholarships."

After a few moments of thought, Tony suggested a place. "What about the Cattlemen's banquet hall? Do you think it's big enough to hold the whole town for Thanksgiving dinner?"

Declan thought about it for a moment. The Cattlemen's Association had their own facilities, and they did have a kitchen and dance hall. But it was pretty small. Maybe a quarter the size of the town hall.

"Unless we wanted to assign times to everyone for dinner, it wouldn't work. Not enough space."

"What about something in Missoula? Surely, there's a space large enough to hold us all there, isn't there?" John asked.

This time, it was Jerod who shot down the idea. "Same issue as if we were to rent tents, there'd be no money left over. No one is going to give us their space. Especially over Thanksgiving weekend. I seriously doubt there is any open space. That's when so many companies and clubs have their own parties."

Marnie raised her hand and cleared her throat. "As one of the newest residents, I haven't been out to the tree farm yet, but what about their barn?" She looked around the table and noticed a few faces thinking about it. "They do have a barn, don't they?"

"Yeah, they do," Declan answered.

Jerod rubbed his chin. "Half of the activities for the entire season are held there already. They can handle the parking."

"And they have already hired a few teens, right?" Tony added.

Dana looked up at the table. She wiped her eyes and sniffed a few times. "They have the largest barn around, but I don't think we can do everything there. Maybe they can handle Thanksgiving Dinner, but I doubt they'll want the live Nativity there. Not when they have so many people coming through to buy trees."

Declan nodded. All of those animals and all of the families milling about, not to mention the carnival that goes up, could spell disaster for the nativity animals. "I think we might be able to host the live nativity on my ranch. Most of the animals will be mine anyways, right?"

"What about parking? Won't that be an issue at your place?" Dana asked.

John looked at Declan, and something passed between the two. Like an unspoken idea that bounced back and forth between the two brains. "What if we asked our neighbors to help out? I highly doubt there will be a ton of people coming. At least not like the Thanksgiving dinner, right?"

"Bite your tongue, John Mason." Indignation had replaced Dana's tears. She stood up and put her hands on her hips. "Just because we are going to tell the story of how Jesus was born doesn't mean that no one wants to see it. I'll have you know that plenty of our wonderful neighbors in Frenchtown and the surrounding areas will jump at the chance to view a live nativity." She sat down hard and crossed her arms over her chest.

"Whoa." John put up his hands in a defensive posture. "I didn't mean anything by it, just that the entire town won't be there all at once, right? You'll have a couple different times you put this on and therefore we only need enough space to handle part of the area at a time, right?"

Dana's posture relaxed and she considered what John had said. "I suppose so. We could break it up into three performances, if there's enough interest. Maybe even sell tickets?"

"Hmm, maybe not sell tickets." Marnie nodded her head and her eyes widened with her next idea. "We could encourage donations and maybe we can get Frenchtown Roasting to host a cart? They could sell their wonderful pastries and coffee drinks?" She closed her eyes as she remembered the taste of chocolate and peppermint on her tongue from the delectable scone she had eaten the other day.

Dana grinned. "They already do that in town at the hall and at the tree farm. But I'm sure Lottie would have no problem setting up a cart for the nativity at Declan's ranch. We might need someone else to run it as I won't have time. I'll have to work with the actors to make sure the program goes off without a hitch."

"Well," Jerod stood and looked at the men, "now that that's settled, what do you all say we go and tackle the barn roof?"

"I'll call Lottie and then see about getting in touch with the mayor's wife. She usually helps with setting up all of the Christmas events. Oh!" Dana held a hand up. "I'll need to contact Santa and Mrs. Claus, too." She put a finger on her chin. "Hmm, they usually like to be part of all of the events throughout the entire Christmas season. I wonder if they'll want to go back and forth between Declan's and the tree farm for one weekend?"

The men stood up and left the room. Marnie looked around and noticed it was just the three little ladies. "Was that a sexist move, or what?" She wasn't sure, but she got the impression that the men didn't want any help from the women. Almost as though they were too weak to be outside in the elements, helping to mend the barn.

Dana laughed and shook her head. "I don't really care. If it means I get to stay inside where it's warm, and the coffee is close." She eyed the fresh pot just waiting for her to get up and take back to the table to top off everyone's drinks.

Marnie laughed and Dana smiled for the first time in what felt like hours and hours. In reality, it had only been about two hours since they had received the bad news about the town hall.

Megan filled her cup with more hot java.

"Alright, first things first. Who is going to speak with Cody about using his barn and farm for all of the town's Christmas events?" Dana asked.

"Not it." Marnie held a hand up. It wasn't that she didn't want to help, it was more that she didn't really know Cody and she doubted he would help her. Why would he?

With a sly smile, Megan volunteered.

Dana giggled.

Marnie looked between the two. "What have I missed?"

"Not much." Megan shrugged.

Dana rolled her eyes. "Except that for almost a year now Megan and Daniel have been dating."

"Ah, I wouldn't go that far." Megan's shoulders slumped and she looked away from the two women.

"Ohh, sounds like someone forgot to tell me her little secret." Marnie narrowed her eyes. "Is this why you were so focused on getting me to flirt with the single cowboys in town?"

"What?" Dana looked between the two. "You never told me you were trying to set Marnie up. Isn't that a little premature?"

Of all people, Dana knew that when a returning veteran began their true healing at the ranch, romance wasn't what they needed. For her, it turned out well. But most of the injured guys that had come through the ranch needed a lot more care and nurturing. Even though Marnie hadn't seen battle, she was severely injured in a way that would affect her for the rest of her life.

Megan raised her hands. "Hey now, I wasn't setting anyone up. It was just a little fun, that's all." She looked at Marnie and tried to keep a straight face. "Besides, I think that she's doing fine all on her own."

Marnie stood up. "Wait a minute. What's going on here? Is this some sort of matchmaking ranch, or what?"

Dana put a hand on Marnie's arm. "Sit down. I think Megan is just a little frustrated. She's not seen much of her boyfriend for the past few months."

"They've been very busy. I shouldn't expect him to pay me much attention when they are still trying to ensure the tree farm doesn't go under." Megan took a sip of her coffee and set it down on the table.

"This is the farm's first year to do a full-blown fall festival, and it went extremely well. They even had a Halloween celebration during the month of October. The local kids loved it." Dana went on to explain the types of booths and activities they had.

"Wow, with making a maze and all of those booths, it sounds as though Daniel must have been working all day and night. It's no wonder he hasn't had much time for dating." Marnie bit her lip, hoping she hadn't said too much. "And now with Christmas? That must be a massive undertaking."

"You have no idea. I spent an afternoon there a week ago, and all I did was work. Daniel barely had any time to even eat with me." A slow blush crept across the counselor's cheeks.

"Mmm hmm. Sounds to me like he did have time for something else?" Dana waggled her brows.

Megan slapped Dana's arm. "Stop that. You'll give Marnie the wrong impression."

"Hey," Marnie put her hands in the air and grinned. "If he took you behind a stack of hay for a little kissing, who am I to say anything."

Megan put her hands in front of her face. "Oh, boy. That man can kiss!"

All three giggled and teased Megan. After a few minutes of acting like high school girls, Megan straightened up. "But all kidding aside, I will gladly go out and see if Cody is willing to let us use his barn for the town's Thanksgiving dinner. I know they have a few area heaters as does the town. So we should be able to keep the barn warm enough. And if we ask the townsfolks to spread out their arrival times just a bit, we should be fine."

"When does the tree farm open for business?" Marnie had never been to a real tree farm so she had no clue. But she did know that back home in Florida the tree lots tended to open Thanksgiving weekend.

Megan scrunched her nose. "Yeah, that might be an issue. They open the same weekend. Black Friday is usually a big day for them and throughout the entire weekend."

"All we can do is ask," Dana said.

And with that thought, Megan prepared to go and see the owner of the tree farm, along with her boyfriend. If he was still her boyfriend. All year long they had spent most evenings texting or calling each other, but the past couple of weeks she'd hardly heard from him. Even though it was his busiest time of the year, Daniel hadn't made much of an attempt to communicate with her. And that had her worried.

Chapter 16

"So, what are we going to do about the nativity?" Marnie asked Dana.

"We keep going as though it is going to happen. Wherever we have the Thanksgiving dinner we will still have the tryouts for the live nativity." Dana picked up her mug of coffee and headed to the kitchen.

With her own mug in hand, Marnie followed her. "Can I help you with dinner preparations?" She marveled at the different designs on all of the coffee mugs and how even with the differences, they still matched in theme. All of the coffee mugs had a cowboy or cowgirl theme. Some were rodeo, some were strong women with various sayings that always made her smile. The mug she had in her hand was one such mug.

The white mug in Marnie's hand had a pair of red cowgirl boots, roses, and the saying: Forget the glass slippers, this princess wears cowboy boots. She liked that even though it was a frilly mug, it still showed that a princess can be tough.

One thing Marnie had noticed since arriving on the ranch was that the women in these parts were nothing, if not tough. Some wore pink and looked all girly, girly, but watch out – they were all tougher than most women she'd grown up with. She figured that if a woman was going to make it on a ranch, she had to be tougher than the bulls.

Until that moment, she hadn't really understood why a ranch was a great place for injured veterans to recover. Now, she knew beyond a shadow of a doubt that what didn't kill you only made you stronger.

Having just barely escaped being run down by a cow, not quite a bull, but close enough, Marnie knew that she was going to not only learn how to ditch her cane but also to be an even stronger woman for all of the issues she had to deal with.

The two women worked on making dinner for the ranch residents, as well as for the helpers from Declan's ranch. They were going to have a full house that night, and Dana needed all the help she could get.

"I had planned on making meatloaf, mashed potatoes, gravy, and steamed green beans for dinner. And I have enough rolls already made that we should be fine. But I think I'll need more hamburger meat defrosted. Can you get another two pounds out of the freezer?" Dana pointed toward the back porch where one of the freezers was located.

The ranch had several of them as they tended to fill up whenever they butchered a cow, went fishing, or a neighbor dropped off extra meat during hunting season. The majority of the residents had chosen not to participate in hunting season the past two years, but with the changing up of men and women they might have an opportunity to do some hunting of their own soon.

"Hey Dana, is bison meat good?" Marnie walked in with the two pounds of ground beef Dana had asked for, but also a package of ground bison.

"I thought we had used it all up. How much is in that package?" Dana couldn't move from where she stood to get a better angle on the package as her hands were wrist deep in the beef. Kneading her fingers through the thick mixture, she continued to mix the seasoning, breadcrumbs, and ketchup along with her secret ingredient, spicy brown mustard. Not much mustard, but just enough to give a little kick without changing the color of the meat or the sauce.

After putting the package of ground beef down, Marnie looked closer at the bison package. "Looks like it's four and a half pounds. What do you use it for? Can it be used for meatloaf?"

"Actually, it can be mixed with beef for a sharper tasting meatloaf, but I prefer to use it for grilled burgers. Some of the men here love bison burgers more than hamburgers." With her hands still deep in the large bowl with the mixture, Dana nodded to the sideboard on her left. "Go ahead and put the bison meat there. I'll defrost it and we can have bison burgers for lunch tomorrow."

Marnie scrunched her nose. "I've heard of them, of course. But really? I thought it was something...nevermind. I shouldn't say anything until I've tasted it." She was about to say something rude about people who ate bison, but then realized that really wasn't what she thought. She'd seen some Internet memes about bison meat but realized it was probably from people who didn't know any better. She'd give it a try and then make her own opinion.

"Okay, what can I do to help?" Marnie asked.

They spent the rest of the afternoon working closely together preparing the meat as well as washing and cutting up the potatoes.

Noticing that Dana had just cut up the potatoes with the skins still on them, Marnie asked, "Why don't we peel the potatoes? Not that I want that job, mind you." She scrunched her nose with the thought of spending hours peeling enough potatoes for their group of rowdy cowboys.

Dana laughed. "Everyone always asks that question. And no one ever wants to peel the potatoes. Neither do I. But the main reason is that most of the nutrients are in the skin. We keep them on here and everyone has enjoyed them so far."

And later when they were all sitting around the table eating dinner, Marnie had to agree that mashed potatoes with the peelings included was quite tasty.

However, before dinner was ready, Marnie turned her attention once more to the guys outside. "So, you think we got the better end of the deal? Staying inside and cooking, that is."

Dana looked out the window and noticed the tree tops swaying in the breeze. Then she checked her phone's weather app and grinned. "Oh, I'd say we got the better deal." She turned her phone to Marnie, who also grinned.

"I think I won't question it again when the guys offer to do the outside work on a freezing cold day." With one more look outside, Marnie noticed the men huddled over next to the barn. "Do you think they'll be alright out there?"

Before Dana had a chance to respond, a shrill ring began and she sighed. If it had been someone she knew, they would have called her on her cell phone. But when it was the house landline ringing, she knew it was business. She glanced at her watch and her brows furrowed. It was too late in the day for anyone from the VA to be calling. And with the storm, she doubted any of the local doctors would be phoning the ranch.

Dana straightened her shoulders and took a deep breath before answering the phone. With a smile on her face, even though no one could see it, she knew they could hear it, so she picked up the phone. "Good afternoon, Crooked Arrow Ranch."

A woman's voice on the other end asked, "Is Jerod Stevens available?"

After a quick look outside the window, Dana notified the caller that he was in fact, not available at the moment.

The woman paused for a moment, then continued, "I'm Eloise Sullivan and I'm calling about Marty Winters. Is he able to make it to the phone?"

Dana picked up on the caller's undertone and realized this person might already know about Marty's accident with the cow. Which was strange since she didn't think Marty had been calling anyone. But, maybe this woman was family and he had phoned one of them? "If you'll hold, I'll check and see if he's available."

Without waiting, Dana put down the receiver and motioned for Marnie to follow her. Once they were out of earshot of the phone Dana told Marnie about the caller. "Do you know anyone by that name?"

With a shake of her head, Marnie said she didn't. "But, to be fair, I don't really know Marty all that well. He's not said anything to me about family, or even if he had a girlfriend."

Marnie thought the caller was more likely to be a girlfriend. If Marty was still out of it, then he probably wouldn't have answered his cell phone should someone have called him on that number instead of the ranch line.

"Okay, I guess I'll have to run to his room to see if he's up for a caller." Dana headed toward the wing of the ranch that housed the residents. Since they had started taking in women vets as well as male, Jerod had moved the female residents into the rooms closest to their master suite, and the guys were all at the far end of the house.

While there weren't really enough rooms to keep any vacant as a buffer between the sexes, at the moment there were a couple of empty rooms that did, in fact, separate the men from the women.

It wasn't that Jerod thought anyone would get up to no good, it was more that women generally preferred a bit more privacy than men did. And their walls weren't thick enough to block out snoring. One thing Dana learned early on was that men tended to snore, and do it very loudly. A quiet ranch tended to make any sounds louder than they would be if she lived in a city and had other competing sounds, like cars and sirens.

One of the best things about living in the country was the fact that other than snores, she rarely heard anything at night. Well, except for when the coyotes decided to pay them a call. Thankfully, that wasn't too often. And then she was glad for the sound because it helped them all to wake up so they could go help protect the animals on their property who depended on the humans for safety.

When she stood outside of Marty's door, she noticed it was open a little bit. She did her best not to peek inside. Instead, she looked at the door and put her hand up to knock. But, when she did, the door opened all the way.

The scene inside was a bit of a surprise. The man was in the process of falling over whilst trying to put on his boots. "Ow."

Without thinking, Dana ran inside the room. "Marty, are you alright?" She knelt down next to him.

"Argh, sometimes I really hate my feet." Marty lay on the ground holding his midsection and trying to breathe normally. While he didn't need an assistive device for his Air Force injury, he did still battle with balance issues. Having only one real foot was a pain he sometimes chose to ignore. His prosthetic was good, but balancing on his left foot wasn't really recommended.

Normally, he sat down to put his boots on, but that day he wasn't in any mood to be careful. Instead, he balanced on his left foot that was a prosthetic from the ankle down, while attempting to put on a boot that didn't seem to want to cooperate.

"Here, let me help you up. You have a caller waiting for you." Dana put her hand out and braced herself for the tall man who was over six feet to use her as leverage to get back up.

"Someone came her to visit me, in this weather?" Marty took her outstretched hand with his left one and put his right hand on the edge of his bed to get enough leverage to get back up. Normally, he could have done it all alone. He no longer had many issues with his balance, since losing his left foot to an IED. But since he had been rammed down by a mad cow, he wasn't exactly up to par.

Dana giggled. "No, someone called the house line for you. Didn't they try your cell phone?"

His head turned to the side table where he had his phone charging. "I don't think so. But I supposed I had my phone on silent and missed it?" Once he was up on his feet, he picked up the cell phone and looked at his history. "Nope, no missed calls."

"Well, there's a woman on the phone asking for you." Dana turned to leave the room and let him finish putting on his shoes in privacy.

"Wait, what woman?" Marty couldn't think of anyone he'd given the ranch number to. His family called his cell when they wanted to talk. His VA doctor was a man, not a woman. But he supposed it could have been a scheduler calling to set up an appointment or something. Although, it was strange they used the ranch line and not his cell.

However, stranger things had happened.

"She said her name was Eloise Sullivan." Dana left and headed back to the kitchen where the phone sat on a tiny wooden table in the corner by the refrigerator. There wasn't a chair there, only a small drawer that held paper and a few pens used for note taking.

This time, Marty sat on his bed and put his boots on the way he knew he should have to begin with. "A woman caller, huh?" He chuckled and hoped it was someone calling to inform him he'd won a million dollars, or something just as sweet.

However, when he got to the phone, he realized it was anything but sweet.

Chapter 17

arnie wasn't one to eavesdrop, but she was working on dinner preparations and Marty was on the phone right next to her. She couldn't help but hear his side of the conversation. And when she looked back at him, she felt sorry for the poor guy. He looked as though he was in pain. And he probably was still in pain from the cow mowing him down, but the expression on his face seemed different.

"I don't think that will be necessary. It wasn't any fault of anyone but myself. You can't anticipate the effect a storm will have on barnyard animals." Marty ran a hand through his already mussed up hair.

She turned back to her task at hand and continued to snap the ends off of the green beans she was preparing for dinner, trying not to listen in on Marty's phone conversation.

When the man was done with his call, he set the receiver back on the hook and sighed. "Well, that wasn't good."

Trying so hard to mind her own business, Marnie bit her lip. Then threw caution to the wind. "What's wrong?"

"It seems our little issue with Bertha made its way to Texas." Marty turned around and screwed up his face. "A woman who specializes in ADA compliance is coming here, to the ranch, to make sure that Jerod and Dana are looking out for us properly."

"What?" Marnie set down the beans in her hands and turned to look him straight on. "What are you talking about?"

Dana was right behind her. "What's going on? Why is an ADA specialist coming here? And when?"

Not wanting to let his frustrations out on the two women in front of him, Marty took a couple of deep breaths before answering. "It seems whomever Megan spoke with about my injury didn't like what they heard. They called someone to come and inspect the ranch."

Dana looked out the window at the men outside and winced. They were coming inside after having spent the past few hours working on the barn. This was not the time to deal with inspectors. She and Jerod had discussed the fact that Marty was the first real injury they had dealt with since opening the ranch and Jerod was worried the VA might not be happy. But he had said they'd been open for more than two years now and since it was a minor injury, he didn't think the VA would have an issue.

"Will this hurt the ranch?" Marnie had put her hand over her mouth and the words were a bit garbled coming out. While she hadn't been there long, she did know that she was in the right place to continue her healing process. Anything that might shut down the Crooked Arrow would most assuredly hinder her progress. That was the last thing she wanted for Jerod and Dana. Or for herself.

This ranch had already helped multiple people to heal and move on to real world jobs. Things that some of them would never have been able to do without the Crooked Arrow. She prayed that this woman, whoever she was, would see the good they had already done and not try to close them down.

The large shoulders on Marty raised up and down and the look in his eyes said more than his words. "I doubt it."

The sounds of boots stomping in the mud room caused all three in the kitchen to turn around.

"You doubt what?" Jerod stood in the entrance to the kitchen looking more like a giant frozen popsicle than a cowboy. His brown hair stood on end and his usually light tan face looked more blue than anything else. Even the beard he had begun to grow looked like it was tipped with frozen icicles.

"Oh, you look like you could use a steaming hot shower and a mug of the hottest coffee we can make." Dana moved to the coffee maker and started to make a fresh pot.

"Is there anything I can do to help everyone? Should I check the fire in the living room and get it going?" With cane in hand, Marnie began to move to the other room, hoping that the fire hadn't gone out yet. While she could start a fire from scratch, it would put off more warmth sooner if it just needed a bit of stoking and a few new logs.

The rest of the men crowded into the kitchen and all of them began rubbing their hands together.

Tony shivered and headed straight to the living room. "I'd like to warm up a bit before showering."

Jerod looked at his wife, then Marnie, and finally at Marty. "Hey, man. How ya feelin?"

"Like I got run over by a bull." Marty grinned, then winced when he tried to stand tall. He took a seat at the kitchen table before the pain became overwhelming. He didn't want to have to take anything stronger than a Motrin, if he could help it. After his time in the hospital he hated pain medication. It always caused other issues that he'd rather not deal with.

"Real close, man. I'm just glad you're standing." Declan watched as Marty slowly sat in the wooden chair. "Or, at least out of bed and in the kitchen with everyone."

Jerod walked up behind Dana and wrapped his arms around his wife as she continued to mess with the coffee maker. "What's wrong? You know I can sense when you're upset."

"Not here in front of everyone." She pushed the on button and stayed in her husband's cold embrace. Even though he had taken off his outerwear, the cold still seeped out of his long-sleeved shirt and through her body. But she would suffer the cold if it meant sharing her warmth with him.

"Alright, while we wait for the coffee, why don't you come with me to change out of these cold, wet clothes." The cowboy's scruffy face rubbed against Dana's soft cheek.

She laughed. "You know, I think I'm starting to like your beard. I wasn't sure at first."

"That's good, because I'm not shaving it again until summer." Jerod pulled back and took his wife's hand in his and they left the room smiling.

Everyone at the ranch was used to the newlyweds and their stealing kisses when they thought no one was watching - someone was always watching. But this time they all seemed to sense something else was up.

Declan turned to Marnie. "Is there something going on?"

"Ahhh," not sure what to say, Marnie turned to Marty with a desperate look in her eyes.

"Well, I guess you'll all hear about it anyways." Marty was the sort who liked to just take the bandaid off quickly and deal with it.

He never liked it when someone slowly peeled the bandaid back. He thought it made the pain last longer. For him, ripping the bandaid off as quickly as possible was the only way to get past it and move on. "An ADA specialist will be here in a few days to assess the ranch and its ability to care for injured veterans, like us."

Everyone stopped their own conversations and looked at Marty. Then they all threw questions at him at once.

Marty held up his hands as if to protect himself from the onslaught of their words. "Whoa, slow down. One question at a time."

Tony spoke first. "What sparked the need for an inspection?" He reached down and felt the top of his service dog's head. Several of the residents of the Crooked Arrow Ranch had a service dog to help for various reasons. Tony was partially deaf and his dog, Buffy, was more of an extension of his body than a dog, or even a pet. Buffy basically served as Tony's left ear. She always stood on his left side and helped to steer him clear of anything that might harm him. Sometimes it was something coming at him from the left, and sometimes, it was when there was too much commotion for Tony to be comfortable.

With his loss of hearing, Tony found it difficult to process some sounds. Usually, it happened when there was too much going on or sounds were very loud. During those periods, his brain would get jumbled up and he would get very nervous. Buffy calmed him and helped him to process anything that would affect him directly.

In times like this, he took solace just in touching Buffy. She always sensed when he needed her. Due to the extreme cold weather, none of the dogs had been outside helping with the barn repairs. Most of the dogs had been lazing about napping, as dogs tended to do on a cold winter afternoon. But the moment Buffy heard her partner Tony in the distance, she had made a beeline for the back door and was standing there waiting for him to enter.

It was amazing the sounds that dogs picked up. And how they differentiated each person's own sounds. They knew when their partner was coming versus when anyone else was coming close. And they knew when it was a stranger who was approaching even before the humans could see or hear them.

Now, she was next to him and offering her support in a way that only Tony could appreciate.

Marnie noticed that the Army officer had been rather stiff and his shoulders had risen considerably until she saw him reach out with his left hand and pet the dog's head. Then, she watched as he visibly relaxed his shoulders. Even his face had fewer lines as he pet his service dog and the dog rubbed up against Tony's left side.

The only other current resident who had a service dog was Dakota Monahan, but she wasn't at the ranch. The moment the storm let up, she had taken her dog and went to see Skeeter at the neighboring ranch.

But even the day before, Marnie had noticed how Dakota and Spike acted as one. The concept of a service dog was foreign to Marnie. She had never seen one in service. Sure, she had heard about them. She had even seen K9 dogs in action while in the Air Force, but she hadn't seen a dog that was specially trained to help an injured, or disabled, person to get around better.

And until that moment, she hadn't really thought too much about it. The realization that there are so many different ways to help someone put a smile on her face, was eye opening. A service dog wasn't what she needed, but who knew what Jerod and his team would come up with for her. One thing was for certain, Jerod, Dana, and Megan were good at what they did. And Marnie was going to support them no matter what. So she tuned back into the conversation in time to hear about the ADA coordinator.

"I didn't call her, nor did anyone I know. My guess is that someone at the VA called her when they heard about my accident. I really don't understand why they overreacted like they did. I'm going to be fine. There won't be any lasting issues. It's all just bruising." Marty did still hurt a lot, but he knew that the pain would go away. It always did. Bruises were nothing to him. Even though he couldn't really talk about his job in the Air Force, he had plenty of experience with injuries that weren't life threatening. It was all part of being in the field.

Marnie didn't like the sound of their interrogation of Marty. The man had been out of it for the most part since he was struck yesterday by the cow. The fact that he was up, dressed, and in the kitchen arguing with the guys really said a lot about how tough he was. "I think that we should give Marty a break. Let's hold judgment on anything until this person arrives. Have there been many injuries on the ranch? Is this just part of the process?"

Tony shook his head. "This is the first injury since I've been here. Well, the first that needed more than a bandage. Cuts and scrapes are part of everyday life on a ranch. Getting run down by a cow? Not so every day, but also not totally out of the realm of normal, either. If only Mike had been here, he would have had the cows in line the moment they showed any signs of distress."

"Mike Blankenship?" Marnie asked.

"Yes, he is, or was, the resident cow whisperer. He now works on a dairy farm about two hours away." Tony, who was obviously feeling better, smiled at Marnie before taking a seat at the table.

With everyone now seated at the table, Marnie went over to the counter and picked up the coffee pot along with a tray full of mugs. She brought all of the items over to the table and let the men choose their mugs. One thing she had noticed was that they tended to use the same mug over and over. There weren't any names on the porcelain cups, but the men did have their favorite. Now that she thought about it, Marnie had a favorite, too.

Looking at the mugs left on the tray, she smiled when she noticed her favorite was there. She reached over and picked up the mug with the cowgirl boots and the saying about this princess wearing cowboy boots. She had used it earlier in the day and hadn't realized that Dana took it out of the dishwasher already. With all of the people in the house, they ran the dishwasher at least once a day, sometimes twice. She should have known her mug would already be clean and ready to use again.

Chapter 18

Instead of stressing over the ADA coordinator's arrival, Marnie got right into the planning for the live nativity. She and Declan spent the next day checking out the sheep, alpaca, and even looking for a donkey that would be tame.

"See, that's the thing with a donkey, they are some of the most temperamental beasts on a ranch." Declan put a finger in the air. "But, if one is generally docile, it will continue to be so, mostly. Just like with people, something could get a bur under the donkey's saddle and cause them to act up."

"So, you're saying that we have to find a donkey that's known for being calm, but also be prepared for it to act up, just in case?" Unsure what to think about donkeys, Marnie didn't know if she really wanted to use one or if she might prefer that they try a pony. Thankfully, they planned to cast Mary with a teenage girl, instead of a young girl as so many nativity plays did.

With a nod, Declan agreed with Marnie's statement. "So, now that we have the animals all sorted, except for casting the right donkey, what do you say we head into town for a late lunch? My treat." He grinned and prayed she'd say yes.

It seemed it was going to be a day of uncertainty for Marnie. She bit the inside of her lip and considered his offer. On the one hand, he had been very nice after a rough start. He was cute and worked hard. The thing that surprised her the most was how very generous he was with his time. Since Marnie had arrived, she'd see Declan almost every day, and it wasn't always about his selling sheep or alpaca to the ranch. He helped out with the barn repairs, which took more than one day, and he ran out to their ranch when the weather was too dangerous to be out driving around in. Especially since he had to drive back county roads that hadn't been cleared of the snow before he left his own ranch.

Declan Walden seemed like the kind of man she would like to be friends with. He was the sort of man who had principles and honor. He reminded her of the gentleman she loved to read about in those regency romance books she always tried to hide from her bunkmate back in Germany. Lola would laugh at her for wanting to read about a time when women were so oppressed, they had to wear metal rods to keep them in place.

That was a bit of an overstatement, but Marnie got her meaning. The women in those days were oppressed, but they found ways to rebel. Ways to contribute to society that was more than just rearing and raising the next Lord Whatshisname that would keep pushing women back in the home.

Marnie shook those memories out and decided that she'd have to pull out a Jane Austen novel soon. Then she focused back on the man in front of her.

If nothing else, she could use the time to get to know him a bit better. While she didn't really need to make friends since she wasn't sticking around Frenchtown, Montana, she did realize that she would be there more than just a few weeks.

When Marnie first arrived in town, she honestly thought that they would either have her all fixed up by the new year, or they'd say she couldn't be helped. Either way, she didn't think she'd be staying past January First.

Now? She was committed to ensuring that she could walk normally. And if that took until spring, then she'd be there until spring. And it wouldn't be awful to have a friend. Especially one that was nice on the eyes, not that she would ever tell him, or even Megan, he was handsome. With her decision made, she smiled at the cowboy. "I'd like that. Thank you."

"Another reason for heading into town this afternoon is to ask about a donkey." Declan grinned but said no more.

Marnie wanted to ask him what he meant, but from the look of his mischievous grin, she could tell he wanted her to ask him about it. Which was something she refused to do. Instead, she changed the subject. "So, does it snow like this often? I mean, I'm from sunny Florida - land of oranges and Mickey. I've never seen a storm like what we just had. And the snow isn't really even melting."

They walked toward Declan's truck, a burgundy Dodge Ram 2500 Big Horn.

"I gotcha." He tapped the brim of his Stetson and opened the truck door for her. Declan put his hand out to help her get inside his larger truck. Once she was settled and had her seatbelt on, he closed the door. Then he went around to the driver's side. "We do get quite a few storms during the winter. Although, I'd say the one that just came through here was a bit stronger than normal. At least it didn't last long. Some of our storms can last for days and days."

All Marnie could think was that they could have been snowed in.

Together.

At one time, she would have enjoyed that. But now? Her foot still had pain where she had lost her toes. The doctors told her she probably would experience pain for quite some time, especially in very cold climates. Arthritis had already settled into her foot, and she wasn't even thirty years old yet. At that moment, she felt much older than what she really was. And she wondered how bad it would get twenty years down the road.

Romance was strictly off the menu for her. Maybe one day she might be lucky and meet a man who wouldn't turn away disgusted when he saw her foot missing all five toes, but for now, she needed to focus on what she was in Montana for, and not on the pearly white smile that sent shivers up and down her spine. No, she wouldn't fall for Declan Walden, no matter how much her heart was telling her to let loose.

"That's a lot of snow. I noticed some ranches have their own plows they put on the front of their trucks. Is that normal in this area?" While Marnie hadn't been out to any other ranches yet, she had seen plenty of trucks driving around with a plow strapped to the front of their trucks. It was something she'd never thought to see before. She had to ask Megan what that was all about. At first, she thought that there was just a lot of construction happening in the area and those were small business owners who had their own earth moving equipment.

She wasn't too far off. They were small business owners. The shovel on the front of the trucks did move earth, although it was mostly in the form of frozen rain sometimes mixed with dirt. But, they were intended to move snow off of dirt roads and parts of the highway that the county or city hadn't gotten around to cleaning before they needed to go somewhere.

In fact, Declan's truck had one such device on it and she had seen him shovel some of the snow at the Crooked Arrow the day the storm ended.

The driver chuckled. "Yup, most people 'round here have their own plows. The city doesn't clean anyone's driveways. And those employed to clear the snow from the roads have a lot of highway and larger city and county lanes to get to. Some of the smaller routes don't get regular service. It is safer for all ranchers to have a truck that they can hitch a snowplow to so they can clean their own driveways and parts of the highway in front of their ranches and farms."

Marnie was amazed at the ingenuity of the rancher and farmer. She never imagined how much work went into providing the world with food. She would just show up at the grocery store and get whatever she wanted before joining the Air Force. Rarely did she not find something fresh that she was looking for. Although, a couple of years ago, she'd heard a lot about the toilet paper shortages.

However, since she was in the Air Force, she never had to worry about food, or toilet paper. They always fed her well in the chow halls. They may not have always had exactly what she wanted, but they never went without food.

And the latrines were always stocked with paper products. She chuckled to herself when she remembered watching a social media video about someone's paper hoarding run.

"What's so funny?" While driving straight, he looked over to Marnie and saw the grin on her face.

Marnie waved a hand in front of herself as if to push the question away. "Nothing, really. Just remembered someone I saw on social media a while back when people were hoarding paper goods."

Declan laughed with her. "I remember that time. Ever since then I've kept a case of TP and paper towels in stock at my ranch. When I open the last case, that's when I buy a new one. I don't ever want to have to drive around to all of the stores looking for who has a tiny roll of paper I can buy." He shook his head.

"I was still in the Air Force back then, and while we did see some of the issues, there was always at least a few squares of paper in the latrines." Her Sergeant had told them to use less and help with saving some trees, but she never felt a big difference. "You know, it's strange we're talking about those days as though they were so long ago."

"I know." Declan thought for a moment while keeping his eyes on the road. "I remember my great-grandparents talking about what it was like during World War II. They had to conserve a lot. Even as recent as the nineties, Granny would save all of the cottage cheese containers and re-use them as though they were her version of Tupperware. When I was still really young, I remember thinking it was normal to save the tubs. I think when Granny passed away, that my Mom went through the place and threw out a lot of weird stuff. Granny even saved the toilet paper rolls. How weird is that?"

With a laugh, Marnie put her hand over her mouth. "My Nanna did the same. Only she added the butter tubs she would get from the grocery store. I don't think she even owned a single piece of Tupperware. My mom tried to buy her a set for Christmas one year, but Nanna had her take it back. She said it was a waste of money. Especially when she had a perfectly good set of storage containers that she could wash and reuse. When one was used to the point of ruin, then all she had to do was pull another one from her cupboard. She saved it all. But my grandparents never did that sort of thing. I guess it was just those who survived the war?"

Marnie then began to talk about how her Nanna would wash out the Ziploc bags and reuse them, even though there was never a shortage for as long as Marnie could remember.

"What about the gas crisis before we were born? Did your parents or grandparents ever talk about that?" Declan asked. He hadn't been born until well after the seventies. In fact, he wasn't born until the early nineties. But his parents still spoke about it, as though it was a huge deal that only made mankind stronger for surviving.

It took a second for Marnie to understand what he was talking about. "Do you mean that time in the seventies when people would line up at gas stations for hours to get just a few gallons of gas at a time? I think my grandma told me once that they were shocked to pay over a dollar a gallon."

Both of them laughed for so long that Marnie started to cough.

"Sorry about that. Can you imagine paying a dollar a gallon? I think when I was a teen, we paid two dollars a gallon. Although, it wasn't all that long ago that gas was just under three dollars a gallon." Marnie thought about how volatile gas prices had been during her short life and wondered what Henry Ford would think if he were alive today.

The two of them continued their odd banter all the way into town. By the time they arrived, Marnie was starting to see Declan as a friend, someone she actually had a lot in common with. Who would have known that the strange things her grandparents and great-grandparents did were actually normal?

"So, you think that surviving the war like they did made most people from the forties and fifties be super thrifty?" Marnie asked when they stepped out of the truck.

"Yeah, I think so. Which only makes me wonder what we are all going to be saying and doing forty or fifty years from now. We survived a worldwide pandemic, which I have to admit does happen every hundred years or so, but we have also had the wars in the Middle East to contend with. Unlike the World Wars of the past, the Middle East wars have dragged on and on." Declan clicked the auto-lock button on his key fob and they headed into the diner.

Marnie's eyes widened. She had been in the diner a few days before the big storm and it had looked like what one might expect from a fifties-era diner. It was red and white with chrome accents that gleamed from constant polishing. Today, however, it was a different diner. It looked to Marnie as though Santa and his merry little elves had come through.

Everywhere she looked it was Christmas. Green wreaths with all sorts of fun décor hung on the wall. Several of the Christmas wreaths were decorated with Coca-Cola ornaments and red ribbon. She hadn't seen that before and thought it was really cool.

All around the booths the owners had strung green garland with red bows, ribbons, and white fairie lights. The place was gorgeous. It really did feel as though it was Christmas, even though Thanksgiving was the next day. She never really did much for Christmas until after Thanksgiving. It wasn't that she was a scrooge or anything, she just loved Thanksgiving and wanted that holiday to have her full attention until it was done. But the moment Black Friday hit, it was all Christmas for her.

So the planning for the Christmas Nativity before Thanksgiving arrived was new for her. As was seeing all of the decorations.

When she was stationed in Germany, the surrounding towns did decorate early. But the base waited until Thanksgiving weekend before most of the decorations came out. She figured times were changing and Christmas would just come earlier and earlier each year. She could only pray that it didn't start coming before Halloween.

Once they were seated in a booth, with the scratchy pleather squeaky noise and all, Marnie opened her menu. "So, what's good here?" She decided not to comment on the Christmas decorations since Declan didn't seem to bat an eye at all. Who was she to rain on a town's Christmas parade?

"Everything." Declan didn't even bother to open his menu. "I usually get whatever is the daily special. But if it's not something that sounds good at the time, then I'll have a bison burger. They're fresh and nothing beats the burgers in this joint."

"You know, before coming here I'd never known anyone who'd eaten bison before. This week, I learned that it's much healthier for you than ground beef." Marnie closed her menu and had made up her mind what to get.

"Did you know that the ground bison meat people get in the grocery stores down south actually only has about sixty percent bison meat? They can legally add in ground beef as a sort of cheap filler and still call it bison." With flared nostrils, Declan shook his head. "They should at least put it on the packaging that they aren't getting real bison, that it's a hybrid product."

Marnie sat back in her seat and watched the man in front of her. For the first time since they met, she saw real anger on his face. It made her realize that Declan could be emotional, but since he always seemed so cheerful, he most likely was a happy man in general. That was until something got his goose. And it seemed the packaged ground bison not being one hundred percent bison meat was one such issue.

She grinned.

Declan deflated. "I got on my high horse, didn't I?"

"Just a bit. Maybe a ten-foot-high horse?" A giggle escaped and she shook her head. Marnie hadn't laughed so much in... she couldn't remember when.

Since arriving at the ranch, she had really loosened up compared to the past year. It felt good to let go of the anger and frustration of all that happened so many months ago. The weird part was that Marnie didn't even realize she had been holding in so much angst. As she felt her shoulders relax, her face did as well. She no longer felt like she was sucking a lemon, instead it felt as though she was enjoying an ice-cold glass of lemonade on a hot summer day.

The feeling of that soothing, cooling drink that always made her go "Ahhh" when she drank it back home was something she didn't even know she was missing. If she stayed in Montana a bit longer, she just might get herself back to where she was, mentally, before the accident. Something she never thought possible.

Sure, the VA had told her she could get her previous mental state back, but she didn't trust they could deliver. And maybe that was part of the problem, she didn't trust the VA to care for her and her needs. So many Airmen, Soldiers, Marines, Sailors, you name it, too many had major mental issues. While she didn't have any contact with the Guardsmen or the Coast Guardmen, she'd bet they had problems with the VA as well. The National Guards were lucky in that most of them had regular jobs and therefore had some form of insurance, besides the V A.

The short time Marnie had spent in a VA hospital after being released from the Air Force, had shown her that the VA was way in over its head in dealing with the injured military. They were understaffed and running on regulations that were decades out of date.

Just like any government bureaucracy, they couldn't make the needed changes fast enough to deal with today's injured veterans. As far as Marnie knew, the issues and lack of necessary funding weren't political. All the past presidents had done a lot for the VA. It seemed to all come down to funding. Money sure was an issue no matter what side of the aisle a president sat on.

Too bad the multibillionaires didn't throw a few hundred million toward the VA to help with staffing and training. Now she was getting on her high horse. Mentally anyways.

"So, I take it you're going to get the bison burger?" Marnie arched a brow. After hearing Declan go on about the bison meat industry, she figured he'd be throwing a few coins that way.

A deep chuckle emanated from the man across from Marnie. It made her feel all warm and tingly. She mentally chided herself. Falling for anyone was not in the cards. She was going to move home and make something of herself. What that was she wasn't sure yet, but she had some ideas. Ideas that involved her working with the local airport and air traffic control maybe.

Although, she'd heard so many bad things about those guys - and gals. The stress levels were horrendous. Maybe working in a tower wasn't for her, afterall. She'd have to meet with a recruiter and see what she could do. Her physical injury didn't preclude her from most civilian jobs, thankfully. But it could cause issues if she wanted to be a pilot.

With her Air Force background and the fact that she had held such a high security clearance and worked on planes, she'd easily get into a flight school. And then have no trouble finding a job as a pilot. Except for maybe her foot. Although, she couldn't think of any reason her foot would be an issue, since she no longer takes pain pills. And if she can walk, she can put her foot on a pedal and guide the plane. Most of the work is done with the hands and pushing or pulling buttons and sticks, but there is still some footwork when it comes to steering and maneuvering the plane.

"Hmm, I don't know. It does sound good. But..." Declan looked around. "They might have some of their Christmas specials on for today. I gotta hear what's on special, then I'll decide."

Marnie tilted her head and looked at the rancher across from her. She would have sworn he'd choose the bison burger just on principle alone. Especially after their talk. Maybe he wasn't as easy to figure out as she thought.

Chapter 19

As it turned out, Declan was smart to wait. The day's special was meatloaf. But it wasn't anything like what she'd ever had. There were cranberries inside as well as a light cranberry glaze on top. She wasn't sure, but Marnie thought she also detected hints of a sun-dried tomato in the meat. What made it so odd was the fact that Marnie didn't normally like cranberry sauce on anything. But on this meal, it was the perfect amount of sweet and tangy.

Oh, and the sides. She wasn't going to need dinner that night. Red potatoes and green beans were the sides. The dessert was to die for - a yule log. She'd always wanted to try one and never got around to it. Not even last year when she spent most of the Christmas season in Germany.

"Oh, wow. This has got to be the very best yule log ever." Marnie's eyes hooded as she took another bite and then licked her fork clean.

A chuckle across the table caused Marnie to open her eyes. "What?"

"You look like you're about ready to marry that cake." Declan took a bite of his Christmas cheesecake then put his fork down.

"You're just jealous I got the last piece of the yule log. I bet your cheesecake," Marnie scrunched her nose and pointed her clean fork at his plate, "isn't anywhere as good as my dessert."

Before he could answer her, something over her shoulders caught his attention. He pointed. "What's going on?"

Marnie turned in her seat, but didn't see what could be the matter. When she turned back around, she saw something on Declan's shirt that had her narrowing her eyes at him. "What did you just do?"

Instead of answering her, Declan shrugged his shoulders as though he had no clue what she was talking about.

She looked down at her plate and knew what he had done. That innocent little boy expression is really what got him caught. Everyone knows that when a man tries to play innocent, he's actually trying to hide something he did.

Something wrong.

Marnie crossed her arms over her chest and glared at him. Her glare was usually enough to get the younger Airmen to fess up whenever she questioned them about anything. And it worked on men her own age, it seemed.

A hand went up in front of Declan and he swallowed what was in his mouth. Then took a drink of his hot tea. "I couldn't resist. You taunted me with your yule log and how you talked about it being the best ever, I just had to taste it for myself."

"Ah ha. So, what you're saying is it's my fault you stole my yule log. The last one they had by the way." Her glare was even more intense, if that was even possible.

Declan gulped. He knew he was in trouble. "It was only a bite, not the entire thing."

With nostrils flared, Marnie didn't have to say another word.

Her stare must have really hit him hard. Declan cleared his throat and rubbed his chin. "How about I order an entire yule log for you? I can bring it out to your ranch on Friday. They're closed tomorrow for Thanksgiving, or I'd get one for you tomorrow."

Not wanting to let Declan off the hook so easily, and certainly not wanting to let him know that he wasn't in any real trouble, Marnie took a moment to consider. "Alright. Deal." In the back of her mind, she knew she'd be inviting him to stay and have a slice with her. Albeit a very small slice, she was raised to be hospitable, and she would do her duty. But boy would it be tough to share that yule log. She put her hand across the table, and he shook it.

The energy that passed between their joined hands sent a shiver down Marnie's spine. The teasing atmosphere that surrounded their little table fled. She felt her eyes widen and noticed his did as well. Almost as though he felt the connection but didn't want to admit it.

Could it be that what she felt wasn't part of her over-active imagination? Did Declan feel something *more* for her too?

It only lasted a quick moment, then Declan pulled his hand back and cleared his throat. "Right, I'll go place that order and pay for our meal. Be right back."

Declan scooted out of the booth seat he was in and high tailed it to the counter where the woman who owned the joint was talking to a few of the older ladies in town. Marnie had been warned about the women. They tended to gossip something awful. She hated gossip, especially when it was about her. She'd been the focus of gossips before and she would rather be boiled in oil and rolled in feathers before she stood by and let someone gossip about her again.

She turned her head so as not to grab their attention, but she did watch them out of the corner of her eye. They all looked at Declan and smiled at him.

The lady with the pink beehive on her head reached out to touch Declan's arm. Marnie wasn't sure but she thought that hairstyle was called a bouffant. Since she was watching, she noticed him back up just a tad bit. Sadly, the older woman didn't get the hint and she moved closer to him. While Marnie couldn't hear the women, she figured the lady was asking him about his "date". They looked back over his shoulder at her and smiled. Usually, when someone looks at you from across the room and smiles while talking to someone else, it means they are talking about you.

She couldn't help it, Marnie rolled her eyes heavenward in a silent plea for God to give her the strength to deal with these women. She knew the Bible said gossiping was wrong, but so was losing your temper. Just because those women weren't acting like Christians, didn't mean she should throw aside her upbringing and get in the mud with them.

But to be fair, she didn't know what they were saying. It could have been something as simple as asking who she was. Or if they were on a date. Not that any of that was their business, but they could be asking something innocent. The warning about those women is what had Marnie's ire up. She had to remind herself to be generous and not jump to conclusions.

Just as she had her thoughts back in control, Declan returned to their booth and slid into his seat. The look on his face told her she had been right from the start. "What's wrong?" Her instinct was to put a hand on his to comfort him, but the moment she moved her hand on top of the table, he moved his back against the edge of the wooden table in front of him.

"Not here. Let's head out to anywhere but here." While ignoring the busybodies at the bar, Declan helped Marnie out of her seat and gave her a strained smile. Out of the side of his mouth he whispered, "smile. Don't give them anything else to gossip about."

Not sure what was going on, Marnie did as she was told. She put a smile on, but she could feel how fake it was. She only hoped that no one else noticed it. While she didn't recognize anyone in the café, she wasn't sure if anyone could read faces well enough to understand what she was truly feeling.

Once outside, Declan let a deep sigh out. Still keeping his eyes away from the café and the chatty Cathies he left behind, he took Marnie by the elbow and led her to his truck. "Sorry about that. Sometimes those busybodies just get under my skin. I know better than to let them do that, but..." He shrugged and shook his head.

Itching to turn around, Marnie had to focus on where they were walking instead of looking back to see if the ladies had followed them outside. "I know how you feel. I hate gossips, too. Most of the time, they just need something to do. Technology has changed everything. Most people feel the need to constantly be doing something, good or bad. We, as a species, can no longer sit still and just enjoy the silence, or read a good book."

"Yeah, I know what you mean. This past summer I hired on a couple of local kids to help out around the ranch and I can't tell you how many times I caught them on their phones. Texting, or checking social media. They can't seem to focus on anything else." Declan shook his head. "I don't know, but sometimes I think it might not be so bad to go back to before we had cell phones."

"I know, right?" Marnie chuckled. "My parents told me that before cell phones were a normal thing, people would call someone's house and leave a message. They wouldn't expect an instant call back. They understood that it could take a day to hear back. But now? Oh boy, if you don't answer your phone right away, you had better call them back within ten minutes or they'll think you don't like them anymore. How strange is that?"

Declan thought about it for a minute. "I don't tend to call back right away. Being out on the ranch, I don't have the best cell reception. In fact, we usually carry radios when we are out in the fields, but only for work use. It's how we talk about the movement of animals or equipment. But I know what you mean. I dated a girl once who always got offended that I never called her back until after dinner."

"We're in the age of instant gratification, and always needing something to do. I wonder what Pink Hair and her gang used to do as kids? They didn't have cell phones, or even computers, why is it that they need to be always doing something or the rest of the town suffers from their gossiping ways?" Marnie couldn't imagine how today's retirees spent their time growing up. They had TV's, for sure. And she had seen a VCR player and knew that the older generation used them. Maybe gossiping was how they spent their time since they didn't have much else to do? Or at least in a small town? She wasn't sure, but then she thought back to when she was in the Air Force and realized that gossip wasn't limited to the blue-plate special club. People of all ages participated in that rotten pastime.

"Pink Hair? I love it. Her name is actually Miss Gladys. Her husband passed away a few years ago and since then, she's been spending too much time at the hairdressers or the café. She and her friends will occasionally help out with the events around town. When they are busy, they don't gossip nearly as much. I wonder who is going to wrangle them into busy work this year." With a deep laugh, Declan's fake smile turned to a real one.

And Marnie relaxed herself. While she did want to know what those women said, she liked seeing Declan letting go of the stress and enjoying the afternoon. "So, tell me, what is this town's Thanksgiving Dinner really like?"

Another chuckle escaped Declan's lips. "Oh, it's nothing like anything you've ever seen before. Words can't really describe it, you have to see it to understand it."

"Well, it sounds as though our entire ranch will be attending, and some will be helping out. I volunteered to man the dessert table." Marnie looked around before continuing. "I understand that there are a few people who will try to steal an entire pie! Can you believe that?"

"Yes, I can." With a grin, Declan's shoulders relaxed back into their normal position and he seemed to have a lighter step as well. She wouldn't call it a bounce, since men don't really bounce. And especially cowboys. But, there was something different about him since they walked out of the café. "About five years ago, Mrs. Henderson began making apply pies with a crumble on top. She also brought cans of whipped cream to put on top of her pies. They are the best pies in the county. She has won blue ribbons at the state fair. And then the next year, a few of the teenagers, mostly boys, began pilfering her pies. So, now there is always a volunteer at the table to make sure everyone gets a chance at the dessert they want most."

Marnie's eyes widened. "Does she really make enough apple pies for the entire town?"

"No, not the entire town. We always run out of her pies, but she does make about ten pies. Most people get a small slice of her apple pie. But there will also be a lot of pumpkin pies. Especially now that we have our pumpkin patch I expect to start seeing a lot of pumpkin goodies." Declan rubbed his mouth and swallowed. "Speaking of pumpkin, we should stop in the coffee shop. They have a fantastic pumpkin spice latte. Have you ever had one?"

"Ohh, I love a good PSL. Count me in."

With that thought in mind, the two of them headed off to the Frenchtown Roasting Company with thoughts of delicious coffee concoctions on their minds.

Chapter 20

Marnie wasn't sure what she expected for Thanksgiving on the ranch, but it wasn't what she was currently looking at. The ranch table, while larger than her family table back home, looked almost identical to the one her parents set every Thanksgiving. They had turkey with all of the trimmings. The only real difference was the fact that they also had a platter of lamb chops and a bowl of macaroni and cheese.

"So, will the community dinner on Saturday be the same as today's?" Marnie asked right before stuffing a fork full of creamy mac n cheese in her mouth. This was so much better than the boxed stuff she usually had back home.

Dana nodded. "There will be plenty of turkey, but also some ham, ribs, and lots of steak. Since we have ranchers here, they will all bring in meat from their own stock."

"You haven't experienced a community Thanksgiving until you've had a Frenchtown Thanksgiving." Mike Blankenship, who had been a resident of the ranch for a few years before leaving them recently, joined them for Thanksgiving dinner. "Even though I'm only a couple of hours away, I won't be here on Saturday. I have to work that day."

"And you will be sorely missed." Jerod slapped a hand on the veteran sitting next to him. "But I'm so glad you found your purpose and a great job." He narrowed his eyes as he tilted his head and looked closely at Mike as the shy man looked down at his food.

Mike wasn't one for the limelight. He preferred to hide behind his cows and have no one take notice of him. The cow whisperer nodded and his cheeks began to turn pink with all of the attention on him.

Skeeter, who had also joined them for Thanksgiving dinner, grinned. "I think Mike has found more than his purpose in life." He waggled his brows. "Did our quiet big guy find a lady?"

"Skeeter!" Dakota Monahan slapped her boyfriend's arm. "Don't tease him like that. At least not at the dinner table. Save it for when it's just the two of you." Dakota hadn't been at the ranch long, but she had known Mike long enough to know that he didn't like attention. And he certainly didn't like it when teased about a woman. She doubted he had found someone so soon since leaving the ranch for his new job.

"Hey, he doesn't mind, do you, Mike?" Skeeter turned his attention back to the man who knew cows better than anyone at that table.

Mike shook his head and stuffed a large piece of turkey with gravy and mashed potatoes in his mouth. He took his time eating his mouthful of food.

Marnie watched everyone interacting with one another and realized that this was a family. They may not have been related by birth, but they had chosen each other to be family. It reminded her of her squad back in Germany. When she was first sent back to the states for medical care, before her medical discharge, she had kept in constant touch with her friends. They came to see her on a daily basis.

When she came stateside, they kept in touch through email. Now? Distance didn't help, but they do on occasion still message one another even if it's mostly in group emails now. Marnie realized it was partly her own fault. As she was going through the therapy stateside, she didn't do enough to stay in touch with everyone.

"Marnie, what do you think about all of this?" Dana, who was sitting next to her, touched her arm.

"Oh, yeah. Sorry. I was somewhere else." She grinned. "This is a lot to take in, but it's also a good thing. It's strange to see how close everyone is. Even those who have moved away. Do you think they'll always stay close?"

Dana took a moment to look at each and every face at the table. When she turned back to Marnie, she nodded. "I think most will. They've all been through so much together and now have a lot more in common with each other than with anyone else they know. Their family can't understand what they've gone through, and their military friends who weren't medically discharged don't understand the shame they felt at not being good enough to stay in. Although, that's not really the case. So far, most have come to realize that there is no shame in receiving a medical discharge. It sucks, true. But it isn't a bad reflection on them."

That was something Marnie could relate to. She nodded. "Yeah, I think you hit the nail on the head with that last one. I have a cousin and she left the Air Force after her four years were up. She doesn't understand why I'm so torn up about being a civvie now. I don't think it's shame I'm feeling, but more confusion."

Dana narrowed her eyes and turned in her seat to look closer at Marnie. "Confusion? About what?"

Marnie sighed. "You know, this really isn't the place and time to talk about this." A soft chuckle escaped. "How about we table this convo until next week? I'd rather focus on all of the fun we are about to have this weekend."

Since there really wasn't much Dana could do, she agreed.

Marnie could tell that her new friend wasn't going to let it go for long. And she wasn't sure she wanted to keep this new thought bottled up inside. It might actually be nice to talk to someone about it. Especially someone with Dana's viewpoint. While Dana wasn't a veteran herself, she was married to one. And she helped everyone here at the ranch. Since she wasn't an actual counselor, she was easy to talk to. It never felt like therapy speaking with Dana.

However, Megan was a different story. When inside Megan's office, it was very evident that she was a counselor. But outside, she was more like a girlfriend. At times it was a bit confusing. But she wouldn't trade it for anyone else. Even though the counseling sessions could be a bit odd, Marnie was comfortable telling Megan everything she was thinking and feeling. She doubted that she'd feel that way with anyone else.

Especially since she never really jelled with her VA or Air Force counselors.

Jerod stood at the head of the table and clinked his glass of iced tea with his spoon. "I'd like to say a toast. And then we have a tradition here at the ranch. We all take turns saying what we are thankful for on Thanksgiving."

Everyone turned to look at the leader of the ranch and put their glasses and mugs in the air. No one had alcohol since it wasn't allowed at the ranch. None of those present had a problem with drinking, but a lot of disabled vets did deal with alcohol abuse in an effort to deal with their pain. Illegal substance abuse or alcohol would get a resident booted from the program. They didn't have anyone on staff trained to deal with those issues, so they didn't accept anyone who had those types of problems.

Jerod smiled and looked at his wife, before looking at everyone around his table. "May you all be blessed this holiday season with love, laughter, and pure joy that resonates deeply within your soul." He raised his glass even higher, then looked at his wife as he took a sip of his tea.

"Here, here!" Everyone yelled in unison before drinking from their glasses.

Once Jerod sat down, he cleared his throat to get everyone back on track. This group was large and could easily get out of hand. "I'd like to start with what I'm thankful for. Then we can go around the table clockwise."

After everyone nodded their understanding, Jerod began, "I'd love to thank my wonderful wife for always being so supportive. I don't think this ranch would still be here without her help." He looked right into his wife's eyes. "I love you and thank God for you every day."

Marnie's eyes began to prick with the emotion the big guy was demonstrating right in front of everyone. Like the rest, she had seen him hug and kiss his wife, but she'd never heard him talk with so much emotion seeping from his every word. It was very obvious that Jerod and Dana had the sort of marriage that she hoped to have one day. Although she doubted a man would be able to get past her missing toes, she still secretly harbored a desire for a love so strong, her deformity wouldn't matter.

As everyone took their turn saying what they were thankful for, Marnie thought about herself. In the past year she really hadn't thought about what she was thankful for, except for maybe still being alive. However, that wasn't really something she wanted to say in front of a room full of macho men.

She continued to listen to everyone else, and then it hit her. She knew what she was truly thankful for at that moment. She smiled when Dana said how thankful she was for Jerod and for him trusting her enough to let her in when he was hurting.

Then it was Marnie's turn. "I'm thankful that I was accepted at this ranch. When I first heard about this place, I just thought it would be a sort of vacation. A chance to see and experience something different. But I'm learning it's so much more." She chuckled.

Tony snorted.

Skeeter hollered.

"Quiet down, let her finish," Jerod admonished.

"I really didn't think I'd be able to learn how to walk without my cane. At least not here. And I'd probably wash out within a few weeks. But since arriving here I see that I do have hope, and a chance at a somewhat normal life." Marnie turned to look at Jerod. "Thank you for starting this ranch. Looking at all of those around this table I can see that there is true healing here. And I am grateful for being allowed to join this wonderful group."

All of those at the table raised their glasses and cheered.

"So, Black Friday? I'm not much of a shopper. And I don't need to buy much, either." Marnie scrunched her nose at the ladies while they were all washing dishes after a very filling Thanksgiving dinner.

"You don't have to join us. It's not a requirement. Some of us just love to go and enjoy the energy of shopping on the biggest day of the year." Dana shrugged.

Marnie grinned at Megan. "So, since you spent most of the day today with Daniel, does that mean that you two are back on track?"

She used this opportunity to get Megan back for all of the teasing and attempted matchmaking she had done recently.

Marnie and Dana grinned as Megan's cheeks turned red.

Marnie was washing, Dana was rinsing, and Megan was drying. Dakota was still bringing in dirty dishes and figuring out what was worth saving for leftovers and what just wasn't enough for even one serving.

"I think Megan's face says it all." Dakota, who held a platter of the last few vestiges of the turkey laughed before setting it down on the kitchen island. "Do you think this is enough to save for maybe one turkey sandwich?" She pointed to the few slices left next to the bones that had been practically cleaned by all of the men, and women, in the house.

Marnie looked over her shoulder. "I'd gladly make a sandwich with what's left."

"So would I," Dana announced.

Megan looked at it and grinned. Then she swiped a slice and stuck it in her mouth. "Mmm, much better than what the guys at the tree farm cooked up today."

"Hey, now there isn't enough for even a sandwich." Dakota almost slapped Megan's hand away, but she was too fast.

"Well," Dana looked around. "Waste not, want not." Then she grabbed a slice and stuffed it in her mouth.

Marnie laughed and felt as though she was home. "I guess if we want any, we need to hurry up and grab a piece." She rinsed the soap from her hands and dried her fingers off as best she could. Then when she turned around, there was only a small piece left. "Hey, where'd it all go?"

The other three women couldn't say anything as their mouths were full.

Marnie chuckled and shook her head. But she did grab the last small piece before anyone else could. "That is so good," she said as she chewed.

A few more dishes ended up being cleared instead of having the leftovers put in the fridge.

When all was done, Marnie slumped back in a chair at the kitchen table. She put a hand on her belly and sighed. "I don't think I've eaten this good, or this much, in forever."

"I've never eaten like this before," Dakota added. "I swear, Dana, you could open a restaurant with how good you cook."

Marnie noticed the pink tinged cheeks and grinned. Her new friend was a fantastic chef. She'd pay to eat her meals. And her desserts. "That pecan pie was out of this world. And I'm not even a fan of pecan pie."

Dana swiped a hand in front of her face. "Oh, stop. You'll give me a swelled head." When she laughed, the others joined in with her.

Marnie noticed that this group of women laughed a lot. She knew laughter was good for so many things, but she'd never experienced a group who were so happy that it bubbled over into laughter. Even though she was in a temporary situation, she knew she had found her place. If she could find a job nearby, like some of the others had, she might have to seriously consider living in Frenchtown.

The question was, what could she do? She was trained for a type of job that wasn't normal in the civilian world. Sure, she knew planes a bit. But she wasn't a pilot, even though she could fly a plane, she wasn't certified. Her training was more like that of a stewardess. She could land a plane if there was an issue with the pilot and copilot, but that was about it. Not to mention her experience was with specific Air Force planes.

But it was a moot point since she wasn't a trained pilot with a license. And it wasn't really what she wanted to do anyway. She didn't know what she wanted, but Marnie knew one thing, she wasn't interested in flying commercial planes. And she didn't want to be an air traffic controller. Not that she had enough knowledge to do that job, either.

No, she wasn't much better than a recent college graduate. Lots of schooling but no real-world experience. She hadn't even had the benefit of doing an internship while in school.

The interesting thing was that until just recently, she hadn't really given much thought to her future. She was so overwhelmed with her present, that the future was more like a sci-fi novel than her own reality.

She could probably teach Russian to kids, but was there any need for that in a small Montana town? Marnie doubted it. Maybe Megan would have some thoughts for her in their next counseling session. Or maybe the guys will in their next group session. But, until then, she needed to get her head back in the game. This was going to be one busy weekend and she didn't want to miss one second of it.

Chapter 21

Instead of heading off to do Black Friday shopping with the others, Marnie stayed behind at the ranch and helped out with the animals. Her cane might have slowed her down, she found herself less reliant on it than she had been only a week before.

The fact that she had run into the barn when the storm hit, and she left her cane at the house, had really hit home with her. Marnie had tried to walk without it a few times and was just too wobbly to continue so she kept using the proverbial crutch.

However, keeping one hand on the tip of the cane wasn't easy to do when one was feeding or brushing an animal. While she kept her distance from the cows, they still didn't seem to like her and it was mutual, she did find that the horses were very calming.

"Aren't you a handsome horse," Marnie cooed to the horse as she brushed his sides.

Dixon, one of the residents who didn't talk much, walked over to Marnie and the horse. "He likes you."

"Huh?" Marnie started when the man spoke behind her. She had been so engrossed in what she was doing that she didn't hear him walk up.

"Jackson, that's the horse. He's pretty tame and likes most people. But his favorite is Zipper." Dixon grinned and put a hand out with some grain for Jackson to eat. The horse was a ten-year-old gelding who was white with brown spots, almost like a leopard, just not as many spots.

The horse nodded his head and snuffled up the offering. Then he whinnied and seemed to preen with the attention he was getting.

Marnie laughed. "He seems to like attention, am I right?"

"Yup, he does. And it's the strangest thing but he and one of the barn cats get along quite well. I'm actually surprised..." Dixon's voice trailed off and a slow smile spread across his face. "Well, there he is."

Marnie turned to look in the direction of Dixon's eyes. There sitting on his haunches with his head tilted was a mangy looking cat. The cat seemed to be watching them just as they were him. His fur was a bit matted, almost like he had been sleeping all day on one side. The other side had a couple of pieces of hay sticking out of him.

"I see Mr. Zipper has been sleeping the day away." Marnie put her hands on her hips. "Have you been earning your keep?"

As if he understood, Zipper lifted one paw and began to lick it. Then he put it down and looked to the corner of the barn where something lay dead on the ground.

A sense of disgust began to pass through Marnie's stomach, but she decided this cat was testing her. He wanted to know what sort of human she was. Would she pass out at the sight of a dead rat? Or would she congratulate the tiny beast on a job well done?

It was an easy choice for Marnie, she chose the latter. "Good job, Zipper. That's what we like around here, isn't it?" She turned to look at Dixon, who scowled.

"Zipper, you're supposed to either eat them, or take them away somewhere that they won't be in the way." Dixon scrunched his nose and spoke to the cat as though he were human. Which was strange.

Marnie looked between the two, then back at the horse who had his head over the gate of his stall watching the little cat. "No, Jackson, that isn't your lunch."

The horse pulled back and shook his head. Then he snorted, almost like he was laughing at her comment.

Dixon did laugh. "No, you got it wrong. Zipper is Jackson's best friend. They usually sleep together on cold nights. Jackson provides the warmth, and Zipper keeps the vermin out of his stall."

With no experience in the animal arena, Marnie wasn't sure if he was telling her the truth, or pulling her leg. "Really? A horse and a cat are best friends?" She'd seen those funny YouTube videos about strange animal friends, but she always thought they were fake, or extremely rare.

"Yup. Why don't you help me put up the garland in here and I'll tell you more about the animals on this ranch." Dixon walked over to the tack room and opened the door to show her several crates full of Christmas decorations.

"Wow. Decorating a house I can understand, but a barn?" Marnie shook her head and blinked a few times. "That's just strange."

"Not really. It's very common around here. And when we're done, we'll need to head over to Declan's place. He's going to show us how to separate the herds and get them to go where you want them to." Dixon pulled out one strand of green garland that had red velvet bows tied on it in equal intervals.

"That's right, the ranch is going to get some alpaca and sheep. But why do we need to separate the herds? Aren't the alpacas supposed to be with the sheep?" With another strand of garland in her hands, Marnie followed Dixon to the other side of the room where they noticed some nails hanging from one of the poles in between the horse stalls.

Dixon put the garland on the first nail, making sure to leave a little bit of a tail to hang down and wrap around the pole. "Yes, and no. When a herd gets too big, and the alphas start to assert their dominance, it's important to separate the herds. We won't have to deal with size issues for a while, and it will be a couple of years before we would have a need for a second alpha. But sometimes we will have to move the herds to different pastures. We need to ensure that there is always plenty of grass for them to chew on."

With a nod, Marnie put her garland up on the nails. She continued to use her cane when walking, but while standing she was able to reach up and attach the garland to the nails without any issue. When she arrived, standing wasn't much of an issue. She used her cane, but it was more like a security blanket while standing. Now, she didn't feel the need quite as much as before.

Besides, she knew Dixon's story. And if a man with a prosthetic leg was able to get around without any aid, then she could certainly stand in place without help.

Dixon noticed her eyeing his legs. "Curious about my bionic leg?"

Her eyes widened and her mouth opened, but then she closed it and smirked. "Bionic huh? Why didn't I get bionic toes?"

He snorted, almost like the horses did just then. "What would you do with one set of bionic toes? Bounce up to the moon?"

She decided she liked this guy. Not in the *I want to date him* sort of way, but in the *he's a nice guy and would make a fun friend* sort of way.

"You seem to have adjusted to your new reality quite well. How'd you do it?"

He finished putting the strand of garland up without answering her. When he was done, he looked at her. "You really think I've done well?"

While Marnie wasn't finished with her garland, she decided to stop and look at him as well. "Yes, I think you seem to be well adjusted. Although, a bit shy. It's taken you a couple of weeks to speak to me." This was the most he had said to her since she arrived. Before then, *pass the potatoes, please*, was the most he had said to her.

"Fair enough. Since the explosion I haven't been very social." Dixon looked down at his feet. He had on cowboy boots. He'd learned that wearing the boots actually helped him with his walk. He didn't walk normally, but with cowboy boots on no one gave his gait a second glance. Most men walked a bit differently when wearing boots with a heel. "You know, I always wondered how women could walk in high heels." He grinned. "Now I know. It's not easy, or fun. But I'm getting used to the boots."

With a glance down at her own feet, Marnie realized she was wearing work boots, not cowgirl boots. "Do you think cowgirl boots with a heel will make a difference for me?"

Marnie didn't struggle with her gait, she struggled with balance. While they weren't too different, the issues were different enough that she wasn't sure adding a heel would help her stay steady.

"Lift your foot. The one with your prosthetic." Dixon watched as Marnie gripped her cane and white knuckled it. He looked at her foot and the shoe she was wearing. "I see you have a good, firm sole on those boots. Are they heavy?"

While they weren't air foam shoes, they weren't cement blocks either. "I don't think so. But I suppose all work boots are a bit heavier than a pair of tennis shoes. However, I've spent the past seven years wearing combat boots, so the weight is normal to me. If I were to wear Doc Martens I might notice a difference, but these are about the same." She pointed to her black boots with thick black rubber soles, not so different from what she wore in service.

"Well, my issue is very different from yours. But I would suggest you give a good pair of cowgirl boots a try. It can't hurt." Dixon shrugged. Then went back to putting up the garland.

Marnie hadn't really thought too much about her shoes. When she first was fitted for the prosthetics, the technician suggested she wear work boots, since she was so accustomed to combat boots. He said it would be more comfortable for her. And he had been right. While the fake toes were similar in size to her real ones, she knew there wasn't an issue with pinching, or anything like that. Especially since she couldn't actually feel those toes.

She still had pain from where she lost her toes. The nerves were damaged, and she might always have pain, but the other patients had said she'd get used to it. It had almost been a year since her accident, and she realized that she rarely used Tylenol anymore for the discomfort she felt. If that was a sign that she was getting used to the pain, then she supposed it was good.

It was strange how fast things were coming together for her since she arrived at the ranch. Never did she think she would be so close to walking without a cane. Nor did she think the pain levels would diminish so quickly.

Marnie wondered, not for the first time, if God had waited to heal her mentally until she arrived at the ranch. It felt as though it was happening too quickly, but it had been nine months since her accident. She should be healing physically, as well as mentally.

When she first arrived, she had thought she might get a service dog, but quickly realized that the dogs weren't for her. She loved animals, but she wasn't in need of a service dog. Even though she thought Pebbles, the black and white collie was the most adorable dog she'd ever met. And Pebbles had taken a liking to her as well. Not that they had spent a lot of time together.

Maybe she could get a job working with Nelly and Sam.

But before she could think any more about that, Dixon spoke to her.

"What do you think about that ADA Coordinator?" Without stopping, Dixon continued to put up the garland. They were close to being done and the barn was looking rather magical with the green garland and red ribbons.

"She seems nice, but her questions have me wondering if she's looking to cause problems for the ranch. What do you think?" Marnie wrapped the end of her last garland around the last horse stall. She smiled when she looked over all of the stalls and their decorations. Christmas was definitely in the barn.

While Marnie couldn't be sure, she thought the horses smiled along with her. She was positive they loved the Christmas decorations just as much as she did.

Dixon stood back to admire their handywork. "Nice. I think we did a really good job. And I agree with you. I get the feeling that she's itching for a fight."

"Well, except for when she speaks with Marty." Marnie giggled. "I think she's got a crush on him."

"You don't say?" The sarcasm dripping from Dixon's voice let Marnie know he was in agreement with her assessment.

It took a moment, but Marnie realized she had done it again. Without thinking, she was walking without her cane. But, the moment she realized it, her legs wobbled and she fumbled for something to hold her upright. Dixon was there with his strong arms and he held her up.

"Thanks. I don't know what's gotten into me lately." She shook her head and stood straight.

Dixon reached down and picked up her discarded cane. "Here. And I think most of your problem is here." He pointed to her head. "Not in your feet."

If anyone would know, Dixon would. Marnie knew that losing an entire leg was so much worse than losing five toes. She couldn't imagine how he had learned to walk so well, and accept all of his changes.

Marnie felt heat simmer up her neck and she used her free hand to rub at the hot spots. "Yeah, you might have a point." She didn't want to dwell on that. Instead, she directed them back to the house so they could get ready to head over to Declan's ranch. She was looking forward to seeing his ranch, and maybe even to seeing him.

Chapter 22

Declan hadn't seen or spoken with Marnie in two days. While he barely knew her, and certainly hadn't seen her every day since meeting her, he did find he missed her when they went more than a day without talking.

Their most recent conversations had him smiling every time he recalled them. Marnie was so much more than a beautiful woman - she was strong, intelligent, and had a fun sense of humor. She also had an adventurous side to her. One that he knew would do well on a ranch. The fact that Marnie had loved all of her new adventures before her injury only enforced the idea that she would love ranch life.

He was getting ahead of himself. Declan had only known her for a short while, and she certainly hadn't shown any interest in dating him. She could barely stand being in his presence only a week ago. The last week had really turned things around for their budding friendship. "That's it!" Declan exclaimed to no one in particular.

"Friendship." Declan patted Ransom's head and gave him the carrot he had brought outside with him. While he waited for the guys from The Crooked Arrow Ranch to show up, he had decided to head to the barn and check on his horse.

"Friendship? Who you talkin' to, boss?" Luis stepped through the barn door and nodded to Declan.

"Oh, you know. Just having a chat with Ransom." Declan grinned back at his young ranch hand.

Juan chuckled. "Is he talkin' back to ya?"

"Of course, he is." Indignation flared within Declan, so he turned his back on his employee. Declan believed his animals understood him. Well, the dogs and horses at least acted as though they understood, he usually had conversations with his horse.

Ransom was a great listener. He never gossiped about Declan, he always gave the man his full attention, except for when carrots and apples were around. Then his attention was focused on those. The best thing about the horse was he never judged Declan. No matter what Declan said, the horse would nuzzle his shoulder, almost like a hug, and let him know all would be fine.

"Old people. Geesh." Juan chuckled and shook his head. "You're just like my pa. He swears up and down that his old horse talks back to him, too." He looked around and lowered his voice. "But I think he's going senile already. He is over fifty, you know."

Declan swung around and arched a brow. "Do you think fifty is old?"

The young man snorted. "Of course I do. Isn't that the time you can start getting senior citizen discounts?"

With a shake of his head and a quick chortle, Declan mussed Juan's hair. "Oh, youth is so wasted on the young."

"Huh?" Juan scrunched his nose and tilted his head.

But before Declan could explain that someone in their fifties may not be busting broncs anymore, that doesn't mean they're old. For most, life really doesn't begin until they're in their forties. At least, that's what Declan's dad always said.

The large barn door opened and in walked a small group of cowboys and one pretty cowgirl. Declan couldn't hold back his grin when he saw Marnie dressed in blue jeans, a black sweater, large winter red coat, and her black boots. The girl really needed to get some cowgirl boots, but Declan didn't feel it was his place to say anything. For just a moment he pictured her in red boots and he felt his lips curl up in a small smile. The image energized him and he stepped forward to greet his guests.

He also noticed she had her cane with her, but she didn't seem to be leaning on it nearly as much as she had in the past. He prayed that she was learning to trust her own feet, instead of that chunk of wood. "Welcome to my ranch. I hope y'all are ready to get cold and possibly wet." Declan grinned when most of the guys looked like they wanted to be anywhere but there.

"Oh, come on. It's not so bad." Juan grinned. "At least it's not hundred and twenty degrees with sand everywhere. Did they really have spider scorpions that were two feet long?" He shivered and shook his head. "No thanks."

Tony Sullivan chuckled. "Well, there were those. But I think I'd take snow over sand any day."

"We used them for target practice." Dixon's talking to a group surprised Jerod.

Even though Dixon had spoken plenty to Jerod, the injured vet hadn't spoken much to others, and it was very rare he addressed a group of people.

Marnie knew part of Dixon's story, and she too was surprised by Dixon taking part and joking around.

"Whoa! Really? They're that big?" Juan's eyes were as large as a dart board. "Do they attack people?"

All of the veterans who had been in the desert shivered, then chuckled nervously.

Jerod was the one who answered, "yes, and you never want to be on the end of their stinger."

Juan put up in hands as if to protect himself just from the image alone. "No, I don't think I even want to see one from a distance, or in a zoo. Those things looked really scary on YouTube."

While Marnie had never served in the Middle East, she had heard plenty of stories and seen pictures from Airmen she knew who had been in the sandpit. It was not something she ever wanted to confront, either. Her stomach turned just at the memory of those pictures.

"Okay, so." Marnie wanted to change the subject without being too obvious. But she needn't have worried, it seemed everyone else wanted to do the same.

"I think it's time we head out and check on the herds." Declan said goodbye to his horse and headed back outside with the group from the Crooked Arrow. "First, we'll start with what we feed them." He headed over to another structure and opened the door.

When everyone was inside, Declan pointed out the different types of feed he had. "We have some hay, alfalfa, various grains, and salt. It's important to mix up what they eat during the winter months when foraging isn't available."

Marnie raised her hand. "But the snow melts and the grass comes out, right?"

"Sorta." Declan rubbed his chin. "We have big storms and little storms all winter long. When the snow does melt, there can still be some good shoots in the ground just waiting for the sheep and alpaca to come by. But we can't count on it. I have a few pastures where I grow hay and alfalfa just for the winter months. We generally put their feed out each morning and afternoon under the shelters we have built for them."

"You don't have to do that all year long, do you?" Jerod asked.

"No." Declan shook his head. "We have a good rotation schedule here on the land and I ensure that we don't have too large of a herd during the winter. The majority of our stock is used for their wool, but we do sell off some ewes at market. Especially if we have a large population explosion like we did this year. Lamb is highly prized and believe it or not, our neighbors to the north love lamb more than Americans do."

Declan went into detail regarding how much to feed each member of the herd and how often. What is the best mixture during winter versus summer and all in between.

Marnie felt like it was information overload, and she could tell her eyes were glazing over. Most of what he was saying was going in one ear and out the other. She really wanted to keep the information in and process it, but it was too much. Like reading an entire volume of the encyclopedia on sheep in one go.

Jerod interrupted Declan. "Okay, do you have literature on this? Or a manual with most of the information?" He looked around at those with him and noticed the deer in the headlights look on his team. "I think we are going to need to study this information like a college student."

Marnie could get behind that idea. She had always been good at studying. Note taking had been the one thing that helped her to excel in college. The professors were always giving too much information or telling it in a way that was boring. She'd go over her notes later and rewrite them in a way that made sense to her, and to her study buddies. She nodded her agreement with Jerod.

After Declan looked around at the group, he smiled and nodded. "Yes, there are plenty of resource materials available on all of this. And I'll be happy to come out when it's time to change things up, too. But the most important thing to do before you start buying any stock is to ensure that you have a few shelters set up, or at least a windbreak. Not all of your fields have enough trees to protect the herd. And when we have storms like what we just went through, the sheep and alpaca will need to be inside a warm barn."

"I read that sheep only need to be inside a barn when it gets below zero degrees Fahrenheit. Is that true?" Dixon sounded as though he had been paying attention and was now asking some very good questions.

Marnie wondered if this was going to be Dixon's thing. Like Mike had found the cows, Skeeter seemed to thrive running a ranch, and a few other guys had found their post-military calling just by recovering on the Crooked Arrow Ranch.

But would she find her calling?

Chapter 23

Saturday morning, after feeding the animals, just about everyone from the Crooked Arrow left early to head to the Christmas tree farm and help set-up for the Thanksgiving dinner.

"I can't believe it's already Saturday." Marnie looked around the space inside the barn where they had all agreed the Thanksgiving dinner - and a few other town events would take place this year.

Megan walked up next to Marnie. "Yup, and we are going to be here a lot." She side-eyed Marnie. "Well, some of us will be here a lot."

"Megan, wipe that grin off your face." Marnie pursed her lips as she watched the woman's eyes and her smile. She could tell that Megan had some plans in her head. Plans that involved Marnie, and probably some ranch hand on the tree farm.

Since the snowstorm destroyed the town's meeting hall, Marnie hadn't had a chance to come out to the tree farm and look everything over. Thankfully, Megan had an in with the farm foreman. Daniel Caruthers was a handsome and tall man. His smile could light up a room, but every time Megan had seen him enter a room, she noticed he only had eyes for Megan.

Megan had voiced some concerns over Daniel losing interest in her because she rarely saw him lately, but Marnie understood duty. This was the farm's busiest time of the year, surely even Megan understood that. But Marnie watched as Megan noticed who just entered the barn.

"Megan, sweetheart." A man who had to be pushing six feet in height and oddly looked a lot like that prince from England with his red hair and scruffy beard, walked up and kissed Megan on the cheek. It wasn't a long kiss, more like a peck.

However, Megan's cheeks turned red almost instantly. She looked down and away from Daniel just enough to hide her smile.

Marnie had plans for payback, but not in front of Daniel.

"Hi Daniel. It sure was nice of you guys to allow the town to move all of their big events out here." She shook hands with Daniel and smiled.

"Marnie, nice to see you again. And it really wasn't a big deal. Besides, we're going to end up getting a lot of business out of this. And, everyone from the ranch won't have to worry about splitting their time between here and town. We were going to be short a couple of volunteers, but now..." A brilliant smile lit up Daniel's face and his shoulders lifted in a shrug. "It's a win-win."

The man had a very warm and inviting smile. Marnie could understand what drew Megan to him. She felt Daniel was a very good guy and she wondered why he hadn't married yet.

Then she shook her head. Marriage wasn't something she even wanted to pass through her head, let alone actively think about. Megan's teasing was getting to her. She had to refocus and get her head back in the barn. Literally.

"Okay, so where do we begin?" Marnie needed to get back on task or her mind would wander to places it had no business going. She had found herself thinking the wrong things lately, and she didn't want those thoughts intruding on the day.

"Well, the guys are setting up the tables right now." Daniel pointed to the stack of folding tables in the corner and at least eight men were over there unloading. "I'd say to join them, but I think they have enough hands right now." He chuckled at his own joke.

For a moment, Marnie wondered if Daniel was making a joke about her hand always being on her cane, then realized he was talking ranch hands, or farm hands. She smiled and nodded. "Should we start putting up the chairs?"

Daniel smacked his hands together. "That's perfect. Thank you. I'll send Gladys and Maybell over to help you."

A strong need to roll her eyes overtook her, but Marnie held back. She was a Christian and would act as such. She'd just have to keep her mouth shut when those gossips were around.

"Great idea." Megan rubbed her hands together. "Let's do what we can to keep those ladies busy. Once the chairs are up, we'll need tablecloths put out and centerpieces. Those ladies will be great at that."

Marnie realized that Megan had had plenty of time to figure out how best to keep the local gossips too busy to talk about others. Her plan was good, really good. "I like it. But I imagine we'll still have to watch what we say around them?" She arched a brow hoping that Megan would understand today wasn't a good day to tease Marnie about, well, anything or anyone.

A quick nod and then the two women turned to leave.

But before they could get away, Daniel turned around. "Oh, I almost forgot. Cody suggested that you hold the Christmas live nativity here. We have the room, and since everything else is going to be here, might as well do that, too."

Marnie grinned when Megan's eyes lit up. "Looks like we are all going to be spending a lot of time here." She winked.

It only took a few hours, but the barn looked more like an event space than anything she'd seen in a while. It wasn't the type of barn with pens for horses or anything like that. Marnie was pretty sure that the Makinaws used this space for their own events and hoped that having the town's Thanksgiving dinner here wouldn't hurt their business. She had heard the story of how they almost lost the entire farm just a couple of years back.

She needn't have worried.

The entire town showed up, and most of the outlying ranches and farms made an appearance as well. She figured that the tree farm would get quite a bit of business tonight.

"Wow, just wow. Cove Hamilton shook his head and grinned. "I think we're gonna have to hold all of the holiday dinners here." He put an arm around his wife, Lottie, who was holding her belly.

Lottie looked around with wide eyes. "Well, it's much easier for me to manage a coffee cart in town, close to my coffee shop. But I must say, I love this space. And the way you used the left-over pumpkins from the patch here on the farm is outstanding. Are those gourds from the pumpkin patch too?" She pointed to a far table that held an assortment of mini gourds.

The tables all had fall decorations. Each table was different, but they all matched in theme and fall colors. The table Lottie pointed to had a cloth covering with pumpkins and turkeys on it and on top sat three large battery operated lanterns surrounded by mini pumpkins and gourds. The tops of the lanterns had orange, red, and burnt sienna colored silk flowers attached along with some creeping vines decorating the top and flowing down along the sides.

Marnie had been so impressed with Gladys and Maybell. They had brought crates full of decorations from the town's storage, as well as from their own homes. When Marnie tried to just put a few pumpkins and some table scatter down, the ladies jumped in and completely took over the decorating.

Maybell said, "We've been doing this for years. Let us handle this part and you two go find something else to do."

"Preferably something that doesn't include décor." Gladys pursed her lips and shook her head. The pink pouf on the top of her head shook like a Jell-O mold. It was all Marnie could do to keep from laughing.

Even with the memory, Marnie still wanted to bust up laughing. She figured she'd eventually get used to the characters in town, but until then, she needed to mind her P's and Q's, or she'd end up offending people. That was the last thing she wanted to do.

"I just love your coffee. I noticed one of your employees showed up over an hour ago and the line has been out the door the entire time. I take it everyone enjoys your coffee?" She couldn't be sure, but Marnie suspected that most of the local ranchers and farmers only drank Lottie's coffee. It was good, there was no doubt about it, but Marnie was used to those chain stores' coffee. And she liked them, too.

"Thank you." Lottie put a hand on Marnie's arm. "You're so sweet to say so. And yes, the town has come to expect my coffee cart at every local event. Even when the rodeo and carnival come to town, they expect me to have one, or two, carts." She chuckled and held her stomach even tighter.

Marnie noticed Cove putting his hand over her belly as well. It did look as though she was pregnant, but Marnie knew to not say a thing unless the woman came out and told her, or she wore one of those cute t-shirts. One that always caused her to smile was: *Caution- bun in the oven. Too hot to handle.*

The happy couple must have noticed her expression because Lottie nodded. "Yes, we're pregnant. My due date is right around Valentine's Day." She looked up at her husband and the love Marnie saw in both of their faces caused a pang in her own heart. In that moment, she wanted what they had.

Then reality set in and Marnie shook her head. "I'm so happy for you both. Quinn must be ecstatic." Marnie knew that Cove was Lottie's second husband. And that she didn't remarry for quite some time after her husband died.

This time it was Cove who answered, "Yes, she keeps asking if she's going to have a little sister. I want a boy, but I'll be happy with either."

"So will I," Lottie added. "But, a boy would be nice."

"Well, next time there's a community dinner here, I highly suggest bringing in two coffee carts." Marnie looked wistfully at the long line. "I guess I better go get in line if I want some before you run out."

Lottie laughed. "Don't worry, we won't run out. At least not of coffee. I can't say the same for the pastries, but there should be plenty on the dessert table."

She waved and walked toward the coffee cart only to be stopped half-way down the line when a hand reached out and grabbed hers.

"Marnie, I saved you a spot." Declan grinned and motioned for her to step in front of him when he let go of her hand.

Since Marnie had been in her own little world, she jumped when he grabbed her. "Oh, Declan." A nervous laugh escaped. "You startled me."

"Sorry, but I called your name and you didn't seem to hear me." Declan shrugged as though it was no big deal.

"Thank you." She got in line with him, then turned around to talk with him. "Do you come to these dinners all the time?"

He nodded. "Yup, I wouldn't miss this for the world. There's no way me or the guys can made such a great spread on our own."

A thought entered Marnie's head and she frowned. "What did you do for Thanksgiving? I never did ask you."

"There's always a family that invites the single ranchers over for dinner. I ended up having a nice Thanksgiving meal with Pastor Mason and his family. It was good, there's no denying that Jeannie Mason can cook." Declan rubbed his belly and licked his lips. "But nothing compares to this community dinner. Everyone always brings such tasty dishes. I usually have a hard time rolling myself home after I'm done eating everything in sight."

Both of them chuckled.

"I've heard so much about the food. But looking around, I have to say I'm impressed with how many people showed up. This place is packed to the rafters. Not everyone can sit down at the same time. Jerod said that people were asked to make room once they were done eating."

Declan sighed. "Yeah, that's the only bad part. The barn is a great size, but normally the event hall is large enough that everyone can sit around and talk all night long. But," he held up a gloved hand. "There is a lot to see and do here at the tree farm. There are also other little spots to sit and chat."

"It's a good thing there isn't snow in the forecast for tonight." A shiver went down Marnie's spine as she thought back to the snowstorm and how much snow was dumped all over the place. She doubted many families would have shown up if that snowstorm had been this weekend.

"True, true. And let's not forget, tonight we are also holding tryouts for the Christmas Nativity." Declan motioned for Marnie to move forward as the line continued to get shorter in front of them. "We are almost there." He pointed to the top of the coffee cart.

"Ah, yes. I can see the sign with the steaming coffee picture. I thought there were pots of free coffee over by the dessert tables. Why is everyone in line for this particular coffee?" Marnie pointed to where she had seen the large silver industrial coffee pots. The kind that held several gallons of coffee.

Declan rubbed his hands together. "Yes, there is the free coffee. And a lot of people will drink it, no problem. But that's just plain drip coffee. Here," he pointed to the coffee cart, "is all of your favorite coffee concoctions, not just plain black coffee."

"Ohh, fancy schmancy. I mean, I knew Lottie would have a cart here, but I didn't realize she would have all the fixings for the espresso drinks. My favorite on a cold night." Marnie giggled but knew she would choose a peppermint mocha over plain coffee any day, no matter how good the drip coffee was.

The time in line flew by as she and Declan talked about past community Thanksgiving dinners. "I can't believe your town's history. This is fantastic. And to think, it all started with wanting to make sure everyone had a decent Thanksgiving dinner when times were tough."

Marnie liked the history and tradition behind the evening's event. She grew up in a city where they had soup kitchens to help those in need. And her family did volunteer over the holidays to help serve meals to those in need, but it wasn't the same. This had turned into more than making sure someone who needed a hot meal got one. This was all about community. The residents all over the area would come together as one and celebrate their town, and its history. People brought what they could, and even if they brought nothing they were still welcomed with open arms.

She knew some of these people rarely left their farms and ranches so it was a huge deal to see everyone there.

Marnie watched as Skeeter and Dakota walked out of the barn hand in hand with smiles all around. They both waved to her as they walked by. When Marnie looked questioningly at their backs, Declan asked her what was wrong.

"Why didn't they stop and chat?" She pointed to the couple's retreating forms.

Declan turned to see who she was talking about. "Oh, Skeeter has to get back to the Henderson ranch. While most everyone will show up here tonight, some are doing it in turns. Especially since there isn't enough space for all to sit down together. I think since the Henderson's still don't have all of their fences back up, the cattle they do have, needs to be watched closely. They are in a small pen."

"Oh, so Skeeter is heading back to check on the animals while the Hendersons come over here for dinner?" Marnie could see how that would be important. Plus, all of the supplies for rebuilding the farm are out for anyone to steal. She figured it was good for most ranchers and farmers to come in shifts.

"Yup, so let's talk nativity." Declan grinned and they moved forward again. They were almost to the front of the line and the tryout were scheduled for an hour from then. He still needed to eat dinner before they began getting the nativity finalized.

Chapter 24

"Well, that went better than I expected." Marnie tilted her head. "Although, I'm not really sure what I expected."

They were both sitting inside the barn to be used for the Nativity later in December. Marnie held a cup of hot coffee in her hands and was blowing on the top to cool it down.

With a chuckle and a nod, Declan agreed. "So, practice starts after church tomorrow. I must say, I'm getting excited to see what we can do." He took a tiny sip and winced over how hot it was.

Marnie leaned in closer and lowered her voice, still not having tasted any of her hot coffee yet. "So am I. I was a bit leery about casting teenagers for the roles, but since we have a real baby, this is going to be awesome."

"But, do you think it's smart to have cast Mark Haskins for Joseph? I mean, you saw how he looked at Susie. If they aren't a couple, I bet they will be very soon. What if they have a tiff before the night of the performance? You know how volatile teenaged romances are." Marnie rolled her eyes and prayed that Mark and Susie would get along until Christmas.

Declan chuckled. "Yeah, I remember those days." He sighed. "But, I know the Pendletons and they aren't going to allow Susie to date Mark. Not until next year. So while they probably do like each other, nothing can happen until Susie turns sixteen. Everyone in town knows that none of the Pendleton kids can date until then."

"Well, I don't know about you, but I had a similar rule and it never stopped me from dating boys before I was sixteen. My parents just didn't know about it. I'd say I was going to the movies with one of my girlfriends when really, I was meeting a boy." She waggled her brows and grinned.

"You can't get away with that sort of behavior in a small town." Declan's lips raised on one side. "You've met Gladys and Maybell, haven't you? They aren't the only gossips in town."

Marnie slapped a hand to her forehead. "What was I thinking?" She chuckled. "Kids always find a way to sneak around behind their parent's back, and stay away from the local gossips. It's part of growing up." She eyed Declan. "I bet you did stuff behind your parents' backs that no one else knew about."

His sheepish grin totally gave him away. "Well, yeah. There are some things. But going to the movies isn't one of them."

She arched a brow.

"What?"

"Confession is good for the soul."

"Okay, miss little goody two-shoes, what about your escapades?" Declan wasn't about to share his childhood shenanigans. Not yet, anyways.

Marnie chuckled. "Oh, no you don't. I asked you first."

"And I asked you second. Two is more than one." Declan winked and showed off his pearly whites.

Marnie couldn't help it, she full out laughed. "Really? You're going with a grade school comeback?" Now, she finally did take a sip of her hot coffee and sighed. "Perfect."

"Perfect?" Declan grinned and waggled his brows. "I don't think I've been called that before. At least not to my face."

Marnie rolled her eyes, resisting the urge to put up her hand in the universal talk to the hand gesture. She didn't do it, but boy was she ever tempted. It seemed this *man* hadn't yet grown up. "Boys."

"What?" With a look that belied his innocence, Declan grinned and sat back to try another sip of his hot coffee. "Oh, I see what you mean." He sighed and took another drink. "Alright, all kidding aside. I think the kids will do well in their roles. They both grew up doing church and school plays, so they should have some sort of knowledge about how to act for the next month."

After taking a long sip of coffee, Marnie looked up at Declan. "I hope you're right. Mary is a key role. We can't hold a live nativity without her."

"Then, should we get an understudy?" While Declan wasn't big on plays and productions, he knew enough to know that having a backup for key roles was important. Even if they never used her, it would be smart to have one.

She took a moment to consider his idea. If they were going to put this production on for days, or even weeks, then they most certainly did need an understudy. But this production was a one night only type of event. Having a backup for the baby was probably something they should do. "I don't think we need an understudy for Mary, but baby Jesus will most likely need a toy baby to step in, just in case. Babies get sick all of the time, so who knows if baby Pendleton will be able to make his stage debut."

Declan rubbed the stubble on his chin and nodded his agreement. "Alright, that's all taken care of. Now we need to make sure that our set crew gets going right away on making the sets."

"Agreed." Marnie finished off her mug of coffee and set it down. Then they both got up and headed outside to speak with the assembled team.

Later that night, after everyone had gone to bed, Marnie lay awake in her room and thought through all they were going to need for the play. "Costumes!" She shot up in bed just before midnight and began pacing her room. She berated herself for forgetting all about costumes.

Her mind swirled round and round with the different ideas and items she still needed to take care of. Then, out of the blue, a sense of peace enveloped her and she took a deep breath. Marnie told herself to breathe deeply and take a seat. She didn't have a desk in her room, but she did have the end of the bed and a notebook she always kept next to her bed.

Marnie closed her eyes and took a few more calming breaths. "You can do this. Just think."

While Marnie had never been part of a production like the Nativity before, she had been to her fair share of plays. She knew that costumes and make-up were needed in addition to sets and the animals. Since they were doing a live nativity, the animals were the first thing they took care of. Earlier that night they had taken care of casting the players. There really weren't too many actors needed for the nativity, which meant not a lot of costumes, either.

As she was thinking about everything they still needed, she stopped and prayed. "Lord, I don't know what I'm doing here. All I know is that we want to tell your story and do it in a way that honors you and your Earthly family. Please give me the knowledge to know what to do next."

Normally when Marnie prayed, she said what she wanted to say and then moved on. But this time, something inside her said to wait. While she couldn't be sure, she thought it might have been the Holy Spirit speaking to her. It may not have been the first time he spoke to her, but it was the first time in a very long time she had heard his leading in a real way.

As she waited for a message, or direction, she kept her head bowed. Sleep was trying to take her away from her meditation on the Lord and His leading. Marnie bit the inside of her mouth to keep herself awake.

Then an image floated through her head. One that had her questioning it at first. The handsome cowboy wasn't what she expected. Marnie thought she might get a few words or even the knowledge to just be there. Instead, the image of Declan Walden smiling at her was clear as a bell.

She opened her eyes and grinned. "Okay, Lord. I'll ask him about all of this in the morning."

For all Marnie knew, the town could have all of the costumes from a previous play that had been held by one, or more, of the local churches. Dana might even have some knowledge on this matter. It was Dana who had begun to set it all up, after all. It was Dana who had originally volunteered Marnie to *help* with the play. Said *help* had turned into totally taking over, but Marnie didn't really mind.

It seemed something was in the town's water supply and several of the local women were now expecting babies. While Dana hadn't begun to show yet, Marnie did pick up on the other signs, like how tired the woman was, and how she had begun to show signs of morning sickness.

Lottie was far enough along that she was showing a decent baby bump, but Marnie wasn't sure how the woman could be due in just over two months and not be totally large. She had heard that some women when having boys have a smaller stomach. It sounded weird to her, more like backwards mumbo jumbo, but maybe she was going to have a small kid? Or maybe her stomach just wasn't showing properly when they spoke earlier? Marnie wasn't an expert, but she had seen plenty of pregnant women over the past ten years to pick up on signs.

Her mind was starting to get all jumbled up again with everything she had to still do.

Then a sense of peace enveloped her again and she went back to bed. Her sleep the rest of the night was uneventful. Well, unless you counted the dream of her and the cute cowboy riding off into the sunset together.

That was most certainly due to her being so tired and her mind totally focused on the nativity. She had, after all, been riding a donkey in her dream.

Chapter 25

Marnie couldn't believe that two weeks had already flown by. The mornings had been spent out at Declan's farm learning about the sheep and alpaca, while the afternoons were spent out at the tree farm going over the play with her cast. She also helped with the sets before the kids got out of school.

Which all meant for very long days, but also a lot of fun. She had learned that the Christmas Tree lot was open seven days a week and, on the weekends, they had a sort of mini-carnival. It was Christmas themed with all sorts of elves walking around and the best Santa and Mrs. Claus she had ever seen even showed up nightly.

It was Friday night and the final set had been put in place. Marnie was standing back and looking at everything they had done so far inside of the barn. Come Monday they would begin using the sets in their practice and then a week later dress rehearsals would begin. She turned her head when she heard the barn door open.

"Mr. and Mrs. Claus. So good to see you tonight." Marnie grinned and headed toward the town's favorite couple.

"Please, Marnie, call me Jessica when the kids aren't around." Mrs. Claus opened her arms for a hug and Marnie stepped right into the woman's sweet arms.

"I know, I know. It's so hard sometimes to remember." Marnie pulled back and then turned her smile on the jolly old elf. "I still can't believe that Frenchtown has the real Santa and his wife living here." She shook her head as she recalled what Declan had told her about Santa just the other day.

"It's not about whether one fat old man can travel the world in one night delivering presents to all of the good little boys and girls, it's about the spirit of the man. Is there someone who inspires belief in what they can't see? Someone who is generous and kind, almost to a fault? Someone who cares more about making a child smile than their own comfort? Or retirement?" Declan grinned and looked off into the distance the entire time he spoke of the merriest couple Marnie had ever met.

Dana had joined them at that moment. "You know, my mom used to always say that unless you believe in Santa, you won't get his special gift on Christmas morning." She nodded.

"And did you get that gift?" Marnie asked, unsure as to how many presents kids got in small, rural towns like Frenchtown.

"Oh, I got it alright. Every year there was a package with different wrapping paper than the rest of the lot." Dana sighed and her eyes got this far away look to them. Almost as though she was reliving one memory in particular from her childhood. "One year I thought I knew what was really going on. An older kid had spilled the beans about Santa and I was going to find out the truth. I remembered that the year before I had noticed the wrapping paper from Santa was different from all of the paper beneath the tree that year."

"Really? How old were you when you noticed different wrapping paper?" It took Marnie forever to realize, and then accept, that Santa wasn't real. And even then, her parents still had a special gift under the tree from Santa. All the way up until she left for the Air Force.

Dana looked down at her hands that were clasped in front of her. "I was...uh...twelve."

A gasp escaped Marnie, but she didn't say a thing.

Declan grinned and watched Marnie without saying a word the entire time.

"You have to understand that growing up in a small town that had its own Santa and Mrs. Claus, well..." Dana splayed her hands out to her side. "We tend to believe longer here than in most places."

Still not talking, Declan nodded his agreement.

"So..." Marnie let the word hang in the air for a few extra seconds. "You were thirteen when you learned the truth?" She arched a brow, waiting for Dana's reply.

"Yes, and no." Dana winced. "I think I knew the truth, but didn't want to so I actually didn't let on until I was fourteen."

"Uh, huh." Marnie bit her lower lip. "I guess, if I had grown up with Chris and Jessica playing Santa and Mrs. Claus my whole life, I'd probably believe a lot longer as well." She wasn't sure how much of that she believed, but it sounded good. And she didn't want to make Dana feel bad for believing for so long. "I guess that's why I've seen so many preteens visiting Santa the past two weeks, huh?"

"Yup. Parents around here like to keep it going for as long as possible. We all know the real reason for the season, but having kids who believe in Santa is just fun."

"Okay, so tell me what you did to discover the whole paper issue." Now, Marnie was getting into Dana's story and wanted the rest of it.

"Well, I decided to sleep out by the tree one Christmas Eve. I supposed my parents thought I'd fall asleep and not wake up when they placed the gifts from Santa under the tree." Dana chuckled. "They guessed wrong."

"Really?" Marnie's eyes opened wide. "What did you do?"

"I was asleep, but something woke me up. Now remember, I wasn't sure yet, so I didn't want to spook Santa if he saw me awake. I barely opened one eye. I could make out the outline of someone wearing a Santa hat in the dark so I quickly shut my eye and scrunched them tight." Dana licked her lips and looked at Marnie. "Then I got brave and opened both eyes, only a little. And instead of seeing Santa leave through the chimney, or even the front door, I saw him go down the hall towards the bedrooms."

"No way! Did you think he might be looking to kiss your mom?" Marnie laughed thinking about the song, and the TV movie – *I saw Mommy Kissing Santa Claus*.

Dana joined in on the laughing. "No, silly. I didn't think that. But I did get up to see what he was doing. When he entered my parents' bedroom there was enough light coming through the door that I recognized my dad's back. He had taken off the hat and I knew it was him."

"But it still took you a year to accept it?" Now Marnie wasn't sure how it all would go.

Dana shook her head. "You see, the man wasn't wearing the Santa hat, nor was it in his hands. And because of that, I convinced myself that my dad must have come out here to see what the noise was and somehow I missed seeing Santa leave. He was supposed to be a magical creature so maybe he didn't need a fireplace to exit the house?" She shrugged her shoulders.

"I see. You wanted so badly to believe that you found a way to convince yourself."

Dana nodded. "Yup. And I suppose it's the same for most of the kids in the area."

"It is." Declan stated. "And I did something similar one year, sleeping out by the tree. Only I slept the entire night without waking up." He chuckled. "A few of my buddies did the same thing. Only one woke up and saw his mom putting gifts out under the tree. We didn't believe him at first. But I asked my mom about it and reminded her that she promised to never lie to me. She told me the truth but asked that I stay quiet and let the other kids believe as long as possible."

"And did you? Stay quiet that is?" Marnie asked. His answer could change how she thought about his character. If he was around thirteen when this happened, and he decided to keep the secret longer, then she knew she could trust him.

He rubbed the back of his neck. "Well, not exactly."

Marnie arched a brow, but said nothing, choosing to wait for him to explain.

Dana crossed her arms over her chest and glared. "Yes, do tell, Declan."

He rubbed the back of his neck and his cheeks grew red. "You see, my aunt and uncle came to visit for New Year's and they brought my cousin who is a year older than me. He was teasing a group of us about still believing in Santa."

Marnie could see where this was heading, and she felt for the thirteen-year-old Declan. That kind of peer pressure had to be tough, especially when being called a baby or any other derogatory thing. Young teen boys always have to prove they are men, way before they are actually men.

"Yeah," Declan sighed. "I can see you pretty much know where I'm going with this story. It's all too common. Boy gets teased, so boy says or does whatever he can to stop the teasing. I just blurted it out like I was some alien monster spewing on the group." He chuckled at the visual he had just created.

While it wasn't exactly what Marnie wanted in her mind's eye, she understood. He was back to that moment and talking like a boy again. Although, she thought back to her time in the Air Force and knew without a shadow of a doubt that most of the men she served with would appreciate that humor.

Even Dana sighed and relaxed her arms.

It wasn't as though Declan intentionally ruined the mysticism of Santa for his buddies, he was just trying to get his older cousin to stop teasing them all and treating them like babies. "So," Marnie asked, "did your cousin ever come back at Christmas time and see Chris and Jessica all dressed up?"

The cutest smirk crossed Declan's face and Marnie's heart did a double-beat.

"Yes, the very next year they came out here right before Christmas to do all of the fun Christmas activities. He had a younger sister and she was probably about eight or nine that year. Her parents wanted so desperately to have her continue to believe. So they spent a week here and I think it must have been another four years before Sally admitted Santa wasn't real. Or at least, the myth that everyone tells their kids."

Marnie could see where Declan was going with this. While Santa wasn't exactly real, the idea of him was. People the world over all throughout time continued to tell his story, and act out his persona. Some may not think it's right to tell a kid that Santa is real, but for most it was just a way to add some magic to the winter.

"I see now why Chris and Jessica do this. The magic they share during Christmas, and really all year long, helps a lot of people." Marnie was thinking about how best to word her next thoughts when she was interrupted.

"And with all of the adults on board, so many donate their time, money, and their own gifts to help others in need. Sharing the joy of the season, and the giving aspect, helps to instill those characteristics in children. And when the cycle keeps on going, then at least one time of the year mankind is a bit nicer and more helpful." Dana smiled and looked out the door when it opened.

She noticed who walked in and her face lit up like the star on top of a Christmas tree.

"Jerod. What brings you out here? I thought you had chores back at the ranch?" Dana walked toward her husband and enveloped him in a big hug.

"I did them all and missed you. Plus," he leaned down and kissed her cheek." It's time you come home for dinner."

Dana pulled back and slapped his shoulder. "I see how it is. You missed me because you wanted me to fix your dinner?" She pursed her lips.

The cowboy's face lost all of its color and he put his hands up in front of him in a defensive gesture. "No, no. That's not it at all. I've got dinner almost all ready. You won't have to do a thing tonight."

Marnie piped up, "Except for clean up your mess, right?"

Jerod grinned. "Well, there might be a little bit to clean, but I'm going to help."

"Mmm Hmm. And what did you make?" Dana stepped back and crossed her arms over her chest.

Marnie watched as the couple went back and forth. She wondered if Dana was really upset, or just playing with her husband. When she noticed the gleam in the woman's eye, she knew it was all fun for her.

Declan sidled up to Marnie and whispered, "so, are they like this all the time?"

"Pretty much. They are just the cutest couple ever. Must be the honeymoon phase lasting longer than most." Marnie knew some of it was the fact that Dana was going to have a baby next year, but since that wasn't common knowledge yet, she kept that part to herself.

Marnie was a grown woman, not a young teenage boy who didn't know how to keep a secret, she thought. Then she mentally berated herself for thinking such thoughts. She knew that for a teenage boy that sort of behavior was expected. If his cousin hadn't been such a bully, she knew that Declan would have kept the secret.

Still, this current secret wasn't hers to share. Marnie would wait until Dana and Jerod notified their friends about the good news before she said a thing.

Chapter 26

Marnie had been working hard for the past three weeks on the nativity and she hadn't taken any time to really look at the Christmas tree farm. Sure, she'd been there almost every day, but when she wasn't working on the play, or wrangling the animals that were now being used for practice, she was wrangling sheep and alpacas on Declan's ranch.

Two days before their final dress rehearsal Marnie was on Declan's ranch helping with the sheep. "You know, I think I'm getting the hang of feeding the sheep and moving them around. I see you need to keep them going so they stay warm."

"Yup, that helps, but having a nice shed or small barn for them to go inside of when the weather is too cold or abrasive, also helps. Their wool really works nicely to keep them insulated all winter long." Declan threw out a hay bale under the lean-to he had made just for winter feeding. In that space he had several long troughs. One was just for water, and two held the feed the animals needed.

Marnie learned that most of the year, they just grazed on the grasses and wheat that grew all over Declan's ranch. When he cut down an alfalfa or wheat field, he would have the herd graze in there for the shoots and leftovers that he and his team intentionally left behind. Then when the snow covered the ground he would put hay, grain, and alfalfa in the troughs that were located underneath the shelters. The animals learned quickly where the food stores would be located all winter.

Declan ran his fingers through the warm, woolly coat of one of his sheep. "You know, it may not look like it, but this wool is going to end up being very fine one day."

Marnie knew there was a long process to make the sheep's coat viable for making clothing or home goods out of the sheared wool, but she hadn't given it much thought. "I know that the wool has to be spun a certain way, but I don't know anything about the process itself."

Declan finished spreading the alfalfa around the two troughs then stood up. He took his hat off and wiped the sweat from his forehead. Even with the cold temperatures of winter, he could work up a sweat from the ranch labor. "Well, I don't do anything past sheering my sheep in the spring and selling the wool. But I do know a local family who does spin the wool and they also create items to sell online. I can ask them to give you a tutorial if you like." He paused. "In fact, it might be a good idea for everyone, including Jerod and Dana. There are many parts to the process of making clothes, and I can see injured veterans finding peace in the process. Shoot, I might even find some peace myself." He grinned.

"Have you seen the process before?" Marnie wondered if Declan had seen it and decided it wasn't for him, or if he'd never taken the time to learn about the wool process from start to finish.

Leaning against the fence, Declan's hat sat at an angle, and he looked the picture of the perfect cowboy. Marnie thought all he needed was a piece of wheat hanging from his mouth. Or maybe a dandelion.

He nodded. "I have. And with that ADA Coordinator here, I'm starting to wonder if she might be appeased by having some of the returning veterans working on processing the wool instead of outside pushing themselves physically all of the time."

That got Marnie's anger flaring, again. That coordinator, Eloise, could take her ideas back to Texas with her where she belonged. The residents of the Crooked Arrow were doing just fine. Sure, Marty had been injured helping her, but that was a one-off type of situation. Anyone could have been injured, not just a disabled veteran.

Eloise had to understand that working on a ranch did have its dangers. She couldn't expect the residents to have the same level of accommodation as they would if they were in an office setting in the middle of a large city. This was a ranch, after all. "Pft, I keep waiting for her to say that we have to put those yellow button things on the ground everywhere and create actual sidewalks all over the ranch." She blew her breath out and shook her head.

Declan chuckled. "I heard her saying to Jerod that he should have chosen a city where they had wide sidewalks and crosswalks that were geared toward the visually impaired."

"What does that even mean?" Marnie scrunched her nose.

"I think it's those crosswalk signs that have the beeping. But, the ranch hasn't taken in anyone who's blind, have they?" Declan thought back to some of the men who had already graduated and moved on. Only one guy had any true visual impairment, but it was only one eye. And Arthur had his service dog, he also had a job as an electrical engineer. If it weren't for his eye patch, one wouldn't even know he was a disabled veteran. He got around so well right before he left for his job.

"I really don't understand why ADA Coordinators swear by those yellow rubber things. They only cause more problems for those with canes." Marnie had been working on getting around without hers, and was making progress, although it was slow. She figured it would have been smoother if she was in the south, where they had paved roads, sidewalks, and no snow. But this was better. If she could get around just find on the bad walks and snow-covered dirt, she could walk anywhere without her cane.

"I really don't know anything about those. I mean, I've seen them and walked over them. I don't like them, but if they help certain people to get into the street properly, then who am I to complain? Sure, it can hurt a person's foot to step on some of them, but I think they're designed to help those in wheelchairs and walkers."

Marnie interrupted, "I know, I know." She waved a hand in front of her face. "I guess I just don't like them. Maybe it's selfish since they don't do anything to help me, in fact, they can make it more difficult for me. But, they do keep the rollers from running away."

"Okay, enough about that. Let's go inside for some hot coffee and I'll call the Andersons to see when we can come over for a demonstration." Declan led the way back inside the house.

"Actually, I think you might want to check with Jerod first. Make sure he's on board with this. And see what his schedule is like." Marnie rubbed her cold hands together in front of the fire once they were inside the house.

After a few phone calls, an appointment was set for the day after the live nativity.

"So, those sets are really great, aren't they? Do you think that the tree farm will want to keep them and use them?" Marnie had been looking at the set decorations. It was their final dress rehearsal and something was bugging her. She couldn't quite put her finger on it, but something was wrong.

Declan looked at her and then at the sets. "I don't see why they couldn't use them. But I can ask, if you want me to. Is there a reason for this?" He chuckled. "Are you one of those who must recycle everything? Or is it you're a secret hoarder?

Marnie shivered at that last suggestion. "No. Spending the past ten years in the Air Force has taught me to keep very little. While the force did pay for my moves, it was always such a pain to have to pack and unpack too many things."

"Okay, then what's up?" Declan eyed her closer and noticed the lines around her mouth. While Marnie wasn't frowning, exactly, she certainly wasn't smiling. He figured she was on her way to frowning and he couldn't understand what had her so upset.

She shook her head. "I don't know. I can't get it out, but there's something here. I don't know if we're missing something or if I just hate the idea of the sets being torn down and used for fires." Marnie sighed. "I don't know."

Declan had felt a little uneasy once the final dress rehearsal had finished himself. But he knew why. After the next day, he wouldn't have the excuse to see the beautiful Marnie every day. He wasn't the least bit worried about the play, but he was sad that he wouldn't have a reason to call Marnie or to stop by with a thought about the play. Sure, they were going to see the Andersons the day after the play for the wool demonstration, but that wasn't going to take a lot of time. And then after that? He figured he'd only see her at church on Sundays.

Jerod and he had just made the final arrangements for the Crooked Arrow to get a few of Declan's herd come spring. So that wasn't even a reason for him to pop in at the ranch. They had both agreed that Jerod didn't have the proper set up yet, and the money from the grants they filed hadn't been awarded yet. The awards wouldn't come out until February.

"I think that the sets will be properly taken care of. And with all of the interest in the live nativity by our town, and surrounding areas, I have a feeling it's going to be something the tree farm will want to repeat next year. I heard Cody telling Jerod earlier today that he was thinking about making it something they did every weekend from Thanksgiving to Christmas. There's been a lot of positive interest here." Declan took Marnie's hand in his.

"There's more to it, isn't there?" He looked directly into her eyes and willed her to say yes.

Marnie's mouth opened, then closed. Then she bit her lower lip. But she kept looking directly into Declan's eyes.

He could feel the tension between them thickening and churning. While Declan knew exactly what he wanted, he knew that Marnie still had a ways to go with her program at the ranch, and the healing she needed to do within. He would never want to get in the way of her finally realizing that she didn't need the cane, that she had it within her this entire time to walk just fine on her own.

Every time Declan watched Marnie grab for her cane and lean on it for support, he wanted to tell her she didn't need it. He'd seen for himself how when she wasn't thinking, she could walk just fine without it. There might have been a wobble or two, but in time he was confident she could relearn her balance, like a toddler. She had to just do it.

This brave woman could do this, if she just believed in herself. But, he wasn't going to try and force the issue for her. Instead, he would stand by her and wait. He would give her the space she needed to heal and relearn how to balance, if that's what she needed.

For just one second, Marnie's gaze swept over his lips and Declan felt himself lean forward when he saw her tongue dart out to moisten her weather dried lips. Instinctively, he licked his lips as well. The second he realized what he was about to do, he pulled back. She was still planning on leaving the moment she could, and Declan wasn't into casual relationships. He had begun to care too much for this woman to kiss her knowing she wasn't going to stick around for the long haul.

When he stepped back, the magical bubble that had surrounded them burst and Marnie blinked. "I... ah... I don't know." She turned and quickly walked away, cane in hand but not really touching the ground as she retreated.

A slow smile crept across Declan's face as he watched her walk away, not relying on her cane for support.

Chapter 27

The night of the live nativity was finally there. Marnie's stomach was in knots one minute and the next it felt as though an entire beehive was buzzing around angrily.

"Hey, there. This looks fabulous!" Dana gushed and came over to hug Marnie.

"Thanks, but are you sure? You don't see anything missing?" Marnie bit her lower lip. She and Declan had just finished doing roll call. Everyone was there, including the baby and his backup. All of the animals seemed fine to her. And Declan had checked them out as well.

"The night is beautiful, no snow or wind in the forecast, just a nice thin cloud layer to help keep some warmth in. And the tree farm is packed with townsfolk as well as a large group from the surrounding cities." Dana leaned in and whispered, "I heard a couple of churches from Bozeman even rented a bus and brought a lot of their members here to see the performance."

"Wow, really?" Marnie looked around, but realized she was in the backstage area and wouldn't be able to see the crowds from where she was. "Do you think the kids will be too nervous to perform?"

Dana shook her head. "Nope. I think they are going to do just fine. Mrs. Pendleton is feeding little baby Jesus now, and so he should sleep for a lot of the performance. His sister is the one who will be holding him when he's not in the little feed trough." Dana chuckled. "You know, I've seen the dress rehearsal almost every time, and still can't stop smiling when I think about the makeshift crib."

"It's a real wooden feeding trough. The Pendleton's brought it after they cleaned it up real nice. Mr. Pendleton even lined it with a real wool blanket, the kind that would have been used back when Jesus was born. I'm so excited for the crowds to see it." Marnie had wanted everything to be as realistic as possible. She knew the Pendletons wanted the baby to have his binky, just in case he got upset, and Marnie didn't want to stand in the way of the baby getting what he needed, so the rest of the set and the costumes had to be as realistic as possible.

The only real concession she made was that the troupe should wear long underwear underneath the robes. December in Montana was so much colder than it would have been during tax time in Bethlehem.

Declan walked over to the duo. "Marnie, are we ready for everyone to get into place?"

Marnie put a hand to her stomach and willed it to stop the roller coaster ride it was on. She nodded. "I think so." Then she turned to look Declan straight on. "Do you think we got everything? Is there anything we might have missed?"

He chuckled. "If we did, it's in the Lord's hands now."

Marnie and Dana both smiled.

"Of course. Alright, let's do this." Marnie gulped and turned back around and walked to the front of the barn where they had erected a stage curtain to cover up the inside of the barn where some of the sets were located.

Over the past few days, the sets had been moved and tweaked until they were perfect. With the venue being in an actual barn, they could act the story quite nicely. Most of the scenes would be outside and the animals would be moving along with the humans along a marked off trail. But the barn, that would be where the best part happened.

"Places everyone!" Marnie yelled out and clapped her hands. Once everyone had stopped chatting and got into place, all thoughts of nervousness fled and her mind was on one thing – ensuring the performers were on their marks and the animals performed as they wanted them to.

Young Mary was in her room, it was a set that had been made from wood and painted to look old and worn. The play began with her on her knees before the angel who visited her one evening. The angel told her to rise and then began telling her what Yahweh had in mind for her. The look of fear that crossed her face for an instant was so much better than in rehearsals that Marnie thought she just might be heading to a real job as an actress.

Then when she heard laughing and a few cries of fear, Marnie turned her head and about screamed herself. She had prayed so hard for a good performance. But she should have known that something would go wrong.

However, a rampaging alpaca wasn't what she expected.

One of Declan's alpacas was trying to eat the straw hat a young boy was wearing. The kid was laughing, but his mom was screaming. The boy was running around with the alpaca in tow. As the audience noticed the boy laughing, they began to relax and enjoy the impromptu show and the scheduled performance was halted.

It almost looked to Declan as though little Johnny Sharpton had intentionally grabbed the attention of the young alpaca, Titus, and led him astray. The alpaca was on the opposite side of the barn from where Mary's bedroom scene was taking place, or rather, had been taking place until the commotion started.

Declan ran to get his young alpaca in line, but the animal had a mind of its own. He had wondered about the choice, he really should have chosen Damien instead, but since everyone was going to be at the tree farm, he wanted Damien to stay behind and watch over the herd, just in case those coyotes tried anything again. Damien was the more experienced guard and alpha, so it seemed wise to leave him home, and bring the young wannabe alpha to work the nativity performance.

Marnie had said the choice was his since the animals were his, but now he really wished they would have discussed it more. Although, to be fair, he doubted anyone would have expected little Johnny to antagonize Titus.

Mr. Sharpton, Declan, and Cody all worked together to corral the agitated alpaca. The moment Titus began to spit at Johnny, the little boy decided it wasn't fun any longer and ran into his mother's arms. As he ran, he dropped his hat which helped to distract Titus.

The alpaca stopped and reached his long neck down to the ground to get his prize. He began to prance around almost like a peacock showing off. Declan figured the alpaca thought he beat the little boy instead of the little boy running away scared. Although, since Titus was still young, he might have thought he did good by causing a little boy to cry. Who knows with alpacas.

A horse or a dog wouldn't have wanted the little boy to be scared or cry. Even Declan's working dogs would have cuddled up to the boy and done their best to comfort him once he was so upset, if they were present. They had also been left behind as extra security against the possibility of the coyotes returning to his ranch.

An exasperated Marnie stood next to Declan, eyeing the young boy. "Maybe he will have learned a valuable lesson. Never antagonize an animal that's bigger than you and spits."

With that, Declan laughed heartily and let loose the tension he had been holding onto. Several of those nearby who heard her comment also laughed.

Cody said, "I think we need a t-shirt that says something to that effect."

Lottie laughed and added, "or a coffee mug."

Declan grinned at Marnie and nodded. "I think we'll be seeing a lot of alpaca coffee mugs showing up in town very soon."

Marnie covered her face. "Oh, please don't say that. I don't want a reminder of tonight's fiasco."

"Come on." Declan put an arm around Marnie's shoulders and led her back to the front of the performance. "Let's get everything going again. At least we don't really need the alpaca for the performance. As long as the donkey is alright, we should be fine."

And the donkey was fine. It did bray at first, as though it was laughing along with the audience, then it began to snort and squeal. Once the donkey was under control, they began the nativity from where they left off. Instead of redoing the angel scene for anyone who might have missed it, Marnie did a very short recap. Then the newly married couple began their long trek to Bethlehem for the census and taxation.

The little shepherd boys had had some difficulties with focus during rehearsals, but with the performance they shone brightly. They were all on cue and said their very limited lines.

Thankfully, the heavenly choir, made up of choir members from all of the local churches, were loud and sounded, well, heavenly. Right on cue the heavenly host sang with the angel, "Glory to God in the highest, and on Earth peace, good will toward men."

And Sheamus Jr. who had the role of head shepherd, spoke loud enough that most in the audience could hear him.

Declan was so happy, and surprised, that Sheammie spoke so well. During the final dress rehearsal, both he and Marnie worried when the boy could barely be heard.

However, today, he spoke his lines loud and clear, "Let's go to Bethlehem and see this thing that has happened, which the Lord has told us about."

Declan watched the O'Callohan family, his neighbors, as their boy spoke his lines and then led the little shepherds to the barn where the scene with Mary, Joseph, and baby Jesus lying in a manger was set up.

Even the animals seemed to realize they needed to do their job and for the most part, were on target. One of the goats was more interested in the hay that was just inside the barn than the baby Jesus, and a dog had ambled up to lick the baby's face. Which caused the audience to laugh.

Finally, Marnie laughed and just shook her head. At this point in the performance, they really couldn't do much. Having a dog jump in and add to the scene, while not planned, did add some enjoyment for everyone. Especially baby Jesus as he was starting to get fussy. Mary was just about to put his binky in when the dog showed up.

"You know," Marnie leaned next to Declan and whispered, "I wouldn't be surprised if God sent that nice border collie in to do his job."

It was all Declan could do to *not* laugh. "You do know who that dog is, don't you?"

Marnie took a closer look at the dog who had decided to stand guard next to baby Jesus as he lay in his little makeshift crib. "Wait, isn't that one of Nelly's dogs? A service dog?"

"Yup, that's Pebbles. Cute little dog, isn't she?" Declan had wondered early on if Pebbles might become Marnie's dog. He supposed that if she never got rid of her cane, then she might get paired with a service dog. But he didn't think that she would need one. Over the past few days Marnie had begun to leave the cane on the side. He noticed her take intentional steps without the assistance of the cane.

"Oh, I know that dog." Marnie grinned and shook her head. "What a great dog. She really knows when she's needed, doesn't she?"

"She does." Nelly Wilson, dog trainer extraordinaire, sidled up to Marnie. "For a while I thought she might choose you. Guess I was wrong." The edges of her brown eyes crinkled with delight. "Nice to know she's so good with babies. I'll have to put that down on her record."

Crinkles appeared between Marnie's eyes. "But I don't need a service dog."

"That's what they all say." Sam Marley grinned and put an arm around his wife's waist. They had recently married and the man who had a reputation for being a grump, always seemed to have a smile on his face. "But in the end, those who are lucky enough to be chosen by a dog are the happiest."

"Hey now." Nelly pursed her lips and playfully slapped Sam's arm. "I thought it was marriage to me that made you the happiest."

"Oh, that's the truth. But for those who aren't lucky enough to have the best spouse in the world," he leaned over and kissed the top of her head, "have to be happy with a service dog."

Nelly chuckled. "You're darn tootin'. Service dogs are the best."

Lightning shot through Marnie's heart. For just a moment, she wished she had a husband. Then she remembered that she wasn't thinking about men at the moment, she needed to refocus on the rest of the play. The kids were counting on her to ensure that everything went smoothly. But later, she would think more about how so many people were recently engaged, married, or just coupled up.

Chapter 28

While the crowd applauded the kids, and a few hooted and hollered their appreciation for the production, Marnie walked to the front of the barn and put her hands up and then down, in the universal gesture to be quiet. "Thank you all so much for joining us tonight. Please, continue to enjoy the Christmas theme here at the tree farm, and if you haven't picked out your own tree yet, I can say with certainty that you won't get anything fresher than a Makinaw Family Christmas Tree Farm tree." She grinned, knowing that the best way to get a tree was to cut one down yourself.

And what better place to do that than a tree farm.

A tall man in cowboy boots, jeans, and a black shirt with a white Roman collar approached her. "Miss Marnie, that was wonderful, alpaca chase and all." He chuckled.

"Thank you so much. I can't believe so many people showed up tonight." Marnie blushed and looked around at the throng of people milling about.

"Yes, well. We Catholic priests do like to keep each other in the loop. I believe your local priest called the Bishop and he let the rest of us in the area know about your production. Everyone enjoyed it immensely. Seeing the live animals, and that dog." He chuckled. "I think the entire congregation will want to come next year. You are going to hold this every year, aren't you?"

"Oh. I don't know." Marnie looked around for some help. She saw Jerod and waved him over. "Jerod, this is Father...Oh forgive me, I don't know your name."

The tall man who would have looked like an ordinary cowboy, if it wasn't for the white band in his shirt collar, smiled and extended his hand to Jerod. "I'm Father Sebastian. Nice to meet you."

"I'm Jerod Stevens, nice to meet you. Are you responsible for bringing one of the buses full of people tonight?"

The Catholic priest nodded. "I am. And boy am I glad I did. This was such a nice treat. I don't remember the last time anyone put on a live nativity. Must be close to a decade now."

"I had never seen one until this year. I must say, the alpaca might have stolen the show." Jerod couldn't help the smile that spread over his face.

"Oh, I don't know about that. I might have to disagree and say the border collie and little baby Jesus stole the show," Father Sebastian stated, ever so congenially.

Marnie sighed. "I think that the show was wonderful overall, improvisations included."

"What a very diplomatic way of addressing the unexpected scenes." Declan smiled and shook hands with the priest. "Father Sebastian, nice to see you again."

"Ahh, the local sheep farmer. Declan, right?" The priest smiled and shook hands with Declan.

"Right you are. How are the sheep doing?" Declan looked to Jerod before telling them all about the sheep that helped the priest with last year.

Father Sebastian rubbed the side of his nose. "Much better since we introduced the alpaca to the herd, based on your suggestion. Thank you for that, by the way."

Jerod looked between the two. "Declan, do you normally suggest to everyone to add alpaca to their sheep herd?"

He nodded. "I do. I think they are very helpful with keeping the sheep safe, but also add a nice bit of variety when going to market, or making your own wool."

"The nuns down the road from my parish take the wool from our sheep and spin it. Then they make the nicest woolen scarves, hats, and mittens. We give them to the homeless in our area, as well as the veterans down at the VFW."

"Really? I'd love to come out sometime to observe, if that's alright?" Jerod asked. "We are going to get our first sheep in the spring, and most likely an alpaca, or two. We don't have plans to process our own wool. At least not at first, but down the road that might be something I'd like to look into. For now, I think I want to get a better understanding of the entire process."

"That's a very good idea, young man. We started out in a similar fashion, but the moment Mother Superior got wind of our sheep, she began looking into wool spinning and dying. She even requested a nun from another region come and help start their ministry. It's been a true blessing to everyone in our area."

Marnie didn't have much experience with Catholics; she was a non-denominational Christian herself. Of course, she had attended the local Baptist church since arriving in Frenchtown, but she'd never been to a Catholic church, or a nunnery. She wondered if she had the terminology correct. It was the only word she could think to describe where nuns lived and worked, out of the public eye.

They continued to chat about the raising of sheep, how it was to learn about alpaca, and how to spin, card, dye, and weave. The priest himself didn't know much about how the wool was handled after his sheep were shorn; he had a very basic understanding of the process.

"Why don't I ask the Mother Superior to reach out to you, Jerod, when I return? We can coordinate an entire day to visit my sheep and alpacas, then head to the convent grounds where you can meet with the nuns who handle the wool." Father Sebastian seemed like a very nice man, the sort to want to do whatever he could to help others.

Marnie liked him right away. It didn't hurt that he brought more than thirty people with him on the bus. Thirty people who were spending money in the gift shop on the tree farm, along with what appeared to be buying handicrafts from the local craft women.

Now that the performance was over, Marnie had plans to come back in the next day or two and check out all of the cute booths where locals sold their goods. She especially wanted to check out the one that had macrame hangings. It reminded her of her grandmother. She used to make macrame plant hangers when Marnie was just a little girl. Her mother would probably love to have one for Christmas.

But first, she had to help take down the sets, or at least move them around so that Cody could have full use of his barn again. With Christmas only a week away, he needed the space.

Marnie couldn't believe how much had happened over the previous month. The amount of information she had taken in was amazing. She felt as though she was back in college, cramming in all of the info she could get her hands on. Only now, it was all related to farms and ranches.

She and Megan were doing their weekly one on one counseling session and Marnie was updating her on what she'd learned since arriving. "I can't believe it, but I think I like sheep and alpaca. I don't know if I want to be a shepherdess, but it isn't turning my stomach like I thought it would."

"That's really great to hear." Megan put her pencil down next to her paper on her desk. "And how is everything going with trying to relearn your balance?"

Marnie deflated. "That's not as easy."

"When you first arrived, you thought it was impossible. Do you still think that's the case?"

"No, I think it's possible." Marnie shook her head. "But I don't know if I'll be kicked out of here before I can do it."

"What makes you think you'll be kicked out of here?" Megan tilted her head and waited patiently for Marnie to get her thoughts together.

"Well, when I first arrived, my VA contact told me I shouldn't be here longer than a few weeks. It's been a month and I'm barely able to take a few steps without the cane before I get all wobbly and need it."

Megan put her elbows on her desk and leaned forward. "But you have done better than that. When you aren't thinking about the cane, you can go quite a distance. I've seen it."

"True." Marnie sighed. "But that was when it was an emergency."

"Don't you mean when you weren't thinking about the cane? I've seen it a few times since you arrived, when you are out of your head, you don't lean so much on the cane, and there have even been a couple of times where you walked totally normal without the cane when your focus was elsewhere."

"But that's exactly it, when my focus is elsewhere. How do I do it even when I'm thinking about it?" Marnie threw her hands in the air and looked like she was about to give up.

Megan pursed her lips and thought about the woman sitting in front of her desk. Marnie had been through a lot in the past year, more than most people will go through their entire life. She didn't have an issue with PTSD, at least so far. From what Megan had seen, it was possible that the condition could show up later in life. But Marnie was too full of life, she thought, to have that come at her down the road. "The cane has become your security blanket. You won't be able to put it down for good until you realize that you really don't need it anymore. I'm sure you did at one time, but not now."

"What makes you so sure of that?" Marnie's hands pushed up from the side of the chair and she stood with both hands on her hips, not even touching the cane. Then she pushed back away from the chair and stalked to the window and looked outside at the snowy white blanket covering the ground as far as she could see.

Megan steepled her fingers in front of her face and leaned her chin on the top of the steeple. "Because you just did it."

"What?" Marnie whirled around, without falling, and glared at the counselor. "What are you talking about?"

Not wanting to say it, but still knowing that Marnie needed to see it, Megan nodded to Marnie's hands.

When Marnie looked down, her eyes widened at the realization that she had moved around, yet again, without the use of her cane. Usually, when she realized what she had done, she wobbled and needed help. But not this time. This time, she stood up straight and after taking a deep breath, took one step. She put one foot in front of the other and then did it again. After taking three steps, she did get a little wobble, but she made it back to her seat without falling down, and without the need of any sort of help.

"I can't believe I did it," Marnie exclaimed.

"Why are you so surprised?" Ever the counselor, Megan turned the question back on to Marnie. Her thinking was to get Marnie truly considering what she had done, and why she could only do it when she wasn't thinking about it.

The shoulders on the disabled veteran moved up and Marnie pursed her lips. After a moment, her shoulders relaxed, and she leaned back in her chair. "Maybe I have some sort of mental block?" Since Marnie wasn't a trained counselor, she couldn't imagine why she could walk normally sometimes, but not at all times.

Megan paused a moment and let Marnie continue to think about her situation. When Marnie didn't seem to be able to say anything else, Megan started giving her some ideas. "Do you think it has anything to do with your own self-doubt?"

"What do I have to doubt? It wasn't as though I could have done anything different during training. It was an accident, a stupid one, but no one was at fault." She hadn't always felt that way. There was a time when she blamed her Captain for not canceling the training that day due to the weather conditions. But she knew now that it wasn't his fault.

Megan arched a brow. "Are you sure that's what you believe?"

Marnie sucked in a breath and considered Megan's words very carefully. It was what she believed in that very moment. But how long had she truly believed it? Was she only kidding herself, and the VA, when she had stated she knew it was an accident just a few months ago?

One thing she knew for certain was that she had never been able to take more than a couple of steps without her cane, before she arrived at the Crooked Arrow. And those steps had been very wobbly. If it weren't for the rails next to her, she would have fallen about only three steps.

But since she arrived, she had begun to move more without her cane. Today was proof, but so was that day when Marty was injured pushing her out of the way of the rampaging cow. Thankfully, he had healed up nicely. But it had caused a stink with a certain ADA Coordinator. The woman had even begun to question what Marnie had been doing out in the barn. Eloise had said that anyone with an assistive device shouldn't be working in the barn, or with animals.

Marnie thought she was nuts, a cane didn't get in the way. A wheelchair on a ranch would be very tough, but they could manage if a veteran who was in a wheelchair wanted to finish his or her recovery at the ranch. Marnie knew enough about the running of the ranch to believe that. But maybe it did take someone who had served to know how best to assist a disabled vet to recover?

Since coming to the ranch it was those on the ranch who helped her the most. Well, everyone at Crooked Arrow, and Declan. While Declan hadn't served in the military, he did seem to have what it took to help her.

Was there more to it? So many different ideas were flitting around her brain, Marnie wasn't sure what she believed in that moment. "I don't know what's going on, but something is changing. Possibly some walls coming down? I don't know." She hung her head, sighed, and squeezed her eyes closed.

After only a moment, Marnie could hear the squeak from Megan's chair as the counselor pushed it back from her desk. A moment later, she felt the woman take the seat next to her and put a hand on her shoulder.

It was another few moments before Megan spoke, "Marnie, what you're feeling right now is normal. This is all part of the healing process. You have to break those walls down and let your emotions in. I know that early on it was necessary to throw up blocks to protect your heart and mind. But now that you know you're safe, it's time to take them apart."

Marnie leaned into Megan's hand just a bit, if only to keep the human contact for a little bit longer. She was tough and wasn't one to cry very often, but since her accident she had found herself much more emotional then she had ever been. In that moment, with Megan touching her arm, giving Marnie her strength, the veteran felt she could let go and accept the help Megan was offering.

Once she had let the tears fall, Megan handed Marnie a tissue. The woman blew her nose and another tissue ended up in her hand. They continued to come until she had cried her last tear. "Thank you, Megan."

"You're welcome."

Chapter 29

Marnie had a lot to think about that night. Once she was done with Megan she went to her room and somehow, Dana knew to send her a tray for dinner. No one expected her to come down that night, and no one tried to coax her out of her room.

After she ate, she opened her door and set the tray outside her door, knowing that someone would take it to the kitchen for her. Marnie wasn't up to seeing anyone that night. She knew her face had to be all swollen and red from crying.

For the past ten years, any time she had wanted to cry, she remembered her drill instructor dressing down one of the other recruits in basic. Emily had cried when she received a Dear Jane letter from a boy back home. Their DI had yelled at her, called her many awful words, then the one thing that had stuck with Marnie all these years was when he said, "Airmen don't cry."

"You were wrong." Marnie didn't normally speak out loud to herself, but she'd let it slide for the night. She was breaking down her walls and letting all of the bottled-up pain out. While she was exhausted, and her eyes burned, she did feel better. Why hadn't anyone told her that letting the tears flow would help her to feel better?

After everyone had gone to bed, Marnie wiped her eyes and decided she was a strong woman, a strong Air Force Staff Sergeant. She hadn't made rank just because of time in service. No, she was resourceful and never gave up. There had been times when she stayed late and listened to tapes over and over to ensure she had the translation correct before submitting it. When dealing with such sensitive information, she needed to ensure her translation was spot on, while not taking too long to submit it.

Instinctively, Marnie knew when to submit and when to rewind and listen again. Something as important as verb tense could make or break a translation. If she reported an event as one still to happen, but it had actually taken place the previous day, she could put her fellow service men and women in danger. And if she said it had already happened, but really was scheduled for the next day, then she would cause the Air Force to miss out on a possible target.

While what she had to do next wasn't the same as translating an enemy communication, she did need to push herself to excel. Marnie Gallagher would do whatever was needed in order to achieve her goal.

Declan had dreamt about Marnie all night long. Every time he woke up, he remembered his dream about her. When he went back to sleep, he'd dream again about the beautiful and headstrong Air Force Sergeant. So when he woke up, the first thing he wanted to do was to go and visit her.

However, he knew better than to head over to the ranch early in the morning. They had a lot of chores, just like he did. The animals wouldn't wait on romance. The thought stopped him in his tracks. He wondered to himself if he really was going to try to woo the pretty lady.

He'd had girlfriends in the past, but he had never met anyone who captured his attention, and heart, the way Marnie had. He'd never fussed over his clothes the way he had that morning when he first thought about going to see her. Could he really be ready to date? Would she be open to his less than skillful overtures of romance?

The only thing he knew to do when calling on a woman one wanted to court was to bring flowers, or chocolates. Since Christmas was just days away, he figured they had plenty of sweets in the house. But he couldn't recall seeing any flowers on the tables the last time he was there. Was that because the women in the house didn't like flowers? Or was it too old-fashioned?

Was it even enough?

The only way to find out was to just do it. Declan Walden was going to bring flowers to the woman who had captured his attention. And pray she didn't throw them back in his face.

"Boss man, what's goin' on?" Luis asked when he came upon Declan just staring into the distance, none of the sheep around. He looked to where Declan was staring but didn't see a thing. "Are the coyotes back?"

"Huh?" Declan shook his head and looked at his young ranch hand. "Sorry, I must have been off in space. What did you say?"

The young man grinned. "Ah, thinking about a pretty lady, I see. I do that all the time, too."

Declan's head turned to the boy and he looked him up and down. Luis was young, but he did seem to have a lot of dates. Declan wondered if he could ask him for dating advice. He mentally shook his head. No, he better not. It wouldn't be right for the boss to ask his youngest employee for advice on women. He'd be better off asking John, his foreman, for advice. The man is, after all, married. Not that Declan was looking to get married. He cleared his throat. "Just thinking. So, what brings you out here?"

Luis laughed. "Yeah, right. I know that look." He patted Declan on the shoulder. "Whatever you say Boss Man. But John sent me out here to look for you. Titus got into Damien's pasture and is causing trouble for his sire."

After a quick eye roll, and a chuckle, Declan headed back with Luis to see how much damage Titus had caused. Or, if Damien still had enough gusto to put a young wannabe alpha in his place.

He never should have doubted Damien. The older and more experienced alpha alpaca had Titus cornered and was spitting in between what sounded like a good put down.

The one thing he had learned over the years since they switched from a cattle ranch to a sheep ranch was that one never wanted to upset an alpaca. They were loyal to their core, which meant they could be meaner than sin when pushed. Just like any male alpha, if another alpaca tried to assert his dominance, the older alpha would do whatever he had to, no matter how they were related.

When Declan sidled up to the outside of the fence keeping the animals in, he noticed John pointing and laughing. "What's up?"

"Those ladies in the field are gossiping about the fight between Titus and Damien." John was of course referring to the female sheep and alpaca that were in the same pasture as Damien and Titus.

Declan even noticed that the animals from the neighboring pen were close to the fence that separated the two and they were watching as well. All of them were busy chewing the cud, so it appeared as though they were chatting up a storm. But, maybe in their own language they were no better than Gladys and her gang of gossips.

However, animal gossips were much more fun than human gossips. Declan grinned. "I wonder what they're saying right now?"

"Oh, I know what they're saying." John shook his head as though he was trying to fling his hair back, like a woman, then in a shrill voice he said, "*just look at that little whipper-snapper. I told him to leave Damien alone, but would he listen to me? No. Boys never do, you know.*"

Luis busted up laughing. "Oh, that's a good one. How about the reply from her friend. "*Mmm Mmm, just look at that Damien and how well he's putting that tuis in his place. He thinks he's a stud, but he's not much older than a cria.*" Luis bunched up the air under his short hair, like a woman puffing up her hair.

Everyone laughed and asked for more.

Declan himself puffed up with pride when he realized how well Luis was learning the lingo. When the young man came to work at the ranch, he though a tuis was just another way of saying Titus, instead of the fact that it's actually the term for a baby alpaca. And when Declan first used the word cria, Luis scrunched his face and thought Declan was cursing in some foreign language. Of course, he had to explain that a cria was a young alpaca, usually when they hit the six-month mark that was the term used for them.

The joking and little show the alpaca, and now the sheep, were putting on was exactly what Declan needed. He felt so much lighter and put aside his worry over Marnie and if she was ready to date him, or not. If the Lord wanted them to be together, they would in the end.

The waiting part was never fun.

Chapter 30

"I always hated waiting for the final few days of the Christmas season." Marnie, who was pacing the living room where the Christmas tree was located, wasn't using her cane. While she still carried it, it was now lying against the chair she had occupied until her nerves got the better of her.

Dana and Megan were sitting in their usual chairs and grinning as they watched her move around the room quite deftly.

Earlier that day, a large box had arrived for Marnie. While she hadn't been on the best of terms with her parents since the accident, they did love her and stayed in touch with her. When she spoke with them at Thanksgiving, they understood she couldn't come home for the holidays this year, her recovery was more important.

But the box had surprised her. Sure, she had sent small gifts home for her family to open up on Christmas Day, but she never expected anything more than a small check or gift card from her parents. That was what they had always done ever since she joined the Air Force.

Even when she went home for Christmas, she didn't get much. Mainly because she had no space to put things.

Barracks living wasn't for the pack rat.

She hoped they hadn't sent her something like a wheelchair, thinking she was worse than when they saw her in the hospital. The box was huge, like a small fort for a kid kind of huge. She had played in boxes like that one when she was just six or seven years old. "What could it be? Should I open it?"

Both of the smiling women jumped up and exclaimed, "No!"

Dana laughed and put her hands on her head. "Are you the type of person who likes to peek at their gifts before Christmas Day? Did you ever unwrap your presents as a kid?"

Marnie looked at everything in the room except for them. "Ah, I plead the 5th."

"That's my girl!" Megan laughed. "I knew I liked you. We're totally kindred spirits."

Marnie sucked her lips in not wanting to admit what she had done as a kid. "Wait, Dana did you ever unwrap your gifts?" She looked straight at the woman who had averted her eyes when the attention was on her.

"No comment." Dana nodded just once.

"Ah ha!" Megan yelled and pointed at the guilty looking cowgirl. "I knew it! Only someone who unwrapped their gifts as a kid would ask that question."

"What do you mean 'as a kid'? She still does it," Jerod joked when he walked into the room with the ladies.

"Hey, you aren't supposed to tattle on your wife." Dana playfully swatted his arm then sat back down on the sofa where there was room for Jerod to sit with her.

The cowboy chuckled. "Last Christmas I caught her red-handed looking through bags on my side of the closet. When I asked her about it, she totally denied it. But the look on her face was priceless!" He slapped his hands together and chuckled loudly. "She looked like the proverbial kid with her hand in the cookie jar when momma caught her."

"Oh, that is priceless!" Marnie relaxed back into her chair and grinned from ear to ear. Sitting around with friends like these through the Christmas season was exactly what she needed. This was starting to feel like home to her. Even though she'd be gone by spring, she still let herself feel as though she belonged here. She did mentally remind herself it was only temporary, but after so many years in the Air Force and not feeling like her barracks was her home, ever, she would take it. Even if only for a few months.

Megan sat back quietly watching everyone laugh and tell stories. She had purposely left her own story out as she just wanted to witness all of this fun. Take it all in. If things went the way she hoped, by this time next year she'd be living in town with her new husband. Lord willing.

"Hey, Megan, what's with that Cheshire Cat grin?" Jerod asked.

Megan's eyes widened. "Who, me?" She pointed to herself and was the picture of innocence. All signs of a sneaky smile gone.

"Yeah, you." Marnie narrowed her eyes and leaned forward in her chair. "What devious plan do you have for us?"

"I don't have any plans for you. But that reminds me, what are our plans for Christmas Eve and Christmas Day? Will all of the graduated residents be coming by at some point?" Megan had done a very nice job of changing the subject seeing how it was exactly what Jerod came in to discuss with the ladies.

"That's what I originally came in here to talk about." Jerod cleared his throat. "As you know, most of our residents and graduates don't necessarily have a place to go. One or two are pretty much tied to the area."

"Like Skeeter?" Dana laughed. "I don't think he'd leave for Christmas even if we gave him a plane ticket to go to Europe."

Marnie grinned. She knew he was head over heels with Dakota. And she seemed to be pretty much the same way with him. They were totally adorable when no one was looking. He tended to kiss the tip of her nose a lot. It was cute. Although Marnie thought about how runny her nose got in the severe cold conditions of Montana and changed her mind about it being cute. It was gross.

"Right." Jerod rubbed his hands together. "As you all know, Dana does most of the cooking around here. Everyone will be here by Christmas Eve for a couple of days, as their work allows. But..."

Dana winced and broke in. "My parents are hosting a small family affair on Christmas Eve. They'll all be here Christmas Day to celebrate with us, of course. But Christmas Eve they decided to have as family time. We're going to open up our gifts to one another. My parents tend to go overboard. It's not always pretty, either."

Jerod shivered. "You should have seen it last year. Wrapping paper everywhere! It was piled so high, we had to send a rescue squad in to find Dana and her sisters. They had been sitting on the ground when the unwrapping began."

Dana laughed. "Oh, shut up. It's not that bad." She nodded, then whispered, "Actually, he might be right."

Jerod pulled her close into his arms and hugged her. Then he kissed the top of her head and the rest of the women in the room sighed. They were the quintessential newlywed couple.

Marnie cleared her throat. "Alright, so does that mean you need us women to cook on Christmas Eve?" She rolled her eyes. The thought that only women could cook a meal was crazy in this day and age, but since she'd arrived, it had been mostly women helping in the kitchen. But to be fair, the men usually went out for the evening feeding of the animals, no matter the weather. It was a fair trade off.

Jerod chuckled. "I take it you think I'm being a bit sexist?"

Marnie wasn't sure if he was, so she shrugged.

"Well, I've been with most of these men long enough to know that you don't want them cooking anything you might want to eat. They can cut vegetables, but that's about it." Dana laughed. "However, I do have an option that is a bit festive and easy. If you don't want a traditional meal two days in a row, that is."

Since Marnie was the new person, she kept quiet and waited for anyone else to say something. When Megan stayed quiet, she wasn't sure if the decision was hers or not. "So, just to be clear, on Christmas Day we're going to have the traditional ham, turkey, mashed potatoes and all the other trimmings, right?"

Jerod nodded. "You betcha. And I'll be up super early helping my dear wife with some of the cooking. And her mother is heading over before the rooster crows so no one else needs to be up early."

"Oh, I'll help. Please I don't want to laze about why others are slaving over a wonderful Christmas meal. I'm just not the best at the big stuff." Marnie grimaced thinking about how she and a previous roommate had once tried to deep fry a turkey for Thanksgiving. Thankfully, the men who lived next door were watching, beers in hand, and laughing. At least until the fire started. Then they ran out and doused it with their beer. And one guy came out with a giant fire extinguisher.

After that, she was told to live on base. The apartment manager wasn't wrong in suggesting she move back to a space that didn't allow more than a microwave in the rooms.

But she could do food prep. That was what she had mostly done since arriving. Well, that and cleaning dishes.

Dana bit her lower lip and looked to her husband for help.

He took her hand and nodded.

"Well, thank you. But that time early in the morning, before anyone else is up, is kind of our time. I hope you don't mind, but my mom doesn't get to spend much time with just me and Jerod. There is always someone else around." She put a hand on her belly. "And with what's coming, she really wanted to have this time with us, just the three of us."

Marnie already felt like a third wheel, or she supposed, a fifth wheel. And not the fun, adventurous type. "I'm sorry. I don't want to intrude on your time. Of course, I'll be happy to sleep in and then you can put me to work whenever you need my hands." She grinned to show that she was on board with their plans and not the least bit offended.

Dana reached over and put a hand on Marnie's. "Thank you. I really appreciate it."

"Think nothing of it." If she was being honest with herself, Marnie was actually glad that she was going to be able to sleep in and not worry about having to cook.

"Great, because I do need you to make the Christmas Eve dinner." The gleam in Dana's eye had Marnie worried that she'd stepped into that one.

Chapter 31

Just before Dana and Jerod headed out on Christmas Eve to her parents' ranch, Dana informed Marnie and Megan that they were going to have a few extra guests at the table, but that it shouldn't be an issue.

"Here." From the back fridge, Dana pulled out a carton of premade mashed potatoes. "If you think you will need extra, just heat these up. And there are a few jars of wonderful gravy in the pantry. I also have a few bags of frozen vegetables you can steam in the microwave. Between this, and what I've already set out for you to make, you might even have some leftovers."

Then Dana whirled around and left the kitchen.

Marnie was standing there, her mouth gaping like a fish out of water. She had no idea who could have been invited. Everyone she knew had been invited was already there. She wondered who it was that had been a last-minute invite. Or more accurately, a last-second, invite. Even Mike Blankenship, who lived a few hours away now, had arrived and was in the other room with the guys getting all caught up.

Megan put a hand over her mouth to stifle her giggle.

Marnie turned to her sous chef. "What do you know about this?" If her hands hadn't been wrist deep in ground beef and all of the spices, she would have put them on her waist. Doing her best imitation of an angry drill instructor, the kind she'd seen on TV only a couple of days ago.

"I don't know anything." Megan shook her head but busted out laughing. "But I can guess."

It was then that the doorbell rang. Just as Marnie was starting to think who it might be, she heard a very familiar, deep, and warm voice from the entry.

"Oh, no. She didn't." Worried about how bad she might look, Marnie took her hands out of the mixture and went to the sink to wash them. She had quite a bit of muck on them from the cranberry meatloaf she was in the middle of making. Dinner wouldn't be ready for another two hours, Marnie wondered why was he so early?

Just as she was drying her hands, she heard the clacking of cowboy boots on the linoleum floor. She turned around to see a wide smile and prayed she didn't have meat in her hair, or something just as embarrassing.

"Mmmm, something smells good in here." Declan grinned and entered the kitchen looking directly at Marnie.

Megan took that moment to exit without a word.

Marnie watched the turncoat leave her alone with the handsome cowboy. Her breathing was a bit shallow as she took in his dark green shirt, black jeans, black boots, and what looked to be a recent haircut. He had even trimmed his beard so it wasn't so ragged. The last time she saw him, she thought his beard was beginning to look like something a bird might nest in. Although, she'd never say such a thing out loud.

"Declan, so nice you could join us." Marnie smiled and decided to pretend it was nice. A part of her was excited he was there, but another part wished she could have had a night without worrying about whether or not he liked her. Or if she liked him. Well, she knew she liked him, but... bother! She was attracted to the cowboy, but she was leaving in a few months. It would hurt too much when the time came to say goodbye.

While she didn't know where she was going or what she was going to do, she figured when she graduated from the ranch, she'd be heading back home to Florida where she could focus on figuring out her next steps.

With the way things were going with Russia, she knew she could put her skills to work somehow. Maybe she could even work for a think tank in Florida. Somewhere in an office so she didn't have to worry about standing all day long. Sitting at a desk, while boring, would be best for her. It would also keep her secret safe from her coworkers.

All they had to do was an Internet search and they'd find out what happened, but maybe they wouldn't be able to discern the extent of her injuries.

"Thank you. I know I'll be here tomorrow for Christmas dinner, but when Dana called and suggested I come over tonight, too, I couldn't pass up the chance to try your cranberry meatloaf. Is it similar to what we had in the diner that day?"

Marnie knew that Declan was referring to the lunch special she and he had had early on in their planning for the nativity performance. When Marnie had come back and told Dana about it, she had done an Internet search and found a similar recipe. Only this one was more like a one-pan kind of deal. The potatoes went into the oversized cast iron Dutch oven pot with the meatloaf, as did the green beans. At least, in the recipe that Dana had found.

But, since they needed to make so much food for everyone that night, Dana suggested that she steam the beans in a separate pan but cook the potatoes with the meatloaf.

The extra mashed potatoes and microwave veggies in the steamer bag were because they had extra guests at the last minute, however it would make for some extra options for each of the diners. No one would want baked potatoes along with mashed potatoes, or at least that's what Marnie thought. Or, she prayed they wouldn't want both types of potatoes.

"It is similar, yes. But, I must warn you, I'm no chef and I've never made this before." Marnie grimaced when she thought back to some of her more creative mistakes. Dana promised her it would be easy enough to make, so she'd give it her best.

"Here," Declan unbuttoned his cuffs and rolled up the sleeves. "Let me help." He went over to the sink and began washing his hands.

A man in the kitchen turned out to be even sexier than a man on a horse. Marnie wasn't sure where her mind was at the moment, but she had to shake herself and stop thinking about how nice it was to have him there with her.

Maybe this was why Jerod and Dana wanted to work alone Christmas morning? But her mom was coming, too. Why they wanted to be alone the next morning didn't really matter to Marnie. She was with Declan at the moment, and she was going to enjoy this. Plus, if the meal went south, she could blame him.

Probably not, but it was fun to think about, and it kept her mind off of the very handsome man now standing next to her.

"Okay, what do I do?" His question broke her train of thought.

"Oh. Um. Let me see." Marnie took the instructions and read them over. "Why don't you cut up the potatoes that will go with the meatloaf in the oven."

"Which ones? The little red potatoes?" Declan pointed to a large bag of potatoes sitting next to the sink.

"Yup, those are the ones." Taking in a deep breath, Marnie turned back to her bowl of meat and dug her hands back in. All was quiet in the kitchen, aside from the light sounds of Christmas music coming from the living room.

For the next thirty minutes she and Declan worked side by side only talking when he needed to know what to do next. Marnie wasn't sure if he was just as nervous as she was, or if regretted offering to help. And Megan seemed to have deserted her. The traitor.

"Okay, time to put the pan in the oven." Marnie went to pick up the heavy cast iron dish, but Declan's hands were there, right next to hers. His pinky lightly brushed up against her.

In a soft voice, Declan offered, "here, let me help." He took the pan while she opened the oven door.

Just as he put the Dutch oven pan into the oven, she leaned against the wall and closed her eyes. Marnie had never felt the fluttering of her heart like she did in that very moment. For just a second, she wondered if she was having a heart attack, but realized it was the fluttering of uncertain emotions pulsing through her entire body.

Even though they had a rocky start, Declan had proven to be a really nice guy.

Marnie had promised herself only two days ago that she wasn't going to let herself fall for the handsome cowboy. She couldn't. It would break her heart if they began dating only to have her leave come spring.

"Marnie? Are you okay?" His worried voice penetrated her thoughts. But before she could answer, she felt his soft touch on her face.

Her eyes fluttered open, and Marnie saw he held a tear on the edge of his index finger. She took in a deep breath when she realized she had been crying. "Sorry, onions." It didn't matter that she had only been working with green onions, not the kind that made one cry when chopping them.

Being the gentleman that he was, Declan didn't push her. Instead, he put his finger in his mouth. Then he grinned. "I'd say it was more like garlic than onion."

"What?" She snorted and shook her head.

He grinned. "How long do we set the timer for?"

"Right." She blew out a breath and looked at the notes. After figuring out how long she needed for the vegetables and mashed potatoes, she set the alarm on her phone. "I'll need to come back in 45 minutes to put the rest of the cranberry sauce on top of the meatloaf, then start the sides."

She headed to the living room with the rest of the group after she had washed her hands, leaving Declan in the kitchen to wash his own.

When she was just about to enter the living room, she saw everyone laughing.

Megan caught her just in time. "Stop!" She raised her hands as an added effort to ensure the woman did stop where she wanted her.

"What's going on?" Marnie put her hands on her hips and chuckled. In front of her were all of the men there for dinner that night, sitting on the floor wrapping presents.

Some of the gifts looked nice with pretty paper and ribbon. Others looked more like a five-year-old who had attempted to wrap something he made at school.

Declan was right behind her and stopped when he got up next to her. "What's going on in here? Dana isn't going to like coming home to a huge mess."

In Megan's hand was her phone. She held it as though she had been taking pictures to prove to Dana what the boys had been up to. Marnie approved wholeheartedly, especially if they didn't clean up their mess.

"Hey, Declan. Look up." Skeeter called out with a wink and a grin.

Both Marnie and Declan looked up to where Skeeter pointed.

It took only an instant to know what had happened, and Marnie's cheek flamed with embarrassment. Hanging above her head was something that wasn't there earlier. In fact, she had remembered Jerod stating that no mistletoe was to be put up in the house. She'd bet her entire month's disability check that it was Skeeter who did it.

While Marnie didn't know him well, she had heard enough tales about his practical jokes to know this had his name all over it.

Those bees that had been buzzing around her gut the other day were back, and they didn't just bring one hive with them, they brought an entire apiary with them.

When Declan turned his gaze on her, she felt the heat in his eyes. Marnie almost melted from the feeling. He leaned in close and for just a moment, Marnie thought there were the last two on the entire planet.

Then Skeeter hooted and yelled, "Kiss her, kiss her!"

The silly cowboy didn't realize it, but if he'd stayed quiet, Declan probably would have kissed her. Instead, he grinned, and lifted his hand to the side of her face. When he touched her, she thought maybe he was going to kiss her after all. Then he moved a piece of stray hair away from her face. "A gentleman never steals a kiss from a lady."

While Marnie agreed, she wanted to tell him it wasn't stealing if she was willing. And she most certainly was willing. But she wasn't about to beg for a kiss, not even a Mistletoe kiss. Instead, she smiled, looked down, and stepped back so she was no longer on the parasite.

"Oh, come on, man. Just kiss the girl already," Skeeter called out.

Marnie felt her entire face heat up. She had to get out of there and cool off, without the teasing of the guys. She knew they meant well, but she and Declan weren't a couple.

As she walked outside, Marnie could hear Dakota telling Skeeter he needed to grow up.

She couldn't agree more.

Chapter 32

Declan could have kicked himself for chickening out. But no way did he want his first kiss with the beautiful Marnie to be in front of a bunch of jokers like Skeeter and Juan. While Skeeter had been the loudest, he heard his ranch hand hooting and agreeing with Skeeter. Bunch of immature boys, those two.

And they ruined his chance at a kiss. Although, he did believe what he said. When walked up and was standing next to her he had no idea they were under the mistletoe. When they both looked up, he grinned, but noticed the horrified expression on her face. He prayed it wasn't just the thought of kissing him, but the thought that everyone would be watching them.

He could understand that.

In that very moment he told himself he wouldn't kiss her until after they had a date. And he certainly wouldn't kiss her in front of an audience, especially an audience of nitwits.

"Juan, I could understand Luis acting out like that, but you? I thought you were a grown man." Declan tsked and shook his head.

Once Christmas was over, he was going to assign Juan all of the worst work for a week, just to let him know he wasn't happy.

"Ah, boss man, it's all in fun. Christmas fun. Come on." Juan threw his hands in the air and deflated when Declan didn't change the expression on his face.

"Dude, give him a break. It's just a mistletoe kiss. It's not like we brought in the minister and set up a wedding, or anything like that." The grin on Skeeter's face changed, and he looked at his girlfriend, Dakota. "I'd never do that, by the way. But a mistletoe kiss is romantic, isn't it?"

Dakota glared at her boyfriend. "It is when the couple both want it. But it's never romantic when a bunch of little boys are hootin' and hollerin' like a couple of banshees." She rolled her eyes and said, "Heaven help me."

Megan laughed. "Hey, I warned you about him, but you chose him anyway."

"Wait, you what?" Skeeter stood up in the middle of the mess he had made. "You warned her away from me?"

This wasn't what Declan wanted to hear so he left them to discuss whatever, and he decided to go looking for Marnie.

He found her outside on the porch, without her cane. It wasn't even within reach. "Sorry about that. I had no idea what they had set up."

Marnie winced. "I know you didn't. You were in the kitchen with me. How could you?" She shrugged then leaned against the banister. "I guess when the cat's away the mice will play? Or something like that."

He snorted. "Got that right. Bunch of rats." He motioned behind him with his thumb. "Aren't you cold out here?" He took off his jacket and put it around her shoulders.

Declan noticed how Marnie leaned her face into his jacket. When she took a deep breath, he smiled. She was smelling his jacket. He couldn't help but match her smile when she looked out at the frozen yard.

"I see the boys had some fun out here." She pointed to an attempt at a snowman. The snow wasn't quite moist enough to make a decent snowman that would last. But it wasn't a bad attempt, just small.

While Declan thought he knew why Marnie was so upset, he had to know. But should he just come right out and ask, or should he beat around the bush about it? He wasn't any good at playing dating games. He'd always been a straight-shooter and didn't think he should change now.

The woman wouldn't look at him, no matter how many times he turned his head to look at her. Something was not right, and he had to know.

They stood there, the tension in the air so thick that Declan knew he could cut it with his pocketknife, easily. He prayed he hadn't hurt her feelings when he almost kissed her. In this day and age, it wasn't right for a man to kiss a woman without her consent, and while he hadn't kissed her, he was on his way to doing so. Even a mistletoe kiss requires consent.

Declan stood tall and turned his entire body to face her. This conversation required his full attention. He was bound and determined to show her he did respect her. He cleared his throat, about ready to speak when she beat him to chase.

"Declan, I'm sorry I ran out like that. It was rude of me." The gulp in Marnie's throat was very evident.

Declan figured she was having a tough time admitting her mistake.

"I didn't think you'd run out on me." He'd actually thought she ran out on the group who were bound and determined to tease her.

Declan couldn't blame her. "Listen, those guys are just a bunch of kids playing around in their dad's clothes."

This elicited a chuckle from Marnie. "I must agree with you on that, but I shouldn't have run out like I did. I was just…" she sighed. "Embarrassed."

Declan blinked. "Why? There's no reason for you to be embarrassed. If anyone should be, it's them." He pointed back to the general direction of the living room.

"Yeah, well, when a guy refuses to kiss you under the mistletoe it is kinda embarrassing." She looked down to the ground and twisted her mouth.

"Refuse? Who me?" Declan shook his head. "I would have gladly kissed you, mistletoe or not, but I didn't want to have our first kiss be in front of a bunch of immature pranksters."

Her head shot up and surprised covered her features. "You would have?"

Declan moved closer and inhaled her sweet scent of jasmine. In that moment he knew he was going to have to buy anything and everything that shared her scent. How was it that he'd never known how appealing jasmine was? With a small whispered, "yes," he leaned down and lightly touched his lips to hers.

Marnie couldn't believe what was happening. She hadn't meant to ask him to kiss her, but here they were, kissing on the front porch. It wasn't anything illicit, just a sweet and simple kiss. But it sent shivers all up and down her entire body. When he pulled back after that first touch, she sighed.

And when he touched her lips again, it wasn't much more pressure, but it was just as delightfully delicious as the first. The best part was when he wrapped his arms around her waist and pulled her even closer.

His warm lips touched hers again and again. Then he kissed one cheek before kissing the other.

She stood there with her hands clutching his chest and her eyes closed. Marnie didn't want this kiss to end. She'd gladly stand there on that porch for the rest of the winter, snowstorms, and all, if Declan Walden continued to kiss her that way. Fear of being caught didn't even touch her mind. Nothing would stop them from kissing.

Declan seemed to want to keep on touching his lips to her. While her eyes were closed, he slowly kissed every inch of her face, and then when he had finished kissing one eyelid, she jumped as something in her pocket began blaring the Hallelujah Chorus from Handel's *Messiah*. Hallelujah screamed at her and she almost swore she was so flustered.

An intense heat warmed her neck and swept up into her face and she fumbled for her phone. "Sorry."

Declan chuckled. "You know, I've been interrupted before, but never by someone singing hallelujah."

His little joke caused Marnie to smile, and she finally looked at him. His eyes were bright, and his smile covered his face. She couldn't help it, she grinned, too. "Yeah, I guess I was just in the mood to set the alarm with a Christmas song that would catch my attention."

"Does this mean that the meatloaf is done?" He put a hand on his stomach. "I must say, I'm ready for dinner."

She laughed. "Not yet. Remember, this is just the midpoint. I have to add more of the sauce and then begin the water for steaming the vegetables and heating up the mashed potatoes." Marnie clicked off the alarm and took one last look at his face. He was so achingly handsome she almost sighed.

Declan took her hand. "Come on, I'll help you with finishing up dinner." He leaned down so that he whispered in her ear. "And we can finish that kiss later."

"Ohh." Nervousness filled her belly, but she would take those butterflies if it meant that she'd get another kiss like that one.

Once dinner was on the table, Marnie looked directly at Megan. "Since you abandoned me in the kitchen, I think it's only fair that you do the dishes."

Skeeter snorted and covered his mouth.

Marnie eyed him and pursed her lips. "And I think that a couple of others should help her. Don't you, Skeeter?"

This time, it was Dakota who laughed. "I think you're right on that one, Marnie." She turned to her boyfriend. "But don't worry, I'll help."

Declan eyed his ranch hand who was doing his best to sink down into his chair and not be noticed. "I think it would be nice if someone from my ranch offered to help clean up as well, don't you, Juan?"

Marnie thought it served them all right. It was probably something that Skeeter organized, but it seemed to Marnie that Skeeter had help. And Megan was one of those who helped. While Juan may not have helped set up the mistletoe situation, she had no problem letting him do dishes.

The best part was that it would give her more time alone, or mostly alone, with Declan. The house was full of people; they had more than a dozen sitting down to dinner. Past residents, current residents, staff, and their dates made it a full house. But, Marnie figured most of them would be too tired from the filling dinner to care about what she and Declan might be up to.

So, when she stood up after dinner, fully expecting to have more alone time for kissing, she wasn't expecting what happened next.

Chapter 33

Daniel Caruthers, Megan's boyfriend, had been invited to dinner, but he only showed up right before dessert. "If you don't mind, I'd like to talk to Megan for a few minutes before she starts her punishment for whatever happened earlier." He stood up and took her hand in his.

Everyone at the table grinned. Marnie wasn't sure what was going to happen, but from the smiling faces around the table, she guessed it was good. "Sure, take your time."

Declan leaned in and whispered in Marnie's ear, "we might want to hang around."

With thoughts of various possibilities, Marnie agreed and prayed Daniel wasn't about to break up with Megan. Not on Christmas Eve.

"Should we follow them?" Marnie asked.

With a little chuckle, Declan nodded. "Maybe, but we shouldn't follow too closely. Maybe hang out in the hallway around a corner from them?"

"What if they go outside?" Marnie's brows raised and her cheeks turned pink when she recalled their kiss out on the front porch. Maybe that was what Daniel wanted with Megan. They hadn't seen much of each other over the past few months, so his wanting time to kiss his girlfriend made sense.

Declan waggled his brows. "Then we should probably leave them alone."

However, when they didn't go outside, but stopped directly underneath the mistletoe, Marnie's brows furrowed. She looked around and noticed most were there, watching with interest as Daniel took Megan's hands in his own.

"Megan, I'm so sorry I haven't been more attentive lately." Daniel looked directly into Megan's eyes.

Marnie wasn't sure if he was just going to apologize, break up with her, or propose. Then it hit her, and she gasped.

"Shhh." Skeeter waved to Marnie, signaling to quiet down.

An unladylike snort escaped Marnie before she put a hand over her mouth. Skeeter was one to talk. He was always getting in the way of things and making a mess.

Daniel took a deep breath. "I love you, I have since we first met."

Marnie noticed that Megan was biting her lower lip, probably to keep herself from saying anything. Then she saw Megan rocking back on her heels and grinning from ear to ear.

"I want to spend forever with you. And I promise to never put work first again. I even spoke with Cody about it earlier this week." Daniel sighed. "This year was supposed to be an easier year, but with less help than last year, I ended up needing to work more than expected. And I'm truly sorry for that." He paused.

Then someone yelled out - not Skeeter Marnie noted, "Just get on with it already, will ya? Santa's on his way while you dawdle."

The group who was watching chuckled.

Marnie noted it was actually Mike Blankenship, the guy who rarely spoke, that egged Daniel on.

Without looking at anyone else, Daniel waved the group away, then took Megan's hand back in his again. He kissed her hands, then let one go as he knelt down on his right knee. "Megan Anderson, would you do me the honor of being my wife and making me the most blessed man on God's green earth for the rest of our lives? I can't promise wealth, or even a house of our own any time soon, but if you'll have me, I will do everything within my power to make you happy."

Megan, who had already started crying tears of joy nodded and pulled him up. "Yes, yes, a thousand times yes. I don't need riches, or even our own house. Just a place where we can live happily."

Marnie wiped tears of joy from her face as she smiled from ear to ear. Daniel stood up and pulled Megan into him, kissing her soundly under the mistletoe. When he pulled back, he pulled out the ring box that he had forgotten to get out before the proposal.

"Sorry, I had this in my pocket and meant to give it to you before I asked." The joy on Daniel's face was so infectious that everyone in the house was smiling from ear to ear.

Daniel opened the lid, held it out to Megan, and she started crying again.

"Daniel, you shouldn't have." Megan took the ring out of the box.

Daniel took it from her hand and then put it on her ring finger. "When I saw you looking at the ring in the window of the jewelry store, I knew that was the one for you."

This time, when the mistletoe did its job, everyone clapped and cheered, and Marnie joined in the happiness.

"Now that's what I call a mistletoe kiss," Skeeter yelled out to the room. Then he took his girlfriend in his arms and kissed her soundly on the lips.

Not wanting anyone to expect Declan to kiss her like that, Marnie turned around and headed back to the kitchen.

"Hey, where are you going?" Declan followed behind her.

"I think it's time to bring out the coffee and the spice cake. Don't you?" Marnie didn't turn around, but she felt his presence behind her as she walked over to the counter that held the coffee maker.

Once the coffee pot was started, he pulled at her hand. "Hey, was that more than you wanted to witness?"

Marnie turned around and looked at Declan quizzically. "The proposal? No, I'm actually very happy I was able to see it. I'm so happy for Megan and Daniel." She grinned and knew that she truly meant it. She was happy for them.

"Then what was it?" Declan prodded.

Marnie rubbed at an invisible itch on her neck. Then she wrung her hands. With a sigh, she looked at him, then turned to look at the door, ensuring no one was there. "It was getting a bit heated with the mistletoe kisses. Having spent so much time in the Air Force, I'm not a fan of PDA."

Declan's brows narrowed. "PDA? What's that?"

Marnie chuckled. "Sorry, I forget that sometimes civilians don't get our military jargon. Public displays of affection. The entire proposal, and subsequent kiss was wonderful..." she trailed off.

"Ah, yes. Skeeter." Declan laughed. "I guess everyone is just used to his antics. And between you and I, I have a feeling that he's about to pop the question to Dakota, even though they've only been dating a few weeks. That boy is over the moon for her."

"I think anyone can see that. While I think he's a...bit too much, I do see how much Dakota cares for him, too. I think they'll make each other happy. Skeeter will keep her on her toes, and..." Marnie stopped short of saying anything else and blanched.

"Hey, it's alright." Declan took her hand in his and squeezed it lightly. "I've noticed that you aren't using your cane anymore. That's a great thing."

Hot tears pricked at the back of Marnie's eyes, but she kept her gaze averted. "It seems my balance has improved greatly over the past few weeks. Maybe all of the physical activity has helped." She shrugged.

"Or," Declan began slowly, "you are starting to accept your situation and your body is adjusting to your new normal."

She looked at him. "Are you a psychologist, too? That's the same thing Megan said to me not too long ago."

He chuckled. "No, I'm not trained in anything so studious. But I do seem to have the knack for reading people."

Marnie turned to look at him squarely. "Oh, yeah. And what do you read about me?"

The cowboy took one step back and rested his chin in one of his hands. "Hmm, I think you need to keep busy, and I also think that you have a previously unknown affinity for animals. You know, they can sense when humans like them, or not."

"Really? And what makes you think they like me?"

"Because I know my animals. And they all seem to look at you fondly and enjoy being around you. You haven't helped out with them enough for them to think you're staff and will feed them all the time, like John, Juan, and Luis. They like you for who you are on the inside. Animals are the best judge of character."

"I must agree." A feminine voice said when she entered the room. "Is that coffee I smell brewing?"

"Hi, Nelly. Yes, I thought after the wonderful news we might all want a cup of coffee and some dessert. I think there are a few coffee cakes, or something along those lines, in the panty for tomorrow. I'm sure Dana won't mind if we take one, or two." Marnie grinned and walked over to the pantry.

"Were you just talking about animals liking you?" Nelly asked.

"Did you hear our conversation?" Marnie wasn't sure how much the dog whisperer overheard, but she felt almost naked having someone else listen in on that one conversation.

"Only that last sentence, where Declan said that animals are the best judge of character. I always listen to my dogs when they get anxious around humans, especially if it's a man." Nelly walked into the small pantry and came out with a package that had Marnie's name on it. "Did you know about this?"

Marnie took the small package and looked inside. Her brows furrowed as she pulled out a note, then three loaves of cinnamon bread. "Marnie, in case anyone has any big news tonight and you need to provide a little extra treat to celebrate, you can use these. If not, then I'm sure we'll use them tomorrow."

She grinned. "Well, it looks like Dana had an inkling of what might take place here tonight."

Declan walked up behind them. "Really?" He looked over her shoulder and quickly read the note. When he laughed out loud, Marnie and Nelly joined him.

"It seems that Dana has her finger on the pulse better than any of us do." Marnie put the loaves on the counter and Nelly helped her to prepare trays to take out to the group with all of the dinnerware they'd need for a celebration.

Chapter 34

"Merry Christmas!" Dana and Jerod yelled when Marnie walked into the giant living room where the tree and all of the Christmas gifts were displayed. On a sideboard to the left of the Christmas tree was a very nice display of coffee and breakfast pastries.

"Help yourself to anything on the table." Dana pointed. "And I heard about your little impromptu celebration last night."

Marnie grinned. "Thank you! You have no idea how much those cinnamon loaves helped. And how much I need this coffee today." She fixed herself a large mug of coffee and then picked through what was left of the pastries. "I see I'm a bit late in coming down." The table looked as though a pack of dogs had run through it. There was a total of four pastries left - one cinnamon roll, one croissant, and two chocolate donuts.

Having had the cinnamon roll from the bakery before, Marnie knew that was what she wanted to start with. It would be filling and help her get through whatever embarrassment she would feel after opening that extremely large box from her parents.

Jerod chuckled. "Yes, it seems even on Christmas morning, the guys can't sleep in. Or maybe I should say especially on Christmas morning. They were all up at their normal time and are currently out there feeding the animals." He pointed to the back of the house, where the barn stood.

"Well, I hope they get a lot of milk today from the cows, I think we're going to need it with all of the people coming today." Marnie grinned, knowing that no one would be drinking the milk from today, but they would most likely be all out of cream, milk, and butter at some point today thanks to all of the cooking and baking over the past few days.

Marnie sipped on her coffee and looked out the back window. The sun hadn't risen yet; it was still fairly early. Even though she had planned on sleeping in, she found she couldn't. It was Christmas morning, after all. She knew the only gift she would have under the tree was that ostentatiously large box from her parents. She sighed and looked back at the tree again. The box was there, sitting to the side of the tree. All sorts of other gifts had been placed around it and on it. It did look good there, but she still didn't know what to make of it.

Jerod and Dana had left the room, and headed back to the kitchen for their preparations. She was all alone in the room and decided to take a look around at the decorations. Something seemed a bit off to her and she wasn't sure what it was.

As Marnie slowly walked around the room, sipping her coffee, and noted the cute little Santas and nutcrackers that had been placed around the room. On one side table was a cowboy Santa along with a cowboy nutcracker. Even the Mrs. Claus that sat on the table, while still dressed in red, was a cowgirl with boots and a pretty red Stetson-style hat with a band of black leather and a gold buckle on it. She smiled and touched the items.

Then she walked to the hearth, where each resident had a Christmas stocking. She grinned when noticed that "Santa" had been there and stuffed all of them with candy and small gifts. Marnie hadn't had a stocking since she was a kid. By the time she hit fourteen, her parents had stopped putting anything in hers. They told her she was too old for it. Secretly, Marnie had always loved the stockings the best. While the gifts were always small, like a travel size bottle of lotion or shower gel from her favorite bath store, there were also little candies and chocolates.

Sometimes she even had giftcards. They were always small dollar amounts, but it was still fun to peek into her stocking and see what Santa had left her. It was like opening a box of chocolates for the first time and checking each and every one to see what types were in there. There was always a piece of peanut butter and chocolate along with something that was mint. But the rest were always different. Almost as though her parents, or Santa, had put her two favorites inside, then told the girl at the chocolate counter to pick out the other three chocolates for the tiny box.

A part of her wanted to pull her stocking down and peek inside to see what Santa brought her this time, but she knew better.

A throat cleared behind her and she turned to see a grinning Declan. "Merry Christmas. Please don't tell me you're peeking at your stocking?" He arched a brow.

She giggled like a schoolgirl who had been caught. "No, but I was thinking about it."

He feigned surprise. "No! You couldn't have been."

Marnie shook her head and slowly walked back to where she had left her cinnamon roll, the one with only one bite taken out of it so far. She sat down and took another bite. "Merry Christmas. I'm glad you're here before we got started."

He looked at the breakfast table. "I'm glad I got here before all of the food was gone."

"Yeah, if you want something, I highly recommend getting it now. As soon as those guys are done with their chores, they'll be in here looking for more food."

"Which is why I have more for the table." Dana grinned and carried a large platter of various pastries.

"Here," Declan immediately stepped closer to the hostess. "Let me help with that." He took the platter and Dana smiled appreciatively at him.

It wasn't two minutes before a loud cacophony of voices broke through their peaceful conversation and a group of smiling and laughing men walked in.

"I told you he'd ask her on Christmas Eve." Tony stated and slapped Mike's back as they entered the room.

"But you never said anything about under the mistletoe," Mike shot back.

"That's only because I thought mistletoe was not allowed here. Not now that we have women living here with us crazy vets." Tony grinned when he saw the table full of pastries again. "Ah, sustenance, just what we all need."

"Ah, ah, ah. Have you all washed your hands?" Dana stood protectively in front of her table.

Skeeter looked affronted. "Hey, of course we have." He scrunched his nose. "There's no way any of us are going to let Mike get his dirty cow hands on any of your delicious food unless they've been cleaned first." He laughed, and the other guys joined him.

Mike was known for always preferring cows to humans, and he never shied away from touching them. In fact, when he was living there, he was the one who milked the cows by hand twice a day, every day. It was an old joke, to make sure he had washed his hands after touching a cow's teat and processing the milk.

"At least there weren't any calves born this morning." Arthur Landbury grinned. He had shown up after dinner the night before and missed all of the excitement, but he'd had to work and lived over three hours away from the ranch.

Everyone who had graduated from the ranch was present, along with those who were current residents. The house was full of joy and laughter on this Christmas morning and Marnie couldn't believe how well she had fit in with this group.

Marty laughed. He'd gone out to do chores with the guys, even though he was still a bit sore from his last interaction with the cows. He'd healed up nicely, and for the most part, stayed away from the animals, but on that day, he said he should help.

Once all of the residents and guests had settled down and were seated in the living room, Dana grinned at everyone. "Merry Christmas to you all. I'm so glad you could join us today. I know last night was a very special night, especially for Daniel and Megan." She pointed to the couple sharing a chair.

Megan's million-watt smile showed how happy she really was with the engagement.

Then Dana picked up where she left off. "It's going to be a bit hectic here today, with so many people, so please, help yourself to coffee, tea, water, and anything that you see out on the counter or table. We won't stand on ceremony here today. The only thing I ask you to steer clear of is the fixings for the traditional Christmas dinner, and the yule logs we've prepared for dessert. I'll put any snacks out on the table against the far wall." She pointed to the back of the room, where the pastries she had put out less than an hour before were already gone, again.

Everyone laughed.

"You know," Skeeter started but Dakota put a hand over his mouth to shush him.

Dana grinned. "Thank you, Dakota. I don't know how you do it, but better you than me."

The entire room erupted in laughter and joking, at Skeeter's expense. The cowboy took it all in stride.

Dana waved her hands to get everyone's attention again. "Okay, so we're going to start with the stockings. All of the residents have a stocking. Sorry, it's current residents only." She looked at Skeeter and raised a brow.

"Oh, I have one for him." Dakota jumped up and ran to the side table and pulled out a box that was underneath. She removed a red stocking that looked homemade. There was a reindeer on it made from felt, glitter, and a couple of puffy balls. "Here ya go. I knew you'd want one too." She handed the stocking to her boyfriend.

"Really? Thank you." Skeeter stood and kissed her on the cheek. "I really appreciate this."

They sat back down and were quiet for a few moments and Dana picked up where she left off.

"Okay, now that that's settled, once the stockings are empty, then Jerod will pass out the gifts under the tree and we'll all open them together. I know not everyone has the same number of presents, but everyone does have at least two gifts apiece. Santa saw to that."

"That's very generous." Marnie said and looked around as everyone nodded their agreement.

"Well..." Dana's cheeks turned pink and she looked down at the ground while waving a hand in front her.

Jerod stood and began walking toward the other side of the tree. "I think once the stockings are done, Marnie should open her gift first.

It's so large and takes up so much space that once it's out of the way, I think we'll have more room here." He grinned.

Marnie felt herself cringe. She knew the box was way too big. If she'd had her way, she would have opened it up the moment she saw it, just so she could keep it out of everyone's way. While the room was large, it wasn't so big that the box didn't take up prime real estate. The moment they got it out of the room, she knew everyone would breathe easier. Well, at least she would. "I could open it now, if you want the space back."

Dana and Jerod exchanged a look, and the pair nodded. Then in a loud voice, Dana stated, "I think it's a great idea that Marnie opens the giant box now. Don't you?"

All heads in the room nodded and looked to the box in question.

"What's in it, do you know?" Skeeter asked.

Sam, who had been quiet so far, spoke up. "It's not a dog, is it? Because that's just cruel."

Dana shook her head and laughed. "No, nothing alive is in the box."

Marnie narrowed her eyes. "How do you know?"

"Because," Jerod answered for his wife. "We would have heard sounds if something in there was alive."

Knowing that everyone was waiting on her, Marnie stood and walked to the giant monstrosity. She looked around for the seam so she could pull the paper. When she found a spot that wasn't covered in tape, she pulled and pulled until the entire box was unwrapped.

"Well, go on." Skeeter egged her on, "open the flap and see what's inside."

With a deep breath and quick prayer, she opened the lid. Then her brows furrowed, and she leaned over the opening to find nothing. "Huh?" She leaned in more when she noticed a small card. Reaching down, she grunted and was barely able to grab it with her fingertips.

She stood up and looked at Dana and Jerod who were both grinning like they knew something. Her first instinct was to question the pair, but she figured she could do that later. Instead, she opened the card and read it. A slow smile crept across her face and she looked up, expecting something.

"Well, what is it?" Declan asked.

Others in the room asked all sorts of questions, but Marnie didn't answer them. Instead, she screamed with delight when two more people entered the already packed room. "Mom, Dad!" She ran to them and they enveloped her in their arms.

"Merry Christmas, Baby girl." Her dad said.

"But, what about the rest of the family? Where are they?"

The smile on her mom's face diminished. "I'm sorry, but they couldn't make it, it was too expensive for us all to come. But we thought you might need us more today."

Her dad patted her arm. "And I thought I needed to see my brave girl today."

Marnie pulled them back into a hug. "Best present, ever." Then she turned around and glared at Dana and Jerod. "You were in on this, weren't you?"

They both nodded and Dana had tears flowing down her face. "Darn pregnancy hormones." She swiped at her face and continued to smile.

Marnie did a double take, as did the rest of the room. While Marnie knew Dana was pregnant, she didn't think the momma-to-be had made the announcement yet.

Jerod shook his head and laughed. "Yes, we're pregnant. We were going to wait, but well." He shrugged.

Dana laughed, again. "Pregnancy brain, too."

Everyone congratulated the married couple as well as went up to Marnie's folks to introduce themselves. Chaos ruled the room until someone got everyone's attention.

"Come on, let's all sit down and get started on the stockings before anyone else opens theirs up." Jerod glared at Skeeter, who had already taken out all of the contents of his stocking.

"What? It's not from you guys, I can open a gift from my girl, can't I?" Skeeter, who looked totally innocent, held up a lollipop before sticking it in his mouth.

Mike said under his breath, "maybe that will keep him quiet for two seconds while the rest of us enjoy this day."

It took almost two hours before all of the presents were opened, even though Dana had wanted everyone to open up all at once, most wanted to take turns so they could see what everyone else was getting.

Even Eloise, the ADA Coordinator, who had decided to not go home at the last minute, had two gifts to open. "Thank you so much, Dana. You didn't need to get me anything."

"I didn't. Santa did it." Dana grinned and pulled her husband's hand. "Come on, I need some help in the kitchen."

Declan walked over to where Marnie sat with her parents. "Hi, I'm Declan Walden, I run the local alpaca and sheep ranch." He put a hand out for Marnie's dad to shake.

Marnie's dad stood up. "Nice to meet you. I'm George and this is my wife, Betty." He motioned to the women sitting next to Marnie.

"Mom, Dad, Declan and I worked together on the live nativity; it was his alpaca that stole the show." Marnie laughed when she thought back to how little Johnny riled Titus up.

George's eyes widened. "Oh, I heard all about that alpaca who spit on people. Do they always do that?"

"Only when they're agitated." Declan chuckled.

Betty leaned close to her daughter and in a low voice, whispered, "he's cute. Is he the one?"

Marnie felt her face heat up instantly. She knew Declan had heard her mother the instant his lips turned up and he looked at her. While her mom probably thought that she wasn't being loud, she was. Her mom was a bit hard of hearing and always spoke in a louder volume than she thought she was. "Mom. Shh."

"What? I didn't say anything bad." Betty looked at Declan, and when realization set in, she scrunched her nose, just like her daughter did. "Oh, right. Maybe I should get those hearing aids after all."

"Betty, I've been telling you that for years." George laughed and shook his head.

The rest of the Christmas celebration went well. There was plenty of food to go around and everyone was cheerful and talkative, even those who normally didn't talk so much joined in.

Later that night, after all of the guests who weren't staying the night left, Declan stood up and put his hand out for Marnie. "Walk me to my truck?"

"Of course." She stood and once they both had coats, hats and gloves on, they stepped outside into the cold December night. "This was a wonderful Christmas, wasn't it?"

"It really was. I'm so glad I got to meet your parents." Declan stopped on the porch in front of the stairs. "I just wish they could have stayed longer so you could spend some more time with them."

"Me too. But I'll see them soon. Once I'm released from here, I'll be heading back home." She stood next to Declan, not looking at him. She felt his sadness at her statement.

"Really? You aren't going to try and find something around here to do?" While Declan knew she had limited time left on the ranch, he hadn't realized she would leave the area. Not many did once they made it to Frenchtown.

"What would I do? I'm not qualified for ranch work." She winced and looked down at her partial foot that was currently covered up by very warm winter boots. To look at her, no one would be able to tell her left foot was missing all five toes. Even now, the stump of a foot didn't look right to her own eyes. But, with proper shoes, no one could tell. However, she would always have to work at maintaining balance.

"Yes, you are. You could work with animals on any ranch." Declan pulled his hat off and ran a hand through his hair. "Shoot, I'd hire you if I had the ability to."

Marnie put a hand on his arm. "Thank you, I appreciate that. Really, I do. But I don't even know what I want to do. My entire world shattered that day, not just my foot. I have to figure out what's next for me, and I don't think I can do that here."

Just then the door behind them opened.

"Oh, I'm sorry. I didn't realize you were out here." Dana grimaced and started to turn away, but Declan stopped her.

"Dana, perfect. I was just talking to Marnie about staying in town. She said she's going home once she's released because she has no clue what she wants to do now. I get that her Air Force job doesn't exactly translate well into a civilian job, but surely a growing town like ours has jobs, right?" Declan pleaded with his eyes to get Dana on board with him.

Instead of smiling like she normally did, Dana tilted her head. "You know, I'm going to be going on maternity leave next summer, and Lottie will be taking off soon herself. I bet Lottie would love to have you stick around and help out while you work out what's next."

"But what about when you go back to work?" Marnie knew most women did go back to work after having a baby. It was normal in this day and age for a woman to have it all.

Dana shook her head. "Nope. Once I leave the coffee shop, that's going to be it." She held up her hands. "There's too much happening here at the ranch, and now that we have a baby coming, I don't want to go back to work at the coffee shop. I want to stay home and take care of my family and this ranch."

Marnie almost said something about having a college degree and working in a coffee shop wasn't a good mix, but who was she kidding. Unless she wanted to go back to school, which she didn't right then, her degree wouldn't get her much more than a receptionist job. If she weren't disabled, she could have easily gotten a job with one of the alphabet organizations, working in intelligence. That had been her plan all along, to stay in the Air Force long enough to learn her job well, and get a good recommendation before joining the CIA or FBI. Or something like that. She wasn't sold on any one of the agencies yet, but she did plan to work for one almost her entire life. But now? Well? Now she had zero clue what to do.

And her degree was only a bachelor's degree. And a Russian studies major would only be worth it if she had a PhD and went into academia, or intelligence. Possibly a DC think tank would hire her once she had her Master's, but she wasn't ready to commit to going back to college, not yet.

"I don't know." She shook her head.

"Why don't we table this until after the new year. Then you can come into the shop and talk to Lottie and see what she has to say. If nothing else, it would be a good job until you do know what you want to do moving forward. We even have a great university not too far away from here." Dana grinned, and patted Declan on the arm. "This big guy went there and he loved it."

Marnie bit her lip and kept her thoughts to herself for the moment, but the minute Dana closed the door, she turned on Declan. "Do you really think I should stay?" She didn't want to add and date you, but that was what she really wanted to know.

He took her gloved hands in his. Looking directly into Marnie's eyes, Declan nodded. "Yes, I do. I want you to stay so we can get to know each other better. I know working in someone else's coffee shop isn't what you want long term, but there are other places to work around here. We aren't too far from a big city." He tilted his head. "Well, big for Montana. Missoula is a good sized city that has a lot of employment opportunities. They are growing like gangbusters."

"And they are less than an hour's drive away. I know." Marnie sighed. She knew that there were opportunities in the area, but in order for her to stay, she wanted more than just a job.

"And, if you stayed, we could really give this a go. What we have between us is something that's worth exploring. Don't you think?" It was Declan's turn to bite his lip.

Marnie hadn't seen him looking so pensive before. Could it be he didn't know how she felt about him? She felt her face soften and she leaned into him. "I do want to give this a try. I can't promise what will happen, but how about we try it and see? If I can get a job locally, then I'll stay here."

Without a word, he took her lips in his and gave her a real kiss. This time when his lips touched hers, it wasn't soft or sweet. His kiss was deep and slow, but oh so wonderful. Had he kissed her like this before, she wouldn't have hesitated to stay. They continued to kiss until another person interrupted them. She swore that if she did get a job, she would have to get her own place. The kind where no one could interrupt such wonderful kissing again.

Epilogue

Spring came, and so did plenty of job offers for Marnie. It seemed baby fever was on the rise and so many women who owned local businesses were looking to train someone to take over for them while they went on maternity leave. Not everyone was going to stay home after the birth, but even Lottie said she'd take at least three, maybe even four months off to stay at home with her new baby when the time came.

Which meant that Marnie had her choice of several jobs.

In the end, she chose to work in an office that had set up shop right in the middle of town, after she helped Lottie with her maternity leave.

Fall had come and she and Declan were still happily dating.

"Marnie, I think God orchestrated your move to Frenchtown. No one else in this area could do what you do." Declan kissed the top of her head as they sat on his porch watching the sunset on Sunday evening.

They had spent the afternoon working together on a list of places where emigrants from Ukraine could find some work. While so many countries around the world opened their doors to those who lost everything in the war, some ended up in Montana hoping to work on a farm or a ranch, like they had back home. They were hoping to start fresh. Somewhere safe, far away from warlords who wanted to harm the sweet-natured people of the Ukraine. Somewhere they could use their natural gifts for raising crops or animals and build up a family.

"I don't speak Ukrainian, but Russian is very similar." She leaned in closer to him. "I know what it's like to have your whole world turned upside down. Although, I don't know the horrors of war, thankfully. I'm just so glad that so many of the Montana ranchers and farmers are willing to give those displaced by the war in Ukraine a place to call home. Even if they eventually go home, they need somewhere safe to live while trying to rebuild their lives and recover from the atrocities they have experienced."

She felt Declan shiver next to her. In a deep voice, he said, "I'm so very grateful that you never saw war. I know it's something that you would have done if called upon, but I know too many who have come home very different then when they left."

"That's what the Crooked Arrow Ranch is for."

Character Page

1. Marnie Gallagher – USAF disabled vet. She was a cryptologic language analyst – Russian. She was an E-5 and received a medical discharge after 5 years of service. Injured in a training accident while in Germany.

2. Declan Walden – Local Frenchtown, Montana rancher. He raises alpacas and sheep for their wool.

3. Pebbles – Black and White Collie.

4. Ransom – Declan's chocolate brown Morgan horse.

5. Marty Winters – Air Force Disabled vet. Just arrived at the Crooked Arrow. He was a Tech Sgt (E6) and served 9 years. His MOS was Tactical Air Control Party (TACP). He was embedded with an Army Ranger unit in the Middle East. He can't say exactly where.

6. Eloise Sullivan – ADA Coordinator from Houston, TX.

7. Jerod Stevens – Cowboy and owner of the Crooked Arrow Ranch. He's a disabled vet and was a special ops soldier in the Army when he was injured.

8. Dana Stevens (Baker) – Wife of Jerod and barista at the Frenchtown Roasting Company.

9. Megan Anderson – Counselor at the Crooked Arrow Ranch. She's dating Daniel Caruthers.

10. Daniel Caruthers – Christmas Tree Farm foreman and Dating Megan Anderson.

11. Arthur Landbury – Former patient at the ranch. He was an Army Electrical Engineer. Recently graduated from the ranch program and moved up to Northern Montana for a job with the power company.

12. Mike Blankenship – Wounded warrior who recently graduated from the ranch. He now works about 3 hrs away at a large dairy farm. He's also known as the cow whisperer.

13. Skeeter Murphy – Another recent graduate of the Crooked Arrow Ranch. He's now working at the ranch next door to the Crooked Arrow as the foreman. And dating Dakota Monahan.

14. Sam Marley – Former resident at the Crooked Arrow Ranch. He's now working with, and married to, Nelly Wilson. They train the service dogs.

15. Nelly Marley (Wilson) – Dog whisperer. She runs the ranch where the service dogs are trained locally. And married to

Sam.

16. Dixon – Resident at the Crooked Arrow Ranch. He was a truck driver in the Army. He's suffering from severe PTSD but making progress. He loves the cows and enjoys the cuddling program.

17. John Mason – Declan's ranch foreman.

18. Juan – Ranch hand for Declan.

19. Luis – Young ranch hand for Declan.

20. Titus – Young alpaca on Declan's ranch who wants to be the alpha.

21. Damien – The alpha alpaca on Declan's ranch.

22. Lottie Hamilton – Owns Frenchtown Roasting Company and is married to Cove Hamilton.

23. Cove Hamilton – Former rodeo star, now married to Lottie, and helps her in her coffee shop. He also still does some ads for rodeo gear.

Cranberry Meatloaf Recipe

Ingredients:

1.5 lbs ground beef*

2/3 C.breadcrumbs

2 large AA eggs - mixed

2 cloves minced garlic

½ C chopped green onions

6 Tablespoons ketchup (or bbq sauce for a little extra tang)

3 Tablespoons A-1 sauce

2 teaspoons Dijon mustard (Spicy brown also works)

1 ½ teaspoons Lawry's season pepper (or you can use cracked black pepper if you can't find the Lawry's pepper)

½ cup cranberry sauce with whole cranberries

2 Tablespoons firmly packed light brown sugar

1 bag of baby red potatoes cut in half, or you can use a mixture of a bag of colorful baby potatoes. Just be sure to cut them in half so they cook faster.

¾ pound of fresh green beans, cut the ends off.

2 tablespoons olive oil

Directions:

Preheat oven to 350 degrees.

Use either a Dutch oven or a large cast iron skillet. It needs to be approved for use in the oven. And it needs to be very large with high sides to hold everything in.

In a large mixing bowl combine, ground beef, breadcrumbs, mixed eggs, garlic, green onions, 2 Tablespoons ketchup (or bbq sauce), 2 Tablespoons A-1 sauce, mustard, 1 teaspoon salt, and ½ teaspoon Lawry's pepper (or cracked pepper) until thoroughly mixed together. I find it easier to use my hands with food grade gloves.

Then in the middle of your skillet or pan/Dutch oven, shape your meat into the traditional meatloaf form. It should look like it just came out of a bread pan.

In a small saucepan over medium-high heat on the stovetop, bring cranberry sauce, brown sugar, 4 Tablespoons ketchup (or BBQ sauce), and 1 Tablespoon A-1 sauce to a simmer (do not boil). Once it's done, pour or brush half of the sauce onto the meatloaf. Put the rest back on the stovetop for use later.

In a large mixing bowl combine cut and washed, but not peeled, potatoes, green beans, oil, 1 teaspoon salt, and ¾ teaspoon Lawry's seasoned pepper (or cracked pepper). Once it's all coated nicely, then divide out the potatoes and put them on either side of your meatloaf form in the oven-proof pan. Leave the green beans in the bowl, covered.

Bake for 45 minutes, then pull out the pan and add the green beans around the meatloaf. Then spread the remaining cranberry sauce on top of the meatloaf. Place back in the oven for about 30 minutes. Be sure to test the meat to make sure it's 165 degrees in the middle with a food thermometer. And check the potatoes to make sure they are tender. If so, then it's ready to take out. Let sit for a couple of minutes, then enjoy!

* Ground beef can be substituted for ground bison. If using beef, be sure to use the lowest fat content. I use 93% fat-free ground beef. But when using bison, be sure to know that you already like bison burgers, at least. Bison has a very strong flavor. You can also mix bison with ground beef for a lower fat content and a slightly stronger taste.

Author's Notes

If you've read the first 3 books in this series, you'll notice A Crooked Arrow Christmas was a bit different. It started off looking as though Marnie would get a service dog. However, after I began writing this book in January, my family dog began going downhill - quickly. I doubted Frankie, who was the inspiration for the service dogs in this series, would make it. While Frankie wasn't a trained service dog, he was smart enough to be one. And at times, he seemed to know when he was needed, and who needed his love.

Frankie passed away peacefully at home with all of us about 2 weeks before I finished this book. I knew that I couldn't write about the bond a human has with their dog while going through what my family and I did. In fact, it's even tough now, writing this part.

But, no worries, the next book will have a service dog. The only question is, will it be Marty or someone else who gets their new partner?

You might have noticed the end, about Ukraine. The war started just as I finished book 3, Love's Healing Balm. It's been a year since that horrible war began. While I don't normally write about current events, I couldn't ignore the atrocities taking place. My heart and my prayers go out to everyone in the Ukraine. This isn't a war between two competing armies, it's more of a David vs Goliath event. I pray that today's David will find a way to save the people.

Now I'm totally going to change things up here. Have you read Jerod's story? If not, then subscribe to my newsletter and you'll get the exclusive story, Wounded Hearts Ranch, free in the second email from me. The first, will give you another free book, Finding Love in Montana.

Keep an eye out for my next book to release. I've also got a new series in the works and will have that start later this year, Lord willing. It's going to be quite different and take place in Arizona. Where I'm currently living.

I wish you all peace and joy,
Jenna

Newsletter Sign-up

Do you love clean & wholesome contemporary cowboy romance? Want more? Then check out Finding Love in Montana today!

By signing up for my newsletter, you'll not only receive this book, but a couple more free stories as well!

If you want to make sure you hear about the latest and greatest, sign up for my newsletter at: Subscribe to Jenna Hendricks newsletter. I will only send out a few e-mails a month. I'll do cover reveals, snippets of new books, and giveaways or promos in the newsletter, some of which will only be available to newsletter subscribers. (https://jennahendricks.com/newsletter/)

Acknowledgements

This book was the first time I've used beta readers in years. I must say, I loved the experience. And I have to say a huge thank you to Susan B and Bonnie R for all of their help! Their insight and suggestions helped to make this a much better read! Thank you so much!!!

Any and all current spelling and/or grammar issues are all my fault.

Contact Me

For those of you who love social media, here are the various ways to follow or contact me:

BookBub: https://www.bookbub.com/authors/jenna-hendricks
TikTok: https://www.tiktok.com/@jennacleanauthor
Instagram: https://www.instagram.com/j.l.hendricks/
Twitter: https://twitter.com/TinkFan25
Facebook: https://www.facebook.com/JLHendricksAuthor
Website: https://jennahendricks.com